RHINO DREAMS

RHINO DREAMS

A Novel

Carolyn Waggoner

and

Kathryn Williams

SHE WRITES PRESS

Published 2022
Printed in the United States of America
Print ISBN: 978-1-64742-333-9
E-ISBN: 978-1-64742-334-6
Library of Congress Control Number: 2021919624

For information, address:
She Writes Press
1569 Solano Ave #546
Berkeley, CA 94707

She Writes Press is a division of SparkPoint Studio, LLC.

Book design by Stacey Aaronson

To lovers of wildlife.

PROLOGUE

The air was electric with tension over their quarrel last night at base camp. They walked side by side across the harsh, dry landscape, both prisoners of their wounded pride and unyielding convictions.

Clare could no longer stand the silence. "But surely eco-tourism in itself is not a—"

Suddenly Eric wheeled around, his fists clenched, his jaw taut.

Clare shuddered at the terrible emotion burning in his eyes.

In a flash she was hurled onto the searing gravel, Eric atop her, his hand wrenching the back of her neck.

"Eric—stop! You're hurting me."

"Shhh," he hissed.

Clare froze. An enormous quiet had fallen over them. Strange. Heavy. Palpable. Even the birds were silent. A mopane fly buzzed softly in her ear. All she wanted was Eric's love, his respect. And now he had her brutally pinned to the desert floor. What had possessed her to challenge him in such a way?

A blasting series of snorts erased all thought.

The earth began to thunder.

"Find cover! A tree—anything!" Eric shouted as he dragged her to her feet. "Run, Clare! Now!"

I.

Earlier that year, Eric Bolton had taken the Land Rover and driven to Windhoek to meet his new intern for The Rhino Project. She was a graduate student who came with the highest recommendation from his former Cornell mentor and friend, Dr. Peter Grant. It wasn't often students were drawn to the austerities of fieldwork in Namibia, particularly fieldwork involving the unpredictable, often lethal, black rhinoceros, so Eric was anxious to meet her.

Eric himself was an anomaly. He had fallen in love with the animal as a child in London. His parents joked that their weekly visits to the zoo were by imperial command, and that Eric, from the time he could barely walk, would make a beeline for the rhino enclosure. His passion for these creatures, now on the verge of extinction, would earn him the title doctor of wildlife biology and eventually bring him to Africa to study them in one of the last truly free strongholds—Damaraland, Namibia. Perhaps his conservation efforts there would help forestall the inevitable.

Interns were an unavoidable nuisance, by and large. Still, they brought funding, and in their own general bumbling way, managed to advance the cause. He had yet to lose one to a rhino, lion, cobra, or elephant. Eric shuddered, reminding himself that there had been plenty of close calls nevertheless. He just hoped this new woman, Stacey Winship, was quiet, nimble, and smart.

After parking the Rover near the arrival terminal at O.R.

Tambo International Airport, Eric entered the nondescript building. To his surprise, the British Airways flight from Johannesburg had arrived early. The terminal was filled with clumps of tourists: loud, cheerful, enthusiastic, wealthy foreigners out to experience one of the most wild and unforgiving regions on the planet. They were easily identified by their crisp, safari-catalog attire. Eric noted brightly dressed Hereros, a bit of local color, their musical voices lilting over the monotone hum in the terminal. He also recognized khaki-clad representatives of various wildlife enterprises, for whom he had little regard, if not utter contempt.

A woman caught his eye, and he exhaled sharply. She stood apart from the clusters of thrill seekers milling about, awaiting their buses to some prefabricated "adventure." She was draped in bags of photo gear. To Eric, she looked as if she were being devoured by an octopus, perhaps several, as she continually adjusted the straps. Tall, somewhat rangier than he usually found attractive. Looked to be late twenties. Blonde, with a delicate aquiline nose. *Damn*, he thought warmly. *This won't do.* Fieldwork was so much less complicated with male interns.

Eric strode toward the woman, who was attempting to consolidate items from one case into another.

"Miss Winship? Stacey?" Eric offered his hand.

She looked up, distracted, then smiled. Eric was utterly disarmed.

"Afraid not," she replied, extending her hand. Eric couldn't help but notice that her green eyes danced as they looked into his.

Just then, a woman shouted shrilly from across the terminal, "Dr. Bolton? Dr. Bolton! Is that you?"

He raised his hand in acknowledgment—then froze, his eyes wide, as a small figure charged toward him, elbowing everyone in her path.

Eric turned back toward the lithe stranger. "Sorry," he mumbled, thinking to himself, *You have no idea.* "My mistake." He drew in a deep breath and turned in the direction of what could only be his new assistant.

2.

While they waited by the luggage carousel, Eric grew increasingly grim as Stacey continued her monologue with narcissistic zeal.

"And the food—the food they served was perfectly dreadful," she droned. "Overcooked sole and undercooked broccoli—I don't even know what was pretending to be risotto."

Eric smiled tersely. This was going to be a very long three months. Did this young woman ever stop nattering? And in such strident, nasal tones. He had met so many just like her at Cornell. Spoiled, privileged, self-absorbed.

"And the movie. Would you believe the in-flight movie was *Elsa's Legacy*? After what happened to Joy Adamson? I mean, really."

Eric interrupted, "I don't think it was ever really proved whether the lions killed her—or whether it was poachers, and the lions, well . . ."

Stacey seemed impervious to conversational nuance. "Oh, there's another bag!"

Eric dutifully pointed to yet more Louis Vuitton luggage, which the porter tugged off the line and added to the growing pile. What did this woman think she was embarking on—a grand tour? More like one of those gawkers who stayed at Lodge at Damara, not a field intern.

Even the way she was dressed reminded Eric of garden parties, the kind his mum would throw in London. Floral patterned chemise, cashmere sweater, matching heels and bag.

Her dark hair was swept up in a chignon. He cast another sideways look of concern, which she noted askance.

"Don't worry. I like to look nice when I travel. I packed for the outback. Cleaned out the entire Patagonia catalog." She patted his shoulder. "Wait'll you see."

Outback? Eric raised his eyebrows. Just exactly what continent did she think she was on?

Without replying, he scanned the baggage area for that attractive blonde, wondering what business she might have in Windhoek. The cameras alone probably indicated a professional visit. If only she and not—*No, focus, Eric.*

"There it is," Stacey squealed. "The last one!"

Eric again pointed, and when the porter retrieved the bag and looked to him for orders, Eric couldn't help shaking his head and rolling his eyes slightly. The porter grinned, obviously delighted at the prospect of a substantial tip.

"You had best freshen up here while we're loading the Rover," Eric advised. "The drive to camp is about three hours, and that's if all goes well."

"This is all so exciting. Do I have time to visit the gift store? I can't remember whether I packed my gum or left it. Do we have water in the car—or do I need to buy some? I do hope they have Evian."

"We never travel anywhere without water, Stacey. Ever. But if you would like some, some Evian for the trip, please, pick up all you think you'll need."

Stacey hurried off, her heels clicking against the linoleum. A group of tourists huddled disconsolately nearby, reminding Eric of nothing more than a small herd of wildebeests, who always looked doleful. Apparently, the luxurious bus to luxurious Lodge at Damara had been delayed. Eric snorted. Big-box tourism. No corner of the earth too remote, too inaccessible for these insatiable, wealthy hordes.

Just then, a deep shout, accompanied by the wave of a creamy-white cowboy hat. "Clare! Over here!" It was Daniel Sypher, entrepreneurial lord of Lodge at Damara, the symbol of everything Eric detested. And whom was he striding toward but the leggy blonde. Daniel swept into a theatrical bow before her, then took her arm. Eric winced in revulsion. He watched as Daniel signaled her trunk to an assistant dressed in the Lodge uniform of an emerald-green polo shirt and khaki shorts. With his hand firmly on her back, Daniel hurried her out of the terminal.

Eric shrugged. What was it to him that Daniel had arranged to meet the woman? That she was leaving with him? Funny, though, how Daniel didn't seem to notice the sorry gaggle of Lodge customers in his hurry to get her into his chauffeured limo. Obviously, the man had his priorities. Eric realized he probably would have done the same. *Damn, that woman was attractive.*

"Ready!" Stacey chirped, beaming, her arms filled with bags of bottled water, magazines, gum, and goodness knows what else. "What an adventure! I can't wait. How long did you say the drive would be?"

Eric wondered whether there was enough room left in the Rover—or whether he might have to lash Stacey and her purchases to the top of the cab, along with the jerry cans of water and petrol.

"Three hours." Eric was already weary of her inattentive chatter. "Take what you think you might need for the trip. I'll stash the rest."

After watching in barely contained alarm as Stacey performed an extended and intensive triage, he grabbed the array of bags and squished them behind one of the spare tires.

"Buckle up, Stacey. We've got a bit of road ahead." Then Eric jammed his key into the ignition, threw the Rover into reverse, and turned the radio up as loud as he could bear.

They sped past the concrete vastness of Windhoek, Namibia's capital, heading north on a two-lane highway. Either side stretched into vast, unbroken grasslands. Occasionally, they would glimpse a cinderblock structure near the side of the road. These unadorned boxes were the homes of the more westernized residents. Often, goats milled about nearby. Otherwise, little else but clear, blue sky and rolling plains the color of dry bones.

The radio blasted pop tunes, and Eric clutched the steering wheel, frowning as he noticed Stacey sigh, then root about in her handbag for something. An Evian spritzer, Eric noted wryly. He wondered what Stacey would make of the local Himba, who never bathed in their lives, water being such a precious resource in this arid, pitiless land. Instead, they coated their bodies in red basaltic earth mixed with fat. Even their simple garments were cleaned by smoking them over a small fire. Stacey spritzed again. Eric frowned—again—and wondered what the Himba might make of her.

Ordinarily, Eric would have driven with the windows rolled halfway down. Never all the way, of course, since cobras had a way of launching themselves at passing vehicles. He liked the dry desert wind blowing through the Rover. He liked the thrum of his wheels against the blistering tarmac. He loved the solitude and the infinite vistas. That is, he usually did. Now he had a passenger, a newcomer, and an apparently fragile one at that. What was Grant thinking to have foisted this frivolous urbanite on him? She'd probably faint at the first sight of a baboon, much less a mamba. Or a rhino.

Eric glanced at Stacey, who had made a pillow of her sweater and was now sleeping, her mouth open, her head lolling to the side. He turned the radio down slightly. No response. Then a little more. Then off. That was good. It would be about two hours to Etosha, where he could buy his last petrol and give the Rover a final check. After that, they would head northwest, toward Damaraland and his base of operations, Rhino Camp.

Gradually, the scenery gave way to jagged mountains and scrubby, low, silvery vegetation graced by an occasional solitary tree. Eric marveled at Stacey's ability to sleep, even after such a long series of flights. More comatose than asleep, actually. He recalled the amazement he had felt during his first journey in this magical, inhospitable land. How he had taken everything in with a hunger he had never before experienced. A passion for this ancient, austere world that was more encompassing than any he had ever felt for a woman.

His thoughts drifted to the blonde at the airport. She and Daniel had a slight head start on them, thanks to Stacey's shopping excursion. He wondered whether the blonde was sleeping—or whether she, like he, was drinking in the enchantment of this alien environment. Whether a passion similar to his own was awakening within her.

3.

As Eric pulled onto the long gravel drive, he continued to wonder at Stacey's capacity for napping. She hadn't awakened, not once, since she first dozed off. Even the occasional jolting rut didn't seem to disturb her. When at last he pulled up to the Rhino Camp facility and turned off the Land Rover, she stirred, murmured something unintelligible, and snorted, but she still didn't wake. It wasn't until two caramel-and-white Jack Russell terriers flew from behind the main building, yapping hysterically at Eric's arrival and flinging themselves with enthusiastic abandon at the vehicle's sides that Stacey jerked wide-eyed from her slumber.

"Whaaa?" she asked in a drowsy panic. "What's going on?"

"Just Rhett and Scarlet. They're friendly. Happy to see us, that's all." Eric opened the door and climbed down. He then kneeled, giving the vortex of canine joy an energetic ear scrunching. "Aren't you, you rascals?"

Stacey, now fully awake, had shrunk to the farthest edge of her seat. "No one said anything about dogs."

Eric paused in clear bafflement. If a pair of fifteen-pound dogs alarmed her, just how might Stacey react to the local apex predators, particularly the lions and leopards?

"Stacey, the dogs won't harm you. You'll learn to appreciate them as you get used to the wildlife here." Eric thought it best not to mention any specifics, like the time the dogs' barking had alerted them to a mamba curled around the outdoor showerhead. Or the old lion who had ventured into camp, starving and desperate. Or the venomous scorpions occasion-ally scuttling across beams in the dining room. Or—Eric imag-ined the countless times these lively canines had saved his and others' lives. "Just think of them as your private security guard. When they're wagging their tails and leaping about like this, everything's fine. If they're both staring in the same direction, tails stiff, you'd best be on alert." Eric suppressed a chuckle as Stacey gasped. "I'll explain more later. Let's get this rig un-loaded and you settled in."

Eric leaned on the horn, giving it a couple of short blasts.

"Where is everybody? You'd think the dogs' racket would have let them know we're here."

He honked a few more times, shaking his head.

Soon, a short, solidly built employee dressed in khaki shorts and a bright orange T-shirt emerged from within the two-story cinderblock and wood structure. Stepping into the veranda's shade, he smiled, wiping his hands on a dishcloth, and waved. He then noticed the figure huddled against the passenger window and looked at Eric with concern. Eric shrugged, shooed the dogs off, and marched around the side of the car to extricate a most unwilling Stacey. Keeping a stern eye on the dogs, he led her toward the porch.

"Hosea, please meet my new, um, research assistant, Stacey Winship. Stacey, meet Hosea." The two nodded, smiling. "He and his wife, Zahara, take care of—run, actually—all of Rhino Camp's domestic operations. Household maintenance, clean-ing, cooking. I doubt we'd get much of anything done without them."

Hosea smiled even more broadly. "A pleasure, a pleasure, miss," he said, insistently pumping her hand. "Welcome to Rhino Camp, miss."

Tears welled in Stacey's eyes. "I thought Professor Grant liked me."

Startled by Stacey's reaction, Eric surveyed the camp where he'd lived for so many years with fresh eyes. Definitely underwhelming. The compound itself was nestled on a rise in a small canyon, entirely surrounded by a tall cyclone fencing, barely disguised by thorn bushes, all topped with coiled barbed wire. There were a few spindly acacia trees on the grounds, but not much else. A few outbuildings and spacious tent lodgings. The entire camp was the same dismal shade of grayish-brown sand.

"Hosea, is Pieter around?" Eric asked.

"No, Doctor Eric. He's out. Back for dinner. I think."

"Wonder why he didn't take the dogs. Unusual."

"Rhino mom and calf. Not far. Mr. Pieter, he worry the dogs—no manners. Scare mom and baby."

"Near, you say? Well, that's exciting. I wonder whether it's Flora. She'd have had a calf a few months back, if I'm not mistaken." He cast a dark look at the burgeoning truck. "But I'm afraid, Hosea, that leaves you and me to unload everything. Let's get Stacey out of the sun. Has Zahara prepared her room?" Hosea, shouldering one of the larger suitcases, replied that she had. "Good. Stacey, I'll give you a tour later. You'll be on the second floor. The first are the more public rooms. Some offices, the great room, the dining room, and kitchen. I'm sure Zahara has some lovely chilled lemonade waiting for us. Why don't we all go in and have a glass."

Just as Eric had anticipated, Zahara stood waiting for them, a pitcher of lemonade dewing on the long wooden table over which she presided. Once the proper introductions had been made and refreshment enjoyed, Eric left Stacey, while he and Hosea went to unburden the Land Rover of its many supplies and luggage collection.

After the third trip between the Jeep and the main building, not to mention the multiple sets of stairs scaled by both men, the two could finally rest.

Hosea shook his head disapprovingly, and softly ventured an opinion. "Doctor Eric, Miss Stacey, she belong at Lodge at Damara. Not Rhino Camp."

"I couldn't agree more, Hosea." Eric gazed across the vast plain toward the eastern mountain range, its foothills the site of that luxurious tourist-filled abomination. He imagined the blonde photographer, now ensconced in an air-conditioned villa, unpacking her delicate things, perhaps showering for dinner. Perhaps—he exhaled deeply—no, it simply would not do. Stacey was here, the blonde was there, and there wasn't a single thing he could do but try to make the best of it.

"I'm a bit tired from the drive, Hosea. Think I'll lie down for a while. Wake me at five? Earlier, if Pieter should show up. And thank you."

"You bet, Doctor Eric. Don't you worry about Mr. Pieter. He be fine." Hosea moved away a few steps and then turned, "Anything else wrong, Doctor Eric?"

"Nothing you or I can solve, thank you."

4.

Clare rested her chin on her hand and stared through the tinted glass as Namibia flew by. How she wished she could have made the trip on her own, stopping to take photos of the children herding goats, the red sands of the Kalahari sifting across the asphalt edges of the highway in delicate waves.

"It's quite impressive, really, if you have a taste for nothingness," Daniel offered. "Once we get to Lodge at Damara country, you'll see that the landscape becomes quite dramatic, especially at dawn and dusk. Those make the best photos for our website and brochures, as I'm sure you will recognize."

Clare nodded absently. Nothingness. What an odd way of seeing. Or, rather, not seeing. For Clare, even the play of light on a frozen sheet of lake was wondrous. And the possibilities of everythingness—of new sight—in this barren world. The interplay of infinite horizon and sky. But she wasn't here for that. Daniel had hired her to make money for him with her photos, not to produce art. Clare imagined plump, pink children cannonballing into plunge pools, their plump, pink parents beaming at them over cocktails from the shade of their individual—how was it the website described them—"villas." Those were the top-end accommodations, layered up the hillside, above the main lodge. She thought of goggle-eyed, chattering tourists rolling around the landscape in customized buses, eager for the sight of reclusive creatures not habituated to humankind. She recalled a video she had watched on You-

Tube, of a traffic jam in one of Kenya's big parks, involving what seemed to be hundreds of Jeeps and Land Rovers. A juvenile cheetah had leapt onto one vehicle's hood. The ensuing chaos, all screams and chatter and roaring engines. Perhaps the cheetah was simply curious. Perhaps it was looking for an easy meal but decided that the ambience was less than desirable. It lay there for quite a while, its long, tufted tail flicking occasionally—the only sign of slight irritation. And all the tourists in the hijacked vehicle, breathless with alarm. A cheetah! Now, had it been a leopard, things might have gotten exciting.

"Wait till you see the Lodge, Clare. Quite impressive, if I do say so." He leaned toward her. "The only five-star in Namibia. We have three bars, four restaurants, a spa, a bowling alley, a movie theater, and a twenty-four-hour fitness room that looks out over the valley. A glass wall with a row of Stairmasters and stationary bikes. So none of our guests ever have to choose between missing their exercise routine or missing, say, an elephant sighting."

"So they never have to leave the Lodge?" Clare was incredulous. "After coming all this way?"

"Exactly. Because we have a number of water holes nearby—man-made, of course—game is plentiful, especially in the dry season, our peak season. It's perfect. And we did get a moderate rating—no small achievement—despite considerable greasing of hands and a number of substantial donations."

"Moderate?"

"Yes," he chuckled absently. "Every tourist facility is rated on a level of high, moderate, or low. For danger. For danger from animals, to be more precise. We would have loved a low, because that really brings in the families, but what with our open safari vehicles, moderate was the best we could do. Most enjoy the 'adventure.'" Daniel used air quotes. "We simply advise parents to keep an eye on children. And, of course, no one sets foot or is driven outside the compound without a guide— and having signed an extensive waiver of liability."

Clare considered how these ratings might be devised. Moderate. Does a facility only lose a handful of guests every so often? Low. One a year? She felt a claustrophobic panic wash over her, sitting in the back of the limo with this garrulous, handsome man. Certainly, she hadn't imagined being confined to the Lodge's spacious, walled grounds for the three months of her contract. Or driven beyond its limits always in the company of Daniel and a driver—or a guide. Surely Daniel would expect her to have some time to explore the region on her own, to take photos that might enrich the world's understanding of Damaraland and its denizens and, in doing so, help to secure some reasonable future for its conservation. She looked at Daniel, his craggy, commanding profile. How confident he seemed in all this luxury. How sure of his place in the world. She was about to speak when she saw her own reflection in the window beyond him. Her eyes looked haunted. She turned away. Now wasn't the time to discuss her freedom.

"May I offer you some champagne? A little bubbly takes some of the tedium away on these drives."

It sounded rehearsed, almost automatic. How many times had Daniel eased "the tedium" just so? And with whom? Not that it was any of her business. Nor would it be.

But Daniel hadn't waited for an answer, having already unwrapped the cellophane of a lovely bottle of Louis Roederer Cristal. Unmistakable. *Tedium, shmedium*, Clare thought as she accepted the fluted glass.

"To a successful affiliation," Daniel proposed as he clinked a toast. He seemed so obviously delighted with himself—and with Clare. He grinned broadly as he took his first deep sip.

"Yes," Clare murmured. "Thank you. To Lodge at Damara." She leaned back into the buttery, soft leather and let the champagne's delicate bubbles tickle her nose. A girl could get used to this.

5.

Clare watched the basalt pan scroll by and sipped her champagne as she listened to Daniel expound on his many fiscal triumphs, Lodge at Damara being the latest. She had to admit his résumé was impressive if one only considered the bottom line, but to Clare it all had a soulless cast. Even the resort, with its ecotourism trappings, seemed calculated, almost exploitative. More about business and profit margins than about the environment. Then again, what was Clare to make of people who would fly halfway across the world, spending thousands upon thousands of dollars only to ogle at exotic creatures from the safety of some 4x4 Jeep or reinforced bus. Hardly the epitome of ecological commitment either. And wasn't she herself implicated in the whole endeavor, having flown halfway across the world and now in the employ of Mr. Daniel Sypher? Sipping expensive champagne in a limousine? Clare felt a jolt of self-recognition—and it wasn't pleasant.

"Everything all right, Clare?"

"Yes. Of course. I'm afraid I'm a bit tired, jet-lagged from the trip. Perhaps I'd better switch to water."

Daniel eagerly reached into the refrigerator. "Pellegrino or Perrier? Or would you prefer still? I think we have Tahiti."

"Still, please. I think I've had enough bubbles for one afternoon." She accepted the bottle gratefully. "Thank you. How soon do you think we'll arrive?"

"It shouldn't be long now. About twenty minutes or so. You might have noticed that we are gaining a little altitude. The Lodge is located on a magnificent hillside. Best site in the country, if I do say. Wait until you see it. Extraordinary."

Daniel certainly didn't seem given to understatement. If he thought she would be impressed, she undoubtedly would be.

And she was.

As the driver slowly negotiated a wide turn, the panorama of Lodge at Damara revealed itself to Clare. A red adobe wall almost twenty feet tall enclosed the area's perimeters. In the distance, she could see small structures dotting the hill. One massive building, four tiered stories high, hung suspended over a vast expanse on the south side of the compound. Its base formed the wall's continuation until it terminated with a cut in the adjoining cliff. As they approached, Clare gasped at the grandeur. Towering wrought iron gates, mounted with "Lodge at Damara" in grand script, swept open.

"Did you by any chance hire the set director from *Jurassic Park* for the entrance, Daniel?"

He laughed wholeheartedly. "Hadn't thought of it. Hope this place is luckier. And safer. But every bit the blockbuster."

A uniformed staff person stepped from a guardhouse and saluted as they passed. The huge gates swung shut behind them, and the limo edged up the hill past a large cluster of small, thatched huts on the north side of the drive.

"Guest cottages?" Clare asked.

Daniel chuckled. "Oh, Clare. Hardly. That's our staff 'village.'" Clare noted the air quotes again, much to her annoyance. Daniel proceeded unfazed. "They live there most of the year. Amazing, actually. Those family members who aren't directly employed at the Lodge make art and other handcrafts for sale. Cottage industry, you might say. We even offer tours, at a small charge, of course. Technically, guests never need to leave the grounds to have an authentic Namibian experience."

Authentically canned and packaged, Clare thought.

Sweeping up a winding curve, the car came to a stop in the broad circular driveway before the main entrance. Clare had seen less impressive airport terminals. Attendants dressed in khakis and green polo shirts rushed to open the limo's doors.

Beaming with salaried hospitality, the staff greeted Daniel and Clare as they emerged from the car.

Daniel turned to Clare and confided openly, "Best paid employees in Namibia." Then, even more loudly, he said, "See that Miss Rainbow-Dashell's things are properly arranged. Be especially careful with those camera bags." He then took her arm and hustled her into the lobby.

Yet again, Clare was astonished by the scale of everything. The vaulted ceiling reminded her of a great bird's arcing wing. Truly magnificent: all space and light. Soon, however, her eyes were assaulted by the assortment of antlers, horns, and striped, spotted, and golden hides decorating the walls. Clare shook her head in disgust. She walked past disquieting masks, propelled by Daniel's enthusiasm, past groupings of oversized leather furniture where guests relaxed with newspapers or each other. They came to a stand before a huge semi-circular window at the far end of the room.

"This is my pride and joy," Daniel exclaimed as he gestured out, beyond the vast window. "You see the water hole out there? And the native trees and shrubs? Built all of that. From nothing. Guests here can see the animals twenty-four hours a day, seven days a week from almost anywhere in the building. From where we are standing. From the restaurant. The bar. The infinity pool.

The gym. The spa. Not to mention the rooms. Nothing like it in the world."

Clare was indeed awed. She admired the clusters of gemsbok and Thomson's gazelle below, sipping daintily, ever alert.

Daniel, noting this, added, "Game's not very exciting during the day, of course. But in the mornings, evenings, and nights. Elephant. Lion. Even rhino. We keep the place pretty lit up. Animals have gotten quite used to it. Not that they have much choice given how dry it is around here."

As much as Clare was repelled by the idea, she could sense already the temptations of captivity. Of ease. A cold rush of claustrophobia raced through her. She felt dizzy and reached for Daniel's arm.

"There now, Clare. A little unsteady, eh? How selfish of me. You must be exhausted. Let me show you to your rooms."

He turned and snapped his fingers. Within a moment, two attendants materialized, all smiles and eagerness.

"Have Miss Rainbow-Dashell's bags been taken to her suite?" They nodded. "Good. Clare, I've taken the liberty of putting you on the third floor. You'll have a spectacular view. You'll also be close to my offices and penthouse on the fourth floor. The elevator is a bit of an inconvenience—too crowded— but at least it's fast. There you go." He pressed the button for 3. Clare noted that 4 was designated "Private. No public access." Daniel continued, "When you've recovered from your journey, you'll probably want to use the stairs. It's peak season now or I'd let you have one of the villas. Sorry about that. The private infinity pools were a real game changer. Booked solid."

"No worries, Daniel. I'm sure I'll be perfectly comfortable. At least I won't be housed in the 'village' and held accountable for any weaving or carving. And I'll be relatively protected from gawking guests wishing an authentic experience." She felt a ripple of pleasure at the dig.

"I doubt you've ever been protected from gawking, Clare," Daniel observed with a sly smile. "Ah—here we are. Just a few doors down. Room 307. I'll give you an hour or two to rest. Then join me for dinner. The tour can wait for tomorrow. Seven?"

Clare accepted, more automatically than enthusiastically. An important lesson had dawned on her: Daniel was a man accustomed to having his way. And Clare was accustomed to making her own choices. Closing the door, she sighed. She could put up with anything for a couple of months. After all, she had signed the contract. Anything? This gilded cage? This good-looking if imperious entrepreneur? Clearly she would have to adjust her expectations. And control her reactions. Perhaps these troubling thoughts were merely the result of travel fatigue after all. She did need a rest, and there were a couple hours before dinner, which apparently was a command performance.

Stretched out on the huge bed, Clare pulled the cashmere throw over her legs and closed her eyes. Images of her parents flooded her thoughts. She recalled when she and Timothy had paid them a visit to announce their engagement. Timothy, typically, had been extremely judgmental of just about every aspect of their alternative lifestyle. He could barely bring himself to articulate even their names, stumbling over "Trip" and "Rainbow" as if he were strangling.

On the drive from their home in Davis to her parents' farm in Sonoma, he had fussed, "Who in the world would call herself Rainbow—not even Emily Rainbow or Genevieve Rainbow—just Rainbow? And Trip—who in the world?"

"Timothy, please," Clare had responded. "We're talking

about my parents here. Theodore Bennett Dashell III, which may be perfectly acceptable in your university professor circle, was less than desirable at the Zen farm where my parents met."

Timothy had snorted and snapped his copy of the *New York Times Book Review* in front of his face.

Shortly after that trip, she'd caught Timothy having an affair. His professorial charm had blinded her to his reputation as a scoundrel and philanderer. But, mercifully, her vision cleared before the wedding.

With a pang, she also recalled the last trip she took to see her parents before coming to Namibia. She'd needed to tell them that her engagement to Timothy had ended and she'd committed herself to a photo shoot halfway across the world. With all her possessions crammed into the back of her battered Honda, she'd made the drive on the little two-lane highway to her childhood home, across Sonoma County, just north of San Francisco, through the rolling green hills and the redwood groves. Fatigued by jet lag, she could still hear the welcoming crunch of gravel under her tires, see the hand-painted wooden sign, "Elendil," always hanging somewhat off-kilter, symbolic of her parents' life together. She had passed the pond where she had spent so many happy hours as a child, her companions noble unicorns and tender dragons. Her childhood had been idyllic. So different from the rigid prep schools and finishing schools her parents had been subjected to.

She stared at the African masks and the thatched ceiling of her room. What was she thinking? To abandon that idyllic place for one of the world's most ancient, unforgiving deserts? For a photo gig in Namibia? She had never heard of Namibia until a month ago.

She smiled to recall her mother's pack of dogs galumphing and howling up to the car, their frantic barks announcing her arrival. Her mother had emerged from the old Victorian, shading her eyes, as beautiful as ever. Tall, thin, with a halo of silver curls. And the diaphanous gown she always wore. Her father, a great bear of a man, with a long graying ponytail and abundant beard, had lumbered out of the milking shed, wiping his hands on his overalls. Even lying in this bed across the world, Clare could feel being caught up in his arms and spun around.

Rainbow had served chamomile tea, steeped in an ornate sterling silver teapot, homemade oatmeal-raisin cookies heaped on a porcelain platter. Clare cherished the anachronisms of her parents' lives, the gentle collision of tie-dye and Meissen.

Turning to look out at the desert, Clare felt the heaviness in her heart. There had been no gentle way to break the news to them, so she'd just blurted it out. "The engagement is off. Timothy never really accepted me for who I am. Never really valued my work. Never wanted me to have a career. Never could promise not to . . ."

"That's a lot of nevers," Trip had observed softly. "You know, you always have us. You could stay here as long as you like. Forever even."

When Clare told them about Namibia, Trip's eyebrows knitted in perplexity. They were obviously crushed, the family circle unraveled so abruptly. She'd assured them it was only for three months. She needed to get away, earn some money.

"You have your trust fund, Clare. Go anywhere you wish, but you certainly don't need to earn money."

But for her it was a matter of honor that she carve out a life for herself as an independent professional. "I know. It's just something I need to do. Don't worry. I will be housed in luxury, quite safe from any ravening beasts—or philandering professors."

Trip had been silent. Then his booming laughter filled the room. The dogs, in sympathetic concert, started keening. The goats, even the chickens joined them. The cacophony was too much. Too silly. Absurd, really. Life was simply too wonderful for tears.

Clare had taken their hands. "I love you both so much. More than you can ever know. I won't be gone long. Promise."

6.

After enduring a formal, many-course dinner, she managed to escape to her room. She slept twelve hours, thanks in part to whatever magic pill Julia had given her when she'd dropped Clare at the San Francisco airport. She would miss Julia, the camaraderie of her classmates, and the freedom and joy of being a student, but this photo gig would be over soon. She'd go back to her life and her pursuit of a bachelor's degree. And she'd go back with a renewed commitment to stay away from men, especially professors.

She showered, surprised by the soft, heavy towels, and dressed, promising herself she'd unpack properly later. Her room was huge, bigger by far than her entire apartment had been. The decor was an *Architectural Digest* spread of exotic Africa: kilims on the floor, masks on the walls, furniture of some lovely, unusual wood. Large windows looked down on the pool and across the barren desert, stretching unbroken to the jagged horizon. To Clare, Lodge at Damara felt more like a space station on Mars.

She went in search of coffee, choosing the stairs over the elevator. No one was in the hall or on the stairs, and an eerie silence pervaded the place. In the lobby, a solitary African stood behind the reception counter. He greeted her in the clipped British accent she associated with India.

"Where is everyone?" Clare felt disoriented at being alone. Part of jet lag, she hoped.

"Most guests are out, miss. They'll be returning for cock-tails. May I order you coffee and muffins? On the veranda?" Clare gratefully accepted his offer.

She looked again at her watch, trying to calculate the time difference, but was pleased to have the solitude. She wandered through the spacious lobby, admiring the art and the rugs. The clerk looked up anxiously a few times, and she smiled. Somewhere beneath this floor, she could hear a buzz of activity, as if the place sat on a beehive. Probably laundry and food preparation.

The lobby opened onto a thatch-covered veranda and a pool, delicately balanced on the edge of the deck. Despite twelve hours of sleep, she still felt tired and stretched out on a lounge chair to finish her surprisingly delicious coffee and muffin. The encounter at the airport with the man she'd as-sumed was Daniel haunted her thoughts. He was—she searched for the word—handsome. But more. What was his name? Eric? He had substance behind his good looks. Clearly, he and Daniel would be acquainted, so Clare hoped she might meet him again. She dozed, her coffee cup tipping precariously in her hand.

"You're awake!" The booming voice jolted Clare, and she was alarmed to see her coffee splash onto the tile floor. "Thought you might sleep the entire day away. People do. Everyone reacts to the flight and time difference in their own way. Never bothers me."

"I've flown a lot, Daniel, a job hazard, but that was a long one." Clare swung her legs down and sat up straight.

"Well, tomorrow we can talk. Today just enjoy the place." Daniel sat down beside her, raised his hand, and snapped his fingers. A waiter materialized instantly and scurried off to fetch something. "I only drink the tea I have flown in from England. Try the swill they call tea here, and you'll understand. Tastes just what it is, a boiled bush. Awful stuff."

The waiter brought a tray with a china pot, two cups, sugar, and cream.

"Give me your cup. Now try this. This is from Harrods. A special blend made for me."

"But the coffee is fine," Clare protested. Reluctantly, she accepted the teacup.

"Coffee they can grow here. Well, not here. Can't grow a damn thing here, as you can see. But Tanzania, Uganda, they produce fine coffee. Took me an age to teach these people to make a decent pot. Not too quick on the uptake." He looked into the distance. "But loyal. Hard workers, if you keep on them."

Clare couldn't understand the unease she felt with this man. He had a big personality, but so did many of the professors and all the magazine editors with whom she'd worked. But this man had an almost indiscernible edge of danger, more than the threat of getting a poor grade or being fired from a project.

7.

D aniel assigned Clare a Jeep and driver to be always available. She needed to complete a form for each trip detailing destination, time out, expected time back, actual time back. She was perfectly fine with the procedure. And though Daniel said it was for her protection, she suspected it also aided his control. Everything at the Lodge seemed under Daniel's control, a textbook case of micromanaging.

Her driver had kept his Himba name, Chioto. Clare liked the musicality of it. And it always struck her as strange that other drivers, clearly Himba, had taken English names: James or Derek or George. In the half dozen trips she'd gone on with Chioto, he'd pointed out the abandoned camps, now piles of rubble, where his relatives once lived before they'd been forced off their land by one of the senseless wars or the government or the game parks. Their land had gradually been taken over by the Daniels and the hordes of tourists their lodges attracted.

There were few Indigenous Africans, the land now peopled with a steady stream of safari groups, constantly arriving and departing. To assume a name of one's oppressors seemed wrong, as if the guides were now assimilated into the business of tourism much as the land and the animals had been. But as Chioto told her, the job paid well—a case of "if you can't beat 'em, join 'em." And the Himba certainly couldn't beat 'em.

This day, Clare and Chioto left before dawn, lunch basket

packed by the kitchen and tucked under the seat. Lunch was a touch of luxury Clare appreciated. Sandwiches, fruit, desserts, one thermos of coffee, and one of lemonade. They headed out the gate in the open Jeep as a hint of daylight etched the far mountains with pale pinks and blues. The dunes around them were visible only by degree of shadow, the crests capturing a few rays of moon and sunlight. The sparse vegetation jutted up like black skeletons. Dunes and mountains now razor-sharp would become dusty and flat when the sun stoked his furnaces. But in this blessed cool, Chioto and Clare wore jackets as they bounced along in silence. Of his many fine qualities, his ability to be silent was the one Clare admired most. No lectures, no advice, no bragging, no flirting.

Chioto and all the trackers had a most uncanny ability to see in near darkness—a heap of brush morphed into a resting lion; a leaf moving betrayed a hyena slinking by. Above, what at first appeared to be a cluster of leaves unfolded as a contemplative buzzard stretching a wing. For Chioto, this was just home, no mystery, little magic. Animals, which tourists spent thousands of dollars to view, were simply denizens of his neighborhood.

Even so, all the trackers respected the danger. All had had friends or relatives or knew someone who had been killed in lion attacks or elephant rampages. Chioto's face was watchful, his body tensed for action. Clare trusted him with her life. They were following a dusty road across the desert, headed for a water hole Chioto thought might still have water. Park managers created some of these water holes and shut off the water when the area became overgrazed, encouraging the herbivores to move on.

As the moon and sun exchanged watch, the sky lightened

and the shadows were sucked up, Chioto stopped the Jeep. "Look, miss, in that tree." He pointed. But it took some time for Clare's eyes to adjust.

"Oh!" She gasped. In an acacia tree, barely distinguishable from the branches, sat a leopard, serenely surveying his kingdom. She grabbed her field glasses. At the movement, he turned ever so slightly to look directly into the lens, through her, beyond her, clearly unimpressed, uninterested.

"Can we get closer?" She tried to judge the distance and doubted even her 500mm lens would bring the cat in close enough for a decent photo.

"Some, miss. Not much. Mr. Daniel says to keep you safe." Chioto started the Jeep and crept closer to the tree.

"This is close as possible, miss. He runs we get too close."

Clare could see the worry on Chioto's face. If he didn't bring her back safely, he would undoubtedly lose his job, and it was likely his wages supported at least one family.

"It'll be okay, Chioto. I promise to be careful." She got out of the Jeep to set up her tripod, though she was wise enough to keep the Jeep between her and the leopard. Her lens would need to be wide open to capture every particle of available light. It was not possible to hand hold it in these low-light conditions.

She affixed the Nikon to the tripod, attached the 500mm telephoto lens, and focused on the cat. Again, he seemed to sense her attention and looked right down the barrel of her camera. She suddenly felt embarrassed, a paparazzo, intruding on this dignified beast. But she clicked the shutter. It seemed an obscene noise—even the insects ceased chattering. The cat merely squinted, looking disdainfully away. The photos she'd taken were good, however. But were they really any better than any photo already in *National Geographic*? Had she in any way captured the danger, the majesty, coiled in this leopard?

Just as she looked back into the viewfinder, the cat slipped like quicksilver down the tree. Her motor drive captured six frames per second, freezing him in time and space.

"Miss! In the Jeep! Quick!" Chioto was pulling her arm, grabbing the tripod, and nearly tipping the camera into the sand.

"Stop it, Chioto! I've got it." Clare's heart was pounding as she looked up to see the cat at the bottom of the tree. She put the camera under her arm and jumped in as Chioto sped off. *One of these photos*, she thought, *one will capture the wildness.*

8.

hree days later, Clare presented a computer slide show to Daniel. "This is good. Yeah, I can use this," he gloated when the leopard appeared, slipping down the tree trunk.

Clare continued on for another fifteen slides before he stopped her at a swimming pool photo.

"And this, this is great. Exactly what I'm looking for." He squinted and appeared mentally to be designing his brochure.

The photo was good. She'd shot it at daybreak, lying on her stomach. The turquoise pool dissolving into the sand and sky, all pale pastels, bleeding one into the other like a watercolor. But it was hardly an Africa shot, not really distinguishable from any scene in any desert. Might as well be Las Vegas. She was surprised he liked it.

"These are good." He looked at her intently and smiled. "Of course they're good. You've got talent." He placed his hand on her arm. "That's why you're here."

She'd read somewhere that touching a person's arm was the most acceptable, least sexual show of affection. But his hand lingered. And it didn't feel acceptable. And it did feel sexual.

"It's just, well, I need more guests in the photos. You know, amazed looks on their faces as they watch a lion from one of our vehicles. Maybe a couple shots of the staff serving a meal, or those fancy drinks they seemed so fond of. Happy smiles, that sort of thing. Like that!" He pointed at the pool where a dozen guests lounged in bathing suits watching an elephant below stroll by with her youngster.

"Okay, but it'll be pretty tame," she replied uncomfortably. "Like a zoo. Not the *Come see the real Africa* that I thought you wanted."

He pursed his lips and looked down for a minute. "Our guests—how do I put it—they want wild. They do not want danger. They pay me a lot of money for that illusion."

"Delusion."

Daniel's look hardened. "Delusion? Perhaps. But since it's my lodge, my brochure, my money paying you, I'd like the photos done my way." He stood up. "How about another try? Say Saturday? That'll give you a week."

Clare watched him walk away. Broad shoulders, slim hips, his dark hair a bit long but meticulously coifed to highlight the silver at his temples. His clothing was pure safari but crisp and pressed. And always, his crocodile leather cowboy boots. He exuded confidence and authority. She thought the guests, particularly the ladies, must find him very appealing.

"My way or the highway, huh?" she mumbled. She sat back in her chair and looked out at the pool, the waiters delivering elaborate fruit cocktails, complete with tiny paper umbrellas. What had she gotten herself into? All her previous work was to bring back photos of birds and reptiles and beasts. Dangerous and difficult work. Getting more difficult with each year. But this job felt like utter nonsense. She studied a bald man in a lounge chair, his drink resting securely atop an enormous belly. She shot the picture, then looked into the screen. "Excellent," she chuckled.

The photo appeared to be of a small bald dune, a larger dune with a drink holder atop the blue pool, and more authentic Namibian dunes in the background. "Definitely a brochure shot. Oh, Lord."

The next few days Clare spent at the Lodge shooting photos of happy staff serving happy meals to happy guests.

Daniel had built a water hole, so photos of elephants, zebras, even lions were relatively easy to get. Was there really any need to leave the Lodge, she wondered. She was finding it difficult to make herself believe she was here in Namibia, that the leopard was real, that he was in fact dangerous. She couldn't shake the feeling that this was a Hollywood set, like the old westerns where towns were fake fronts braced by 2x4s.

As requested, Clare accompanied the guests on their outings in Lodge at Damara Land Rovers, Disney contraptions with tiered seating, accommodating up to fifteen tourists. Safely. Everything was safe. Lions, if they looked up at all, seemed to have concluded long ago that these treats-in-a-can were impossible to access.

Daniel was pleased with the photos, even snickering at the chubby tummy photo. "These are good. You're on the right track now." He slipped the cursor back and forth through the slide show.

Clare had worked with many editors. They each had a vision of the brochure, the article, or the advertisement they wanted. Her work was to interpret that vision, which was always nebulous even in their own minds, and produce a photo to fit it. *Perfect lion. Yes. But not exactly the lion I had in mind.* It was frustrating work.

Daniel rejected photos of animals that looked too wild, too dangerous. He rejected others because the animals weren't wild enough.

"You don't have a rhino." He leaned back in his chair, contemplating the ceiling. "I'm going to take you myself tomorrow. We'll find us a rhino."

"Okay," Clare replied. "Should I alert Chioto to have the Jeep ready?"

"Nah, don't need him." He stood, smiling up and down at Clare. "Three's a crowd."

9.

At daybreak, they left. Clare was relieved to see the picnic basket tucked in the back. Daniel looked every bit the Ralph Lauren safari explorer—except for the cowboy hat and boots. Clare wished Chioto were coming along.

Once on the dusty road, Clare felt a bit more comfortable. Daniel appeared competent. In an hour, they encountered a herd of oryx, grazing peacefully. With their single, long spiral horns, Clare grinned at a vision of them all painted in pastels like My Little Pony characters.

Clare shrieked in alarm when Daniel suddenly drove straight at them.

"Watch 'em run!" He had the gleeful look of a child chasing pigeons. "Get your camera ready."

Careening in the Jeep, Clare had to shoot at her fastest shutter speed. As the spooked oryx abandoned their lunch and ran, she prayed she'd get one usable frame of these mystical unicorns with their long tails flowing. They galloped effortlessly, as if not on the cobbled ground at all but sailing above it. Then they were gone.

"Wahoo! Sometimes this place is just like Texas, and I'm a cowboy again."

Clare couldn't invent a suitable response. She doubted he'd ever been a cowboy, and that certainly was not the word she'd choose to describe his behavior. They sat in silence for the next couple hours, driving farther into the desert.

"The water hole I'm headed for is near that ridge, but let's eat here." He had a way of issuing orders even if they were couched as suggestions. He maneuvered the Jeep into the shade of an acacia tree and pulled out a blanket and the basket.

Clare felt uneasy at the sight of the blanket. She and Chioto always ate in the Jeep. But her stomach overruled apprehension.

The kitchen had supplied Daniel with a picnic far more sumptuous than the ones she and Chioto usually enjoyed. Clare watched him pull out package after jar after bottle like a magician from a top hat, half expecting a live rabbit as the finale.

"Oh, my!" Clare knelt beside Daniel on the blanket and was amazed and delighted as she inspected the bounty. Pâté, pickled crab apples, cheeses she'd only seen in France. Crackers, olives, jams, rolls, butter cookies like edible art, exotic fruit.

"Allow me." Daniel popped the champagne cork and poured them both a glass. "To your health. To your beauty. To our success." With studied nonchalance, he brushed her cheek with his fingertips.

She stiffened, imperceptibly she hoped, then clinked her glass to his. "To Africa, to elephants, to rhinos, long may they roam."

A brief shadow cut across his face. "Yes, to the rhino." He sipped champagne and surveyed the desert around them. "You're new here. I don't know what you've heard or read, but I've been in Namibia for nearly twenty years, and I can tell you this: the country and the rhino and the elephant are better off since I, and other men like me, arrived and tourism boomed. The Himba slaughtered the beasts because they were a pest to the ten scraggly-assed goats they kept or because the elephants trampled their miserable gardens. Or because they could get money from the tusks or horns of either beast." He opened a jar of tapenade, casually spread it on a cracker, and held it to her lips. Clare turned her face, then took the cracker with her fingers.

"Men like me came and built lodges to attract tourists, and then the villagers realized money came easier leaving the rhinos and elephants alone. Sometimes they can't get it through their thick skulls that people will pay big money just to look at the animals, but when they start getting paychecks, then they understand." He had rearranged a few jars so as to sit closer to Clare, his shoulder nearly touching hers. She moved, busying herself with plates and silverware.

After getting a few inches from Daniel, she ventured, "But they've had to give up their way of life." She looked up at him, felt his strength and confidence. "Most men haven't waited tables, but it's awful, an awful job. Doing anything with or for rich people who think they've paid for you, that's demeaning."

"Right," he said, with an angry, sarcastic edge. "More demeaning than watching your family starve because this land won't support agriculture? These poor bastards were shipped out here years ago because the Germans and Brits thought it was cheaper than wasting all those bullets shooting them." He turned to face her. "Can you hear me? This land is only suitable for the very few animals that can live without water for days and eat shrubs, poisonous shrubs. And for very rich tourists!"

Clare recoiled. "Europeans and Americans come over here for amusement, because we can, because we have enough money. Just to pester the animals. Doesn't that seem a bit bizarre?"

"No! It does not seem bizarre because if we weren't here,

the Asians and the Arabs would wipe the rhinos and elephants off the face of the earth for their horns, their tusks. What is it that you can't understand?"

"Tourism is the only solution to poaching? And aren't we changing the animals? Just our being here, isn't that changing them?"

Daniel squinted suspiciously at her. "Have you been talking to that nutcase at Rhino Camp?"

"No, what nutcase?"

"I saw you talking to him at the airport when you first arrived. Clare, he's nuts. He can be here studying rhino, but no one else is allowed. And for the record, we follow the rules he chiseled into stone when we take groups out. How close we get to the rhino, whether we're upwind, or it's a pregnant female, and so on for thirty pages. Does that satisfy him? Nope. The only thing that would satisfy him is our handing over the country to him. Of course he doesn't have a bean to pay the villagers to be park rangers so they'll protect the animals. But he doesn't credit us for that."

"Let's stop arguing. Ruins my appetite. You're right. I haven't read enough to have an informed opinion. And you certainly have more experience." She couldn't decide if he was a passionate conservationist or a fantastic salesman—or both. That he was passionate, she found appealing. Holding her glass up for a refill, she gazed into his eyes, dark as midnight velvet. "Let's do justice to this picnic."

The champagne was delicious, buttery hints of toast plus grapes, everything she loved. The bubbles slipping down her throat reminded her that she and Timothy had celebrated their engagement not so long ago. But now she was on the opposite side of the planet.

"That's not the look I hoped the wine would inspire." Daniel gazed at her, his eyebrows raised in question.

"No, no, it's lovely." She sampled the cheese and sardines. "Eat! You have to stay sober to drive."

"You're right. Traffic's a nightmare out here. Look, there's a gridlock of termites." He leaned against the tree, stretching his long legs, grinning widely, king of all he could see.

"Quite the boots."

"Handmade. Genuine saltwater crocodile. See the yellow? It's a juvenile. Not that easy to come by."

"*Was* a juvenile. And, yes, I've heard crocs, especially the yellow ones, get irritable when someone skins them."

Daniel topped off their glasses and leaned his head back. "In Texas, we might call you a bunny hugger."

"That where you're from?" He had barely taken a bite, but Clare was starving as usual. She attempted to keep herself in check, nibbling delicately at crackers, though she could easily devour the entire feast.

"Yes, ma'am, born and bred." Finally, he ate a couple crackers and a few of the tiny apples. "Miss a few things. Have to say, though, Namibia comes close to looking like a lot of Texas."

"So how'd you get here?"

"I like a woman with a healthy appetite. Want some tea with that cookie? Don't know how you keep that girlish figure." Daniel pulled a thermos from the basket and poured tea in the tin cups.

"I know. I love food. Thank God, I'm blessed with good genes. But that's some picnic they gave you."

"They didn't *give* me anything. They may have packed it, but it's all bought and paid for by me." He sipped his tea with an appreciative sigh, added a third sugar cube, and ate the remaining cookie. "They'd take it from me if they thought they'd get away with it." He smiled slyly. "But nothing at Lodge at Damara happens that I don't see. Nothing."

"Wow." Clare couldn't believe that was the most intelligent retort she could make. But the champagne had gone straight to her head. She wished she could say that he seemed somewhat paranoid, and really, would it matter if they took some food?

Her parents had occasionally hired help around the house and in the garden. No one stole anything because her parents paid so much no one ever wanted to leave. But it was possible Africans didn't have the cultural prohibition against taking things. Maybe what belonged to one belonged to the community. She understood that Daniel couldn't very well run a business on that premise.

"I read your bio online," he said. "Not married. Never married? Looking? Running?"

"You didn't answer my question," she stalled. "How'd you end up here?"

Obviously pleased with her interest, he smiled and settled back. "Well, I didn't exactly grow up in the Bush family compound. My dad took off, and my mom was useless, weak. At ten, I got tired of church folks' charity and wearing hand-me-downs. Always stressed that some kid would recognize my shirt used to be his. So I got a job shoveling shit out of barns and chicken coops. At sixteen, I was bucking hay bales to feed myself, my brother, and my mother. Soon as I graduated high school, I got out. Joined the military. They sent me to Saudi Arabia, and when they let loose of me, I flew with some buddies to Johannesburg. And I just never left Africa."

Clare couldn't even insert the obligatory "uh-huh" or "oh."

Clearly he had memorized this narrative and wasn't interested in any interruptions. But she thought it was better he talk than if she allowed her champagne brain to divulge too much of her own history.

When he finally finished with the Lodge at Damara portion of his story, she asked, "So, do you see your mom or brother? You ever go home?"

He looked sharply at her. "No. This is my home. I had to provide my own. This is it, my first and the last." He began packing up the food, expertly arranging things in the basket. "You look like a girl who's always had a home. And I suspect, a damn fine one."

"I was lucky to have loving parents who, indeed, provided a very fine life for me." Why did she feel embarrassed that she had it good? Doting parents, money, education. Clearly Daniel had had none of her advantages, though he was obviously wealthy now. She felt a mild sympathy toward him. Maybe this controlling exterior was just a reaction to his hard-luck childhood.

"Let's go find a rhino." She smiled up at him.

"Yes."

His look softened as he helped her load her gear into the Jeep. Gently, he held her by the waist before she could step up. He tucked a strand of hair behind her ear, and she felt his large belt buckle pressing against her. "Enough of the past. Now's what we got. And I couldn't ask for more attractive company."

A wave of panic washed over Clare and subsided only when he released her, apparently satisfied with his attempt at a romantic overture. And his display of dominance.

Daniel steered the Jeep back onto the dirt track, which took a bit of skill, as the ruts had worn deep from some long-ago rain. The sun beat on the roof as they headed toward the water hole. Clare was grateful Daniel's Jeep had air-condition-ing. Though it failed to lower the temperature much, at least she didn't feel her eyeballs baking into little green marbles as she sometimes did when out with Chioto. Luckily, conversa-tion was impossible over the engine and AC, and Clare enjoyed the quiet. Daniel was a good driver, intense and focused, a man on a mission, though taking in nothing more than the road ahead.

She, on the other hand, felt like a child transported to an-other world. A startled herd of zebras flashed by, their stripes fragmenting into an Escher drawing as they thundered away in unison. She could almost feel herself flowing beside them in that indiscernible pattern they followed. Chioto had told her these were Hartmann zebras, less shading between their stripes and their stripes narrower than those of their cousins to the east, the Burchell zebras.

As the herd veered away from the Jeep, a red oven of sand closed in behind them, and Clare felt an unearthly peacefulness settle on her. This land had been scrubbed by sand and fired by heat until only the essential remained. The clutter of her life in California now seemed almost impossible to return to.

"Stop here!" she shouted over the engine.

"For what?"

"A photo." She gestured to her camera.

He shrugged with the impatience of a man interrupted from his task but stopped the Jeep and got out. "I don't see anything." His arms wide, he turned in a circle. "Nothing. That's what you want to photograph, nothing? That's not what I'm paying you for. Why didn't you get the zebras?"

"I already have zebra shots." Clare climbed down, grateful to stretch her long legs. She walked a short way into the desert, surveying the undulating sand so reminiscent of waves petrified on a great red ocean.

"Okay, but make it snappy." Daniel walked in the opposite direction toward a mopane tree. "I'll be right back. Call of nature."

Stretching her arms over her head, she filled her lungs with the hot, dry air. It felt healing, as if it were cleansing mold and mildew. But unlike mild California with her soft, easy bosom to rest upon, Namibia was as happy as not to reduce her and every other creature to dust. The desert required hard-edged moxie. And Daniel had buckets of the stuff.

Affixing a polarizing filter, she spread a ground cloth on the hot sand, lay on her belly, and shut down the lens as narrow as it would go. She wanted the greatest possible depth of field, so a grain of sand on the far hill was as sharp as the one beneath her hand.

"My guests mostly know there will be sand in the desert." Daniel knelt beside her and settled his hand on the small of her back. Clare felt suddenly vulnerable. And as unreasonable as it seemed, she felt in danger. Using her motor drive, she fired twenty frames in rapid succession, then quickly moved to her feet. The landscape was unimportant now. This was a man who might not wait for an invitation.

"You're right. Let's keep going." She returned to the Jeep and packed her gear.

Daniel didn't move but stood studying her. She smiled and got in the Jeep, keeping her eyes down. Her heart pounded. She wished she had a better defense than the girlish don't-hurt-me smile. But he was like a wolf: direct eye contact equaled challenge. And she was certain Daniel did not tolerate challenges to his authority. Or to his desires.

Clare's thoughts, which earlier had roamed widely across the landscape and cavorted with the zebras, now closed in tight, circling her well-being. She would complete this project, collect her pay, and return to a life where she was in control. The academics, students and professors alike, were stuffed toy animals compared to this man. But when she glanced over at him, his chiseled jaw and flashing eyes, a sudden surge of arousal surprised and disgusted her. *Power is an aphrodisiac,* she reminded herself. One she was obviously vulnerable to.

For another hour they drove, until finally reaching the water hole. Clare was impressed he could find this small spot in the vastness of the desert. She stood beside him, watching as he scoured the ground for the large paddle prints of a rhino.

"Fresh lion pugmarks. Looks like a pride. Probably means the rhino skirted around." He looked out across the sand. "The rhino I'm hunting might have a baby, or so the genius at Rhino Camp says. *Warns,* I should say. She wouldn't risk a lion encounter with a baby in tow."

He headed back to the Jeep, leaving Clare to trot after him. "We'll drive down there, toward those two trees."

They stopped randomly and searched the horizon for the mother and baby. Daniel was obviously getting frustrated, looking at his watch, driving too fast over the swales. Clare clung to the grab bar to keep from bashing her head on the roof.

Just as they were about to turn back, Clare spotted them walking, a bullet-shaped speck on the valley floor with a small dot behind her, like a punctuation mark. The mother walked resolutely toward two euphorbia trees.

"Set up your tripod," Daniel instructed. "See what you can get with that big lens of yours."

Thanks for the tip, thought Clare wryly.

"Okay," she replied, "but they're too far. They're going to look like what they are, two dots, a big dot and a little dot. We need to get closer."

Daniel looked at his watch and then through the binoculars at the mother kicking up small puffs of red dust with each step. "We might be able to get upwind of her, force her to run back toward the water hole."

"You said she'd avoided it because lions were nearby. For God's sake, we don't want her in trouble just so we can take her portrait." Just then Clare felt, for the rhino's sake, that she had to calm down and handle Daniel diplomatically, make him think it was his idea to abort this trip. But she struggled to tamp down her outrage.

"Let me try the photo again." She swung the camera around on the tripod to frame the rhino, but even for this lens, she was too far. Clare studied her through the viewfinder, a mesmerizing force of nature, moving as if a treadmill were propelling her. The little one wandered off, a bit this way and that, inspecting the scenery on the journey, just as any child would do. But the mother never wavered, never waited. She marched purposefully ahead, leading with that great sweeping horn, intent on their survival.

"I think I got something." Clare unclipped her camera and folded the tripod.

Daniel scowled at her, then back at the rhinos, who were making impressive progress away from them.

"You sure?" he sounded doubtful. Resigned. "Okay, we'll go. I like to preside over dinner. The guests expect it." When they got in the Jeep, he turned to her, his eyes hardened. "Get me a usable photo of that rhino and her baby, understand?"

She swallowed an angry retort when she heard her father, Trip's, voice. *Pick your battles, Clare. You can't win 'em all.*

"Understood," she replied.

Daniel sulked the entire drive back, though it didn't much matter, as conversation was impossible. It was hardly her fault he couldn't have acted the cowboy and lassoed the rhino and her baby. And if it was, she was glad. Despite her prowess, that mom needed all her energy to find food and water for herself and her baby. She did not need to be caught up in Daniel's advertising campaign. Yet even with the black cloud of a man sitting beside her, Clare was able to soak in the natural beauty. The sun hung low in the sky, casting long shadows, and the desert that had seemed so flat was now an etching in gold and black. How could such a stark landscape feel like home to a girl from lush northern California?

When they arrived at the Lodge, the garage staff rushed to attend to Daniel, though they seemed wary to Clare. He barely turned off the Jeep before exiting, leaving her still sitting there.

"See you at dinner," he threw over his shoulder. "Six o'clock. Sharp."

"Bali, Sahib," she muttered to his back. Chioto materialized at her side to help unload and carry her gear. Though she could manage, she felt the need for a pleasant soul to walk with.

Chioto deposited her bags with the porter, and she went to her room. The shower, an octagonal tower constructed to give the illusion of a cave, was divine, but Clare rinsed off quickly and wrapped herself in one of the impossibly thick towels. The whole place was a mirage.

The clinking of glasses and laughter drifted up from the patio. Cocktail hour. She was in serious need of a cocktail after this day and dressed hurriedly into the only fancy outfit she had brought. The indigo silk sheath accented her blonde hair and complemented her shapely legs. She fastened Nona's pearls around her neck and winked at herself in the mirror. *I can handle this. I can handle him. I hope.*

Downstairs, the staff bustled through the lobby with trays of drinks and hors d'oeuvres. She admired their grace and ease. They seemed to possess the ability to become invisible—a thought that unnerved her momentarily.

Instead of joining the guests, she waylaid a server with a tray of what seemed to be a fine Meursault and another server with crab cakes. The events of the day still had a hold over her, and she needed a moment before switching on her social self, always a struggle for her rather introverted nature.

The central room of the Lodge was empty except for an elderly couple who sat reading in the deep armchairs, cups of tea on the brass tables beside them. Congolese masks adorned the walls and were lit from beneath, lending them an even more frightening countenance. Exactly what the carver intended. Europeans may use these as decor, but the Africans imbued them with life and power and danger. The masks appeared very much as if they could spring from the wall and thrust a spear clear through the ample bosom of the elderly lady sitting beneath. Clare took another sip of wine.

Her empty glass forced Clare out to the patio. Guests had apparently bonded over their adventures. They clustered like the antelope Clare had seen earlier, chatting and swapping tales. The setting sun cast an orange glow over the group, making the night even more festive. Tin Moroccan lights twinkled above, and candles glowed on tables by the pool. Clare hoisted another glass from a tray, this one a rum concoction, and prayed Daniel would announce dinner before she landed face-first in the pool.

A new, jolly Daniel now wearing a white dinner jacket was weaving amongst the guests shaking a hand, kissing a cheek. He was captain of this ship sailing on the ocean of sand. Eventually, he sidled up to her. "You're looking refreshed."

"Refreshed? That's good, I guess."

"Well, you look a lot more than that." He ran his fingers over her shoulder. "You got some color. I think Namibia becomes you. Hope you had a good day out there. With me, I mean. Saw a lot, didn't we?" He rocked back on his heels, smiling at her and surveying the scene in front of him.

Clare arranged a suitable look on her face but couldn't quite manage to keep the confusion out of her eyes. Had he altogether forgotten his temper tantrum about the rhino? His threat that she better get their photo, or else? Perhaps, she concluded, he actually believed this Fantasy Island thing he'd created here, safe from the lions and hyenas and Africans. A kingdom where he could be whatever he wanted whenever he wanted.

"Interesting day, yes," she answered, quickly changing topics, "and what a beautiful evening."

"Oh," he said, leering at her, "the evening's barely begun. I've put you beside me for dinner." He whispered this last comment in her ear as though afraid of offending a captain of industry or some other royal who had been promised a seat at the captain's table.

She rummaged in her fuzzy brain for words. "That's good. I'll have to make an early night of it, though. Afraid—well, long day."

He frowned, his old self slipping back, then launched off to join a welcoming group of well-heeled guests.

10.

On the day of Eric's return and Stacey's arrival, Pieter Van Alstyne leaned forward in the Jeep and rubbed his tired eyes, blinking in disbelief. There in the shimmering distance was the object of over a month's searching and speculation. Flora, a mature black rhino, whom Eric had first noted as pregnant. And a tiny calf, barely visible, at her side.

The seasoned Afrikaaner knew he had to content himself with only a sighting from afar this late in the day. He couldn't risk spooking the new mother—or provoking her.

The two were ambling purposefully northwestward, toward a water hole, Pieter was sure, as rhinos prefer to drink at night or in the cool of early morning. He estimated their position and tapped the coordinates into his GPS. As he did so he smiled, his leathered face wrinkling as he recalled sleepless vigils near other water holes in Kruger and Tsavo, the squealing and snorting carrying on for hours in the darkness. Such was the rhinos' delight at this precious substance. Even the elephants joined in the celebratory racket, rumbling and trumpeting. Evidently, Flora felt confident enough to bring her baby along for an evening dip and perhaps some company.

He wondered where Flora had kept the calf hidden for so long. Probably in some thicket of euphorbia or thorns, hiding the vulnerable calf to the ever-seeking eyes of lions and hyenas. Not that many would dare take on a mother rhino. There were far easier, less potentially fatal meals to be had. A young gemsbok or a debilitated wildebeest would satisfy any local predator. And that, in the scheme of things, was fine with Pieter.

He marveled at the silvery dots, one large, one tiny as they glided along the horizon of the flat, barren pan in the deepening crimson light. The grace of these magnificent giants. As if they were floating rather than navigating the rocky, cobbled terrain. Pieter sighed as they receded into nothingness, and then he climbed into the Land Rover to head back to camp.

IT WAS QUITE late before Pieter returned. Zahara and Hosea were just finishing with the dishes. Stacey had already retired for the evening. But Eric was up, concerned for his friend. Excited about what might have kept him out so long.

The dogs announced Pieter's arrival with their customary enthusiasm. Eric bounded onto the veranda and down the steps.

"We'd begun to worry, old chap. No good tooling about in the dark by yourself, you know."

"Yes, Eric. Yes, I know." Pieter shook his head in mock contrition but kept breaking into a grin. He couldn't hide his exhilaration.

Eric stared into his face, its craggy shadows deepened from porch floodlights. "What is it, Pieter? Rhino?"

"Better than rhino."

Eric tipped his head, puzzling.

Pieter burst out laughing. "Rhinos, my friend. Rhinos. Flora and her calf." He punched Eric's arm in gleeful exuberance. "Only two hours' drive. North, near the rimrock. She's done a fine job keeping herself hidden from us, hasn't she?"

"Wonderful news! Extraordinary. We'll get an early start tomorrow." Eric clasped his friend's shoulder. "Hopefully, we can get close enough for some photos to be able to sex the calf. But you must be famished. Let's get you some dinner. Zahara!"

Eric beamed at his friend slurping down the delicious stew Zahara set before him. Both men were obviously consumed with excitement over the find. They had been looking for Flora and more tangible evidence of her long pregnancy for well over a month. Eric had estimated her at almost fourteen months at last sighting. Then she seemed to have disappeared from the bleak face of Damaraland. Of course Eric was concerned for her welfare. So many dangers in this harsh world. And any time a calf was born to this most precarious species there was cause for immense hope. So many had been decimated by the recent decades of poaching that had claimed over 90 percent of their former numbers.

"Well, what about the new girl?" Pieter asked in between bites. "Will she make it?"

"I have my doubts, to be honest." Eric sighed. "No idea why Grant would have recommended her. Stacey's soft. Wealthy. And privileged. The luggage—I've never seen anything like it. Dear God!" He groaned at the day's unnerving revelations. "This woman should be studying, I don't know, polo ponies. Not rhino. I'm thinking family money. Namibia, land of mystery and glamour. Brangelina nonsense. The heavy hand of endowments, regardless of sense. Grant probably didn't even have a say."

Pieter shook his head, then paused. "Don't tell me she'll be going with us tomorrow."

"I'm afraid it's unavoidable. Maybe she'll enjoy the adventure so much that she may not want to leave the compound for a while." He winked.

Pieter seemed less than pleased. "Well, that's that, then."

"Quite so." But Eric couldn't hold back his overall glee. "And Pieter—congratulations! Can't wait to get a look at them. We'll leave no later than four thirty. I'll let Zahara know she can sleep in. Breakfast's on me."

II.

In the still cool of early morning darkness, Eric tapped on Stacey's door. "Up and at 'em, Stacey. We've got something special in store for everyone today. Real excitement." He heard a soft groan in response and the sound of Stacey flopping over under the covers. Then silence.

"Be down for breakfast in ten, you hear? Stacey?" Eric tapped again, more insistently. "If you're not, we're leaving without you!" He realized he was shouting.

"Okay, okay! Stop banging. I'll be down."

Eric had prepared a simple breakfast of porridge, eggs, bacon, toast, and orange juice. He'd packed a cooler full of sandwiches. He glanced at his watch, then at Pieter. No Stacey. The men began to eat in silence. Fifteen minutes later, they heard a muffled clumping on the stairs. Soon a very rumpled and swollen-eyed Stacey emerged and plopped down at the table.

"Espresso? Latte? I'll take anything," she flatly announced.

Pieter choked on a mouthful of toast.

"Afraid the barista is on break. Here you go." Eric reached over and filled her coffee cup, which she lifted wordlessly to her lips. He had to admit he preferred this groggy, more subdued version of his assistant.

When he saw her eyes were finally more than half-mast, Eric spoke. "Stacey, I'd like you to meet my longtime friend and associate, Pieter Van Alstyne, the most knowledgeable rhino man in Africa, if not the world. Pieter, Stacey Winship, my assistant for the next three months."

"A pleasure, miss." Pieter's tone indicated nothing of the sort.

Stacey mumbled something unintelligible in response, then slowly began to ladle porridge into her mouth. "This is disgusting," she pronounced. "Blechhh. Pass the toast?"

"Tomorrow there'll be croissants—promise." Eric couldn't contain himself as he passed the plate to her.

The men stole disbelieving glances at the young woman as she nibbled away. She was dressed entirely in spanking new Patagonia sportswear. Eric had never seen clothing with so many labels. Or in such an array of bright colors. He could only guess at the expense of the ensemble, what it might have enabled in terms of conservation efforts, however slight. What the woman's entire trip would have enabled. But there wasn't a thing he could do. Fitness gym chic, not fieldwork. Not Namibia. Probably scare a cape buffalo in that getup. Well, today at least, fashionista Stacey would stay in the Rover. A small consolation, but a consolation nevertheless.

"Eat up, Stacey. We've got to move out. Pieter found our new mother with her calf yesterday."

"Cows?" Stacey looked puzzled.

Pieter lifted his bushy eyebrows in alarm.

"The mother rhino and her baby," Eric corrected. "Pieter spotted them yesterday. We'll have to see if we can do as well today."

Stacey looked up from her plate and nodded, Eric wasn't sure at what.

"Off in ten, then," Eric announced as he rose from his seat.

He and Pieter left the table to load the Rover and do a quick mechanical check. Stacey sat at the table, a piece of half-eaten toast in one hand, her cheek cradled in the other, and began to drift off. "I'd like to order a buttery croissant and a foamy cappuccino," she muttered to a non-existent Starbuck barista.

It was still dark when the group departed, Stacey splayed against a cooler in the back seat, the two men up front.

Eric drove angled against the rising sun. Eventually, the gravel roads gave way to uneven tracks littered with rocks of every size imaginable. Each time they hit a rut, Stacey awoke with a snort but soon fell back to sleep.

"You're doing that on purpose, aren't you?" Pieter chuckled.

"Just don't like to waste petrol, that's all," Eric replied, steering for another hole.

They bumped and skidded and roared along, the black sky giving way to bluish gray. At last, Pieter signaled to Eric that they had arrived.

They were positioned on a small plateau overlooking a vast pan, dotted with dark-green euphorbia and lollipop-canopied mopane trees, all still in deep shadow. The morning air felt crisp, and all was quiet, waiting for the scorching day to come.

"I saw them last from over there." Pieter was pointing to a brushy area about a half mile away. "By my reckoning, she should be visiting the water hole we mapped last year."

"Let's drive on. I don't want to risk annoying our new mum, but I do want to get as close as possible."

"There's a dry riverbed down there she might be using. More cover. We could take a look."

Eric threw the truck into first gear and nosed down the hill.

They had only cruised along the riverbed for a few minutes when Pieter spotted a pile of what looked like semi-deflated footballs. Rhino spoor.

Eric stopped the Rover; then the two men stepped out, scanning their surroundings before approaching the fragrant mound. Perhaps because of their extreme nearsightedness, rhinos use dung as a way of identifying others, as well as marking territory. After eliminating, they often scuff and stomp repeatedly, coating their hind feet with the scent. It was obvious a number of animals had used this spot.

"Communal latrine—and fresh," Pieter observed, wrinkling his nose.

"You think it would be odd for Flora to contribute, the calf so new and all?"

"Not necessarily. Not with a water hole nearby."

The men fanned out, instinctively, in opposite directions, circling wider and wider as they sought fresh tracks. Especially certain fresh tracks.

"Unbelievable! It's her," Eric exclaimed, pointing toward the ground.

Pieter joined him. There, in the talcy sand, were the unmistakable three-toed tracks. Some, the size of dinner plates. Others, saucer sized. Side by side. Meandering, to be sure, but meandering with purpose toward what could only be the water hole nearby.

Pieter looked up expectantly. "Shall we leave the Rover and follow on foot, then?"

"No, I don't feel comfortable leaving Stacey for too long. Her first time out. Let's drive a bit farther."

Pieter shrugged. "I'll track them. You follow me."

He slowly made his way along the riverbed, pocked and ribboned, the Rover grinding slowly behind him. At one point, he lifted his right hand to signal Eric. He had seen something. The rhinos?

Eric watched breathlessly as Pieter scanned the desiccated trees and shrubs lining the riverbed. Was something lurking there, hidden in the sparsely dappled shadows? Lion? Leopard?

This last stop finally jolted Stacey from her slumbers.

"We there yet? What do you see?" She wiped the sleep from her eyes and began energetically spritzing Evian. "See anything? What is it?"

`Eric didn't care for the impatience in her tone. If there was any single quality the desert required, and the black rhino demanded, it was patience. And respect. And, from Eric's perspective, a kind of reverence.

"We drove all this way to look at sand and dead trees?" She leaned over the front seat and gave a huff, clearly disappointed.

"Don't know. Hush. Pieter's seen something."

Eric and Stacey peered from the cab as Pieter approached a branch overhanging the path and inspected it. Satisfied by the 45-degree angle at which the end had been severed, he waved them on.

They proceeded in the now rosy light, Pieter leading the way. Finally, he stopped and pointed to his left. Tracks, leading out of the riverbed. The difficulty would be getting the Rover out as well.

Eric scanned the bank disapprovingly and beckoned Pieter to join them. "I think we'll have to drive a bit farther. Flora is making this rather difficult, isn't she?"

Pieter nodded his agreement. "I'll follow the tracks a bit. Then wait for you."

Eric nursed the vehicle forward. He forced a smile as Stacey, who had joined him in the passenger seat, newly invigorated from her slumbers, began to chatter. Eric so wished he had packed cotton wool.

Finally, Eric spotted a passable opening in the bank and eased the Rover, lurching and scraping, onto higher ground. He was astonished to see Pieter kneeling beside a rock not a hundred yards to their left. Eric quickly shut off the ignition. Pieter's pose could mean only one thing. Caution.

He turned to Stacey as he opened the door. "You stay here. It's too dangerous."

"But I don't see anything," Stacey protested in a querulous whine. "I didn't come all—"

Eric cut her off. "You stay here, in the Rover." He was looking anxiously in Pieter's direction. "If it gets too hot, get out. Find shade. From the Rover. Leave a door open and stay near it. Just in case. Understood?"

Stacey scowled and crossed her arms. Her cheeks were flushed the same hot pink as the fitted shirt she wore.

Eric stepped from the vehicle, then carefully closed the door. What was it that Pieter saw? The plain seemed infinite horizon. Only parched, dwarfed vegetation adorned the vast expanse.

As he slowly made his way toward Pieter, Eric noted his focus. Taking a small cloth bag from his pocket, he gave it a gentle shake. The talc drifted away from the direction of Pieter's gaze. Good. Both men were downwind. Eric kept himself low and moved with cautious deliberation until he reached his friend, then crouched beside him.

"There," Pieter mouthed, tipping his chin slightly ahead. Eric saw nothing. He waited. Then, to his amazement, Flora, rising as if from the earth, pulled by invisible strings. Then her little calf. The pair seemed to float along, oblivious to anything but their singular purpose. Water. And there was something magnificent in their obliviousness, in their purposefulness.

For who or what would challenge these undisputed rulers? These glorious giants who reckoned little beyond their own strength and will. For millions upon millions of years, their ancestors had reigned supreme over this desolate kingdom.

The men knew that, even downwind, they couldn't risk entering the mother rhino's forty-yard bubble of sight. Nor could they risk an alarm sounded by the watchful oxpeckers riding along Flora's broad, dusty back. Yet neither could they waste this precious opportunity.

Pieter gave a quick smile. "Stay low. If we move slowly, I think we can get close enough for some photos."

"Low? I'll crawl if I have to." And he meant it.

12.

Pieter and Eric cautiously made their way toward the watering hole, keeping a wary eye on the rhino pair. It wasn't easy. Each footstep had to be carefully calculated, avoiding the baseball-sized rocks cobbling the ground —all while trying to maintain the lowest possible silhouette against the horizon. The sun rose relentlessly. Soon, however, their efforts were rewarded.

The men watched breathlessly as Flora and her calf approached the water hole. She lifted her massive head, receptive to any audible danger, breathing in the scene as her ears rotated. A defensive measure, to be sure, but also grand, as if issuing a challenge to any foolish enough to threaten her and hers. Then she lowered her head and drank. The calf splashed about clumsily, never leaving her side, and soon began to nudge and suckle.

Eric was crouched behind a boulder about fifty yards away, snapping photo after photo. Half kneeling next to him, Pieter smiled and drew the biological symbol for female in the red basalt grit. Eric nodded assent. The calf was indeed a female. The best possible news. The more breeding cows, the more secure the population.

Eric turned to his friend and whispered, "Flossie? What do you think?"

"I was hoping for Fiona."

"Next one. Fiona. Promise."

The two men watched in wonder as the mother sipped,

then periodically scanned the periphery, smelling, listening. Satisfied that all was well, she would resume drinking, her paintbrush tail casually flicking away mopane flies. The hitch-hiking oxpeckers continued their ministrations on her back. After slaking her thirst, she slowly backed out of the shallow water's edge. Ever alert, she swiveled her tufted ears and nuzzled her infant, who greedily nursed in her mother's shade. The water hole slowly became alive with other denizens. A small band of ostriches paraded past, looking for all the world like high-stepping ballerinas. Springbok and Thomson's gazelles tiptoed to the life-giving water. Piebald crows bathed in feathery flurries. And Flora presided over it all.

Eric scarcely noticed the time passing but soon became aware of the baking heat. Flora, too, decided it was time to snack on a few nearby acacia branches before seeking the shelter of a thicket or tree. She gently butted the calf, and the two moved away from the water, not on the same path they had come.

For whatever reason, Flora had chosen another direction—toward Eric and Pieter. Not directly, but at an angle that if maintained would bring the pair dangerously close. The mood changed immediately. Eric and Pieter exchanged glances and began frantically to retrace their steps. The ease with which the rhino climbed the slope was astonishing. Such bulk. Such grace. And she was surely gaining on them. If either man lost his footing or so much as gasped, there was little doubt that Flora would charge. At thirty-plus miles an hour.

The men cast anxious looks for sheltering boulders, termite mounds, or trees. The landscape was despairingly barren. A stealthy retreat anticipating the rhinos' direction was their only hope.

Suddenly, a savage noise shattered the tense silence.

HONK! BLAAT! HONK! Blaat-blaat-blaat! BLAAT!

It was the Land Rover. Stacey was furiously honking the horn.

Flora galvanized. The calf next to her stiffened and pressed itself defensively against her flank, its little head raised in alarm. Flora cast her massive head about, every sense straining for information.

HONK! Blaat! BLAAT! BLAAT!

Flora snorted, lifted her tail, and blasted out two spurts of urine, a signal of imminent combat. The men, still downwind, winced when the acrid mist wafted over them. Then she lowered her daggered head and charged.

The men froze. There was simply nowhere they could hide. So dire was their situation that Eric became deaf to the insistent honking. Every fiber was tuned toward the two thousand pounds of wrath careening toward them.

Without warning, the rhino skidded to a halt and wheeled. Then wheeled again. The noise obviously agitated her but was nothing within her ken. She was unable to identify the source of imminent danger to her and her calf. Even the oxpeckers, who had flapped away, began to flutter down and settle. The baby mewled and scrambled toward her. Flora stood panting, still uncertain whether to fight or flee.

Neither Pieter nor Eric dared move. Even their breathing was tremulous, shallow.

Flora snorted in rage and frustration. The source of menace was both everywhere and nowhere. The horn's blaring continued unabated. Flora's ears spun continuously, radaring toward the unfamiliar noise. Suddenly, she made her choice and trotted toward the calf, pushing her away from the frantic honking. In her primal mind, perhaps a zebra was in mortal agony nearby. Best move away. Now. Get her baby away from the ghastly confusion assaulting her senses.

As the rhino picked up speed, the calf struggled not to fall behind. They broke from a fast trot into a gallop and soon disappeared into the relative safety of the riverbed, leaving a cloud of chalky dust in their wake.

After the shock of the crisis had passed, Eric and Pieter exchanged relieved looks and gulped. Both men were drenched with sweat and breathing heavily. As if awakening from a deep sleep, Eric returned to the world, slowly. Yes, the honking. Was it his imagination, or had it grown more faint?

"Christ!" Pieter swept his brow. "What's the matter with that woman?"

"No idea. Took the keys. Habit." A look of concern clouded his countenance. "My God—the battery!"

The men sprinted toward the fading noise. Once the vehicle was in range, Eric trained his field glasses on it. He turned cold at the sight.

The Land Rover was surrounded by a troop of Chacma baboons, perhaps fifty or more. A few perched on the hood, staring intently through the windshield. Others sat on the roof, tearing at objects Eric couldn't identify.

"Bloody hell," he finally breathed.

"What? What is it?"

"Baboons. A troop of them. Appears the Rover is under siege." Eric lowered his binoculars. "Don't know how our friend managed, but it appears the cooler is out and the apes have looted it. Among other things."

Pieter was incredulous.

Eric continued, "Probably just curious—then, well, an easy meal. Compliments of Miss Winship."

Incredulity turned to indignation. Pieter blurted, "Yeah! My meal! I say we let her stew a bit longer."

"No. The battery. Enough harm's been done. Besides, it's getting too hot. She must have the windows rolled up."

"Right." Pieter cupped his hands to his mouth and shouted, "Dear God, woman, STOP! We're coming!"

At that, the two men whooped, raised their arms, and raced toward the beset vehicle. Eric and Pieter knew they had just one chance to terrify the beasts, so it had better be effective. Neither wanted to use his pistol. If they couldn't startle the baboons into a retreat, they would have little choice but to pummel them with rocks. And that meant pummeling the Rover as well. Neither desired that degree of collateral damage.

As they neared the chattering, howling chaos, the men began to scream and flap their arms about, each attempting his best impersonation of a baboon demon.

The uproar abated. A few baboons hooted a warning. Then every razor-fanged head turned.

13.

A shoulder's width apart, Eric and Pieter strode toward the marauders, emanating what they hoped conveyed deadly intent. Make yourself big, as big and as menacing possible was their unspoken mantra. Eric noticed with dismay that, in addition to reducing Stacey's "picnic" to a war zone, the baboons had also done considerable damage to the Rover. One appeared to be munching on a wiper blade.

All eyes were trained on the men.

Eric tensed as the enormous alpha male gave a warning double-bark hoot. A few larger apes formed a wary phalanx behind him, and the group began a stern, knuckled advance. It was obvious they had no intention of relinquishing their prize without a fight. Eric could see the menace in their small, coppery eyes, the hackles rising along their spines. He tried not to imagine the canine teeth, longer than a lion's, hidden in their wide doglike snouts.

"Bigger," Pieter advised, as the distance between them shrank.

Eric began to whip his arms in threatening circles. Pieter joined him. This unexpected gesturing gave the lead male pause. But the group didn't retreat. They meant to defend their booty.

Eric could see Stacey's face pressed against the glass, her eyes wide, her mouth a silent, screaming O. Thankfully, she had stopped honking the horn.

"What do you think?" Pieter asked, panting.

"I say we pick up some rocks and charge. If that doesn't work—you've got the pistol. Not that it would make much difference."

"Make it good then, mate," Pieter said, stuffing some baseball-sized hunks of basalt into his pockets.

"On the count of three. One. Two. Three. GET THE HELL AWAY FROM MY TRUCK, DAMN YOU!"

The men sprinted toward the beasts, who were clearly agitated and had halted in a nervous cluster. Pieter hurled a chunk at the largest male and hit him in the leg. The animal shrieked in pain. Eric missed his first throw, but his second grazed another's face. The men continued bombarding the advance group, as the animals leapt about, yelping and hooting in confusion and pain.

The men advanced, Eric continuing to pelt the group with painful accuracy, but still they wouldn't budge. Pieter drew his pistol. Eric knew Pieter had no intention of killing or even wounding any of them. With nothing to lose, he fired three shots into the air.

That was it. With a resounding whoop, the male signaled retreat, and the animals fled in confusion, crying out to the rest to do the same.

Eric and Pieter watched as baboons careened about and plunged off the vehicle, scattering as they raced for the safety of some nearby trees, which they clambered up. There they perched, observing the humans with angry, indignant eyes.

As the men surveyed the crime scene, Pieter's face took on a murderous expression. Eric nudged him gently with his elbow and pointed to the gun. "You'd best holster that. Or perhaps I could just take care of it for a while."

Pieter set the safety and shoved it away, snarling, "Wouldn't waste a bullet on that—"

"Easy." Eric smiled grimly as they drew alongside the truck. "What a bloody mess." He rapped on the glass. "Stacey, you can unlock the doors now. You're safe. Relatively speaking."

"You think they'll come back?" Stacey whimpered, unrolling the driver's window a mere inch. "I can't believe what they did. I . . . I just wanted a little lunch. It all happened so quickly."

"Stacey, unlock the door. Now," Eric commanded. He wanted to be stern, to scold her, to punish her for all the damage and annoyance, but she was so pale, so obviously shaken. In unresponsive solidarity, he and Pieter began to sort through the litter surrounding the truck, stuffing most of the mangled debris into the cooler. Reproach blanketed their every move.

Stacey reluctantly emerged and leaned against the cab, too traumatized to take part in any of the cleanup. Then she began to sob. "I thought you'd never come. They were everywhere." The men continued to ignore her; the sobbing grew more dramatic. "They even took turns urinating on the windshield. Right at my face! Disgusting."

"I'll tell you what's disgusting," Pieter blurted fiercely. "People like you who have no sense, no business out in the bush. Parading around as if you were in . . . in a damn shopping mall. Putting us all at risk like this. Just so you could have a bite to eat. You're. Not. Home."

Eric looked at his friend. "Easy, Pieter. Damage done."

"Well, she can just enjoy the view through the piss, because we don't have any wipers." Pieter dangled a mutilated blade as if it were a dead cobra, then tossed it into the growing pile in the cooler. "Jeez! And not just piss—bastards shat all over the truck." Pieter cast a withering glance toward the baboon-festooned tree as he and Eric heaved the cooler into the back. "This will be a real treat to clean up. Maybe you'll donate some of your fancy spritzy water to the task, girlie." Pieter spat into the dirt.

"Enough, Pieter," Eric said. "Let's just hope we've got enough juice to start the truck up."

Pieter snarled, "We'd better."

Stacey shot a look at Pieter, then at the tree, then hurled herself into the back seat, where she huddled in a perfect misery of self-pity and dread.

After a few heart-stopping attempts, the engine finally turned over.

"Christ!" Pieter bellowed, as they all breathed in the acrid stench of baboon waste flooding the cab. "Open the windows, for the love of God!"

Stacey meekly obeyed, but only a few careful inches.

Eric glared at her in the rearview mirror. "No air-conditioning. And if I see a spritzer, even once—" He turned his eyes back to their surroundings and, swinging the bespattered, fragrant Land Rover in a wide turn, saw hundreds of eyes watching warily from high in the tree. *Clever buggers,* he thought. *You'll stay in your tree. It'll soon be dark. And leopards will be hunting.*

14.

Eric and Pieter were as excited as new fathers in anticipation of another sighting. Neither had slept well the night before. The two had set off at first light to find Flora and her baby, hoping she was somewhere near where they'd last seen them. Zahara had brewed coffee for their thermos and packed a sack breakfast and lunch. Each baby rhino provided precious hope for the species. But babies had died before, despite having among nature's most intimidating parents.

The men were silent in the early morning cool, each lost in thought. Much of their work ended in frustration, sometimes tragedy, and sometimes, though rarely, joy. Maybe this day would be a joyful one. Even so, they could not overplay their hand. Flora needed a lot of space. Frightening her could cost her and the new baby a vital chance at food, water, or rest.

Pieter drove. Eric contemplated the desert he loved. Shadows carved sharp-edged sculptures from the hills and rocks. By midday, the sun would be overhead, flattening the landscape. Dawn was Eric's favorite time to be out, the ravines black slashes in the red desert. The mountains were illuminated, almost blinding, on one side, dark as deep space on the other. Grasses etched fine lines like brushstrokes in the sand. Those small bushes and scrubby trees provided life to the myriad strange creatures who lived here. And nowhere else on earth.

Scanning the area from a hilltop, searching for a rhino who might be roaming an area bigger than Yellowstone, prowling water holes at night to witness the lions sauntering in, watching all the beasts nervously jostle for a drink—these pursuits nurtured Eric's spirit, made his loneliness almost bearable. Almost.

For the first time, he'd not made his annual trek to England to see his family and friends. Probably that had been an error. In London, he spent too much time walking off restlessness and the urge to be back here. Still, he apparently required time with his family and friends. Friends who spent each day behind desks, who went home each night to a wife and children, whose only adventure was a week at the beach. To them, his life was exotic, filled with danger and excitement. He agreed, but he longed for someone to share it with.

Lately, a nagging emptiness haunted his nights. How long had he been in Namibia? Ten years, maybe more? Ten years sleeping on a single cot, often atop a truck. The day was approaching when there'd be no going back. He'd be like Pieter, hard-baked by the sun, indistinguishable from the desert beetle with its armored shell. Just as solitary.

He was roused from his ruminations when Pieter stopped the truck on a hillcrest. In the distance lumbered Flora and her baby. Scanning the area through his field glasses, Eric spotted a cluster of euphorbia. "That's probably where they're headed." Eric pointed out the trees to Pieter. "Get a snack and some shade."

"So our visitors are probably headed there too," replied Pieter, gesturing to his left. Eric swung his binoculars around only to see a huge cloud of red dust billowing up from the Lodge's damnable circus truck. Apparently, Daniel was driving. And with a full load of tourists. And that blonde photographer from the airport. Eric lowered the glasses with a deep sigh.

"Cut them off."

"Right away, Mr. Boss." Pieter turned to Eric. "But you'll just get your knickers in a knot and accomplish nothing." He started the truck and rolled down the hill to intersect the tourist mobile. "No denying you have your ideals, ones I happen to share. Also no denying you're about to create an entertaining explosion. But all you're going to accomplish is raising everybody's blood pressure." Pieter paused to navigate around a rock. "Except mine. I've been out here long enough to know that Namibia is inevitably being dragged into the civilized world. One day soon, it will be tamed, neutered, domesticated beyond recognition. And if our beloved rhino cannot adapt, well then, they will vanish."

"What you fail to understand, Pieter," began Eric in his most annoying and professorial tone, "is that if we tolerate these bastards, they'll keep on breeding." Eric's glare went from Flora to the bus. "One day, some American will decide rhinos are cute and build a Disneyland here. Have rhino rides and rhino shakes, rhino fries. Crap."

Pieter's eyes narrowed. The tour bus had spotted them and waited. Pieter barely got the truck stopped before Eric was out, charging very like a rhino. Daniel, too, was headed over, attempting to cut Eric off before their inevitable altercation disturbed his clientele.

Eric strode toward them. "I don't know how you found that mom and baby, but you can't go closer. She's headed to shade and needs a rest. Turn your circus wagon around. Now!" His face reddened.

"We found her because we have excellent trackers." Daniel kept his voice and gestures down, letting Eric appear to be the lunatic. "And we have no intention of alarming her. We're not amateurs. And you are not the Great White Savior of Rhinos."

"You most certainly are bloody amateurs! And I've seen you scare animals plenty of times. This rhino has a vulnerable baby with her." Eric poked his finger at Daniel's crisp safari jacket. "You jeopardize her or her baby, and I'll see the park shuts down your obscene resort."

"You have no authority and we—" At that moment, the blonde from the airport joined them. The tourists all stared, clearly alarmed.

Daniel put his hand on her arm, but she shook it off. "What's going on?"

"He's concerned we'll startle the rhino. In case you weren't aware, he owns Namibia and all the animals in it," replied Daniel.

"I don't want to startle her." The woman looked into Eric's furious gaze. "I want exactly the opposite. A photograph. And not one of her rear end."

"There are a billion bloody photographs already." Eric attempted to still his flailing arms, but his emotion was too strong. "Why are you so special that you get to intrude on Flora? What exactly do you think you have to add that a thousand photographers missed?"

"That's ridiculous. That's like saying because there are so many books in the library no one needs to write another. Who's Flora?"

"That's entirely different!" Actually, Eric couldn't say why it was different. He felt like a seventh grader. Again. That Flora's name had slipped out made him even angrier with himself.

"Enough." Daniel put his hands up. "We're not turning around. What besides that would satisfy you?"

Eric's brain smoldered from the confrontation.

At that point, Pieter stepped up, and speaking to Daniel said, "See that rise? Stay behind us, and we'll drive up there. We'll be downwind but close enough your clients can watch, and this woman can get a photo."

"Fine. And her name's Clare." Daniel strode back to the group, trying to put on a pleasant face.

"Flora?" Clare looked at him with more kindness. "You named her? Honestly, I do *not* want any part in upsetting her." His expression didn't change. "Our very existence seems to upset you, but . . ." She shrugged.

"There! That shrug." Without willing it, Eric poked his finger in her face. "I've seen that shrug. It says, 'Oh well, there'll be other rhino babies if this one dies.' Shrug. 'I have a job to do.' Shrug. 'We're not really hurting anything.' Shrug. 'We paid ten thousand quid to get here.' Shrug."

Clare forced herself to take a deep breath or she'd slug him. "You're kind of a bastard, you know that?"

"No, your friend's the bastard. He just dresses it up, those tidy, clean khakis and all that conservation bullshit."

Clare stared at him for a heartbeat too long and then whirled around.

Eric and Pieter watched her stride away until she'd gotten into Daniel's vehicle.

"Oh, you charming devil," said Pieter. "You are a smooth one. For sure she'll be sneaking into your tent tonight." He got in the truck, leaving Eric still staring at the circus mobile, which had begun to back up. "Come on, let's go."

15

Eric had been shocked to receive a note from Clare asking if he'd take her out to look for Flora. It had been a week since the encounter with Daniel, and he was certain his outburst had ruined any chance of seeing her again. Good news, altogether.

Eric parked his Land Rover just inside the obscenely ornate Lodge at Damara gate, arriving later than he had hoped. He'd asked the guard to call the Lodge to let Clare know he'd arrived and was waiting. As she walked down the drive, Eric took stock of her. Long hair pulled back, clothing appropriate for the bush and clearly not bought at the lodge's gift shop, sturdy boots that appeared to have seen many miles of trails. She shouldered a heavy pack, so he walked up to help her. She was even more attractive than he remembered from the airport. However, he was still convinced that the chances were slim she'd endure the trials of Africa long-term with her fair skin. That hair, for starters. In the rainy season, maybe there'd be enough water to wash all it, but not in the dry season when water was barely sufficient for drinking and cooking. Of course, the Lodge would have water to waste.

She dropped her bag and fumbled to pick it up. "Thanks for agreeing to take me out." Stuffing a lunch bag into the jeep, she dropped her water bottle. "Guess I'm a bit off today—bad night's sleep."

Eric retrieved her bottle from behind the front wheel. "No worries. Ready?" He started having second thoughts. This was going to be worse than he imagined. If her nerves couldn't take this little bit of fuss, what would she do in camp? What would she do when faced with a rhino? Go back where she came from. And take Stacey with her.

The sun was climbing, promising yet another blistering day. "What should I call you? Eric? Dr. Bolton?"

"Eric's fine." As he helped her into the Land Rover, he thought her hand the softest he'd ever felt. "We'd best get going. Making a late start as it is."

Eric's tension dissolved with every passing mile. He pointed out a giraffe, and they smiled at each other as the creature ripped off an acacia branch, tilted its head, and eyed them under thick lashes, as if they were the curious creatures. After an hour, they exited the paved road and bounced off down a red dirt tract to nowhere.

Occasionally, Eric studied his passenger, who clung fiercely to the grab bars as they drove around boulders the size of small mountains and over potholes deeper than most lakes. She'd wound a white scarf over her head and had on sunglasses that made her look exactly like Audrey Hepburn in some movie classic he'd seen. But more than pretty: Eric was thrilled by the way she gazed with awe at the great expanse that was Namibia. He'd half expected she'd be demanding to be returned to the Lodge by now. Instead, she smiled at him, the wind and motor precluding any conversation. He smiled back. The brief minute of their encounter at the airport, he'd promised himself he would feel nothing more for her, and if he did feel desire, he doubly promised himself he'd not show it. She'd never stay in Africa. This was a woman who could break his heart.

But in the instant he took his eyes off the road, he slammed into the sharp edge of a large rock, and a tire exploded. Clare screamed as the Land Rover toppled onto its side, and the engine died. Eric held tightly to the steering wheel to avoid crushing her with his weight. He felt his shoulder hard against hers and looked into her frightened eyes. Using the open window, he struggled to pull himself up and climbed out. Reaching back in, he took her hand and guided her over the gear knobs and out the window. He held her waist, amazed that his hands nearly circled it, as he eased her to the ground.

Clearly shaken and near tears, she yelped, "What happened?"

He huffed in frustration. "Tire. The tire blew. We'll be okay. Don't worry. Everything we need until help comes is in the Land Rover. I'm so sorry. I guess I lost my focus." Eric climbed back into the truck. His heart sunk when he saw the radio had been smashed. He stared at it, too stunned to think. He emerged to see a now furious Clare staring up at him. "Are you hurt?"

"You planned this!" Tears ran down her face, but when he reached to touch her shoulder, she slapped his hand away. "To test me. Punish me. I don't know."

"I *planned* this? I *planned* to be stuck out here instead of on my comfortable cot? I *planned* to eat stew from a can instead of eating a good meal in camp? Oh, yeah, great plan." He began unloading the truck, flinging a cooking pot out, then a tent. "You tell your boss where you were going?"

"No. He warned me about you, your unstable personality. I decided it'd be better to ask forgiveness than permission. A decision I now regret."

"Completely understandable. He'd have five servants and . . ." Eric took a deep breath. "You look shaken. Go sit on that rock. Rest a bit. I'm accustomed to setting up a camp."

At the click of the shutter, Eric whirled around. "What are

you doing? We're not playing a game out here. We're stuck in the middle of nowhere, a very dangerous nowhere. It's going to get dark, and out here, it gets dark fast. And you're playing tourist?"

"Sorry! I wanted a photo of a mighty African explorer." Clare hopped down from the rock and rubbed her backside. "I'm okay now. Give me a job."

And thus it begins, thought Eric. *What would take me twenty minutes to complete will now take an hour. Twenty minutes to explain, twenty minutes to undo, and then twenty minutes to do it myself.* She looked even more pale than when he'd picked her up. "Unload that bag. Lay everything on the ground exactly in the order it comes out. It's the tent."

"*The* tent? We only have one tent?"

Eric looked at her for a moment and just shook his head. "Normally, we'd sleep on the top of the truck, but as this is clearly not possible, we'll have the truck at our backs for protection."

The sun hovered low in the sky, and a trace of pink glowed just behind the distant mountains. Eric glanced at her now and then, trying not to be obvious, not to admire her perky rear end as she bent to take out the poles, the stakes, the tent, doing it exactly as instructed. He chastised himself: *Damn it, Bolton, it's up to you to make sure we survive the night. You don't need such distractions. Bury your feelings, for God's sake!*

The last time he glanced at her, she'd finished and smiled at him. And without willing it, he smiled back, feeling the muscles in his jaw relax. He gave a quick nod at the job she'd done.

"Take this corner and we'll lay the tent out. Let's get it up quickly. We'll need it soon."

In the next thirty minutes, they'd set up the tent. Eric retrieved a small propane stove and lantern. Clare wished for a fire, but all she could see were a few scraggly camelthorn trees.

"Be back shortly." Eric grabbed an empty canvas sack.

"You're leaving? Where are you going?"

"I need to look for fuel. Don't worry. If you need shelter, get in the tent."

Eric returned with his bag filled with small sticks and dried manure.

She watched him pull it out. "Poop? You're going to burn poop?"

"Yeah, lucky I found some, eh?" he replied without sarcasm. He set up the twigs in a pyramid, and when the fire got going, set what looked like a cow patty on top. Soon, they were sitting in the glow of fire.

It got dark fast, no lingering dusk, from oven to refrigerator quickly."

"Coastal fog rolls off the ocean, off the Skeleton Coast, each evening. That exchange from hot to cold provides about the only moisture the creatures out here have." He watched her hug herself, wishing he could put his arms around her. "Do you have a jacket?"

"No. Foolishly, I thought you'd get me home before dark." Clare perched on a rock still warm from the sun.

"You've been at the Lodge how long? And you still don't get it that this desert is wildly unpredictable?"

"I didn't get it that your driving is wildly unpredictable."

"I deserved that. Here, take this." He blushed, handing her a waxed canvas jacket.

"No, I'm fine." Clare hugged her arms around her knees.

"You won't be fine soon." He wrapped the jacket around

her shoulders, lingering a moment. But right now she was about as cuddly as thistle.

"Thanks."

Eric fussed with the stove. The very rock that blew the tire now made a convenient table. Soon he had water boiling for tea.

"This will warm you." He sat beside her, and they drank their tea looking at the far mountains outlined in a faint violet glow.

"Beautiful, isn't it?" said Clare.

Eric glanced at her, surprised by this kindred spirit, another being who could love this vast, empty place. "Yes, it is. I'm sorry this happened. You have every right to be angry. I lost my concentration. A flat, that happens. But I've never tipped a truck."

"Well, I came to Africa looking for adventure. Lodge at Damara is awfully civilized, sanitized even, so maybe I should be grateful you drive like crap."

Eric chuckled. "I was hoping you'd come to that view." A wisp of her hair had escaped from her scarf, and the light from the fire made it glisten gold. Eric practically had to sit on his hands to keep from touching it. "Think I heard one of staff say you're from California. What did you do there?"

"So, I'm part of the rumor mill? I'm flattered."

"Don't be too flattered. We're pretty hard up for entertainment out here. Daniel provides most it with his annoying convoys of tourists and his schemes for a theme park."

"Your new assistant must be grist for the rumor mill. She's caused a buzz."

"Ah, Stacey." He grinned uncomfortably. "Yes, well unfortunately for us, our lives are now in the very iffy hands of that very Spacey."

"Stacey," Clare corrected.

"Right. I just hope she'll notice I didn't come back to camp and send one of the trackers out. That, however, may not occur to her for a week or so."

Clare looked alarmed. "Seriously?"

He paused. "Sorry I scared you. Stacey's my backup; Pieter is my camp boss. He's wicked smart and an Afrikaaner. He'll have someone to us as soon as daylight comes." Eric studied her upturned face. "You didn't tell Daniel you were out with me, did you?"

"I should have! Another stupid blunder like no jacket. He'd gone to the airport to collect another herd of tourists, and I thought we'd be back before he returned. Not likely."

16.

The sun set as if a light switched off. Eric had prepared the camp and lit a lantern. Normally, Clare
would have offered to help, but she enjoyed seeing
him busily making sure everything was safe and reasonably
comfortable. She suspected he felt guilty about the tire and
decided she'd let him.

"I'm sure Daniel sets a superior table." Eric put down two
tin plates and cups.

"Yes, he does. However, I do give you credit for ambience."

He bustled about, boiling water and pouring in dry pack-
ets of food. "Dinner will be served momentarily, mademoi-
selle. If you would be so kind as to come to the table." Placing a
rag over his arm, he bowed.

"I suppose. The table looks rather low, rather dirt-like. And
what is this dinner you've prepared? It didn't seem to take
long."

"We have wine, white of course. Fruity but definitely not
overwhelming." He filled their cups with water. "And tonight,
we begin with reconstituted desiccated chicken noodle soup.
Fittingly, we also finish with reconstituted desiccated chicken
noodle soup. In between, we have sparkling water without
those irritating bubbles—and a twist of nothing. And for
dessert, we have nothing flambé. I beg you, take a seat."

"Where?"

"In the dirt, of course. Like all fine restaurants."

"I often have raspberry coulis with my nothing flambé, if it's not too much trouble."

"You're being rather difficult."

"Well, at these prices—"

Clare looked into his blue eyes. She didn't dare stare long enough to decide anything but that they were beautiful and kind. How had this man she thought so rigid become a delightful clown? He'd almost become human. The glance lasted a second or two longer than it should have, and she felt her heartbeat racing.

Eric sat in the sand beside her. "I'd like to propose a toast to that wily Van Alstyne. May he get his skinny arse out here in the morning before it gets too bloody hot."

"Here, here!" Clare added. They clunked their tin cups together. In the sudden chill of the evening, the hot soup tasted good. She was still unaccustomed to the lethal heat of day being overcome by chill coastal air. This place—schizophrenic in the extreme. Nothing about this country was normal. And Clare had traveled to some wild parts of the world.

"Perhaps the finest reconstituted chicken noodle soup I've ever had."

"We aim to please." He looked over at her. "You chilly? It does get cold here. Too bad we can't store the heat like so many of our fellow creatures." He went to the truck and returned with a blanket, which he draped over her.

His large hands were surprisingly gentle. Clare ruefully thought that Timothy, if he'd gotten a blanket at all, more than likely would have wrapped it around himself first. "Thank you. That's better. Do we have enough blankets to keep warm overnight?" Clare rather hoped the answer was no. That they'd have to cuddle to stay warm. At the moment she could imagine nothing better than to be curled up, spooning, pressed against his strong thighs.

"Think so. I've ended up stuck out here before, though I wish I hadn't dragged you into this." He looked at her. "Have to admit, you're a trooper, and I really appreciate it. Not many women would be laughing right now."

"I photograph wildlife, Eric, most of which lack the consideration to live in Manhattan where the restaurants and plays are so good. Plus, with all its dangers, Namibia is blessedly devoid of mosquitoes." She placed her hand on his arm. "It's exciting to be out after dark—and on a school night. And it's beautiful. Daniel is rightfully concerned with staff or guests leaving unaccompanied. People get so testy when their relatives are eaten. But I didn't come here to be safe. I came to experience Namibia, and that's not really possible in a cage." She smiled up at him. "That does not mean I won't be very happy to see Mr. Van Alstyne."

"If you need to, um—to use—to pee, let me know. The facilities are a bit rustic. Not Ralph Lauren rustic. Snakes and insect rustic. Some beautiful specimens, mind you."

"You are a romantic fellow." Clare leaned into his shoulder playfully.

"No, just, well, I come highly recommended as a discreet toilet guard."

"I'll keep that in mind. For now, I'm quite happy watching the burning poop." Clare paused. "Daniel says you've been in Namibia for years. That's quite a sacrifice. Away from home, England, I believe. Away from family and friends." Clare shifted her legs and longed for a chair.

"Sacrifice isn't the word I'd choose." Eric looked out at the vast darkness. "Being here has been a lifelong dream for me. I won't go all New Age on you, but it's as if I've come home, not left home. And the friends that I have here, they're my family. So much depends on whom you're with here, whether you succeed or not. Survive or not." He, too, straightened his legs. "Like everyone, I'm fascinated by the animals, the lions and hyenas. But a long time ago, I got it into my head that the fate of the world hinges on the fate of our black rhino. Tough ole bugger. Should be king of Africa, but his bloody great size doesn't allow him to slip slide around humans like the others can."

"Daniel's camp brings people here, people with the clout to help the rhinos."

"I know. And I want their help too. Only I want them to send it from whatever suburb they live in instead of using precious resources for the amusement of coming here to pester the rhinos. And everyone else."

"That's not terribly reasonable," Clare replied.

"So I've been told, told many times by your friend." Eric stirred the fire and put on another scarce piece of poop.

"Boss, really. Maybe friend. I'm not sure yet." Clare thought Daniel rather more pompous since she'd been with Eric. But wasn't Eric tilting at windmills, a naive idealist?

"Well, he's got more to offer you, but I'm not quite the Don Quixote I'm accused of being."

Clare was startled and a tad embarrassed that he'd read her mind.

Eric ventured, "When we're out of this, maybe you'd let me take you to Rhino Camp, spend a day there with me." He poured sand into the pot to scrub it clean and set it on the warm rock. "Your suite awaits, if you're tired, and I imagine you are." He motioned to the tent set up against the chassis of the truck. Clare crawled in, surprised at the comfort, despite the scent of petrol.

"Okay in there?" Eric stuck his head in. "I'm right here outside the door."

Clare poked her head out the tent flap. "Come in. Despite early evidence to the contrary, I don't bite."

"That was my first worry. The second was leopards—the third, lions."

"What exactly are you intending to do if a lion attacks? You don't have a gun, except for that little pistol."

"Well, I would shoot a poacher if I had to, but otherwise, I view myself as a guest here. Shooting the host seems so rude. However, they aren't fond of fire or light, so I'll keep it burning." He smiled as she peeked out from the tent flap. "They're adapting so quickly to the incursion of humans that I anticipate one day seeing a hyena stroll by with a Coleman stove he'd ordered online from REI."

"Okay, I'll leave you to it. But take this blanket. There's another in here. And Eric? Thank you. For dinner. For everything. Almost."

He laughed softly. "You're welcome, Clare. Sleep, if you can. Seriously, I have this under control."

17.

Inside the tent, Clare shook the blanket, then checked the corners of the tent for scorpions. Lions killed you. Scorpions just made you wish you were dead. She curled her long legs under the too short blanket and wadded her pack into a pillow. But her eyes refused to stay shut, snapping wide at every sound. When Eric rustled around, she was calm. When he was still, she worried, but resisted the urge to call out.

As a diversion, she ran various scenarios. She lying beside him. He would stay on his side of the tent, ever the gentleman, then perhaps a noise would frighten her, and she'd move closer. Their hands would touch, an explosive desire would overwhelm them—and on and on her fantasies went until she actually dozed.

She awoke suddenly, not certain where she was, her hip aching from the hard ground. And then she heard it, quiet, but an unmistakable rumbling growl. She bolted up, clutching the blanket around her shoulders, listening with every fiber of her being. Nothing. Had she been dreaming? Crawling to the tent flap, she peered through the slit. Where was he? Her heart thudded against her chest. Then she saw him walking back to the camp. "What was that?"

"Lion. Not sure how close. Not sure how interested in us. You sleep any?" He'd moved a gas can from the truck and was perched on it.

"Surprisingly, I did. A little. Until our visitor arrived. Our visitor who hopefully is *not* interested in us. Who in fact finds us very, very dull."

"I can be dull. I've been told so." Despite his attempt at humor, Eric sounded distracted, obviously worried.

"Haven't noticed. Yet." Clare smiled nervously and moved to sit cross-legged just inside the open tent flap. How the tent would keep a lion from eating her wasn't quite clear, but it gave her a small sense of security.

"At least you're dull and skinny. I'm dull and meaty," Eric offered.

The banter settled Clare's nerves, until she heard the slightest movement. She'd been in close encounters with apex predators before, but always in the company of a few people, at least one of whom toted a proper gun.

"Eric, I appreciate your principles, but for the love of God, why can't you carry at least a tranquilizer gun instead of that Nerf gun?"

"Good idea. After she kills us, she can take a nice nap. Let us get used to being dead before we become food."

"Seriously, I'm scared. We're sitting ducks. Even a geriatric lion could kill us out here." Clare debated about leaving the safety of the tent for the small comfort of being closer to Eric. She compromised by leaving the tent flap open but sitting beside him. The fire still burned fitfully. "We're running out of fuel."

"Yeah, not good." Eric had never been stuck overnight without being at least on top of the truck. And rumors had been circulating of a rogue lioness who'd mauled a village child. Once animals realized humans were mostly hot air and bluster, as well as soft and chewy, they became lethal predators.

"We need to get into the truck. I just caught a shift of

shadow. Could a lion. Could be a hyena—not much better, but better.

Clare heard the lion growl again. This time closer, very close. "The truck's on its side. How do you propose we get in?"

"Quickly." He pulled her to her feet, her hand so small in his. "We'll be easy pickings crawling in. I'll get you up first." Then he held the lantern aloft and illuminated a glint of golden eyes and a flash of fangs. The lioness gave a deep throaty chortle, readying herself to uncoil like a steel spring, a deadly projectile. Still fifty feet out. But with her speed, she'd be on top of them in seconds. "Too late. Stay behind me."

Clare was terrified, frozen. Her legs barely able to hold her up. She had nothing, no weapon, not even a stone to throw or a stick to wield. Nothing. And she could not hold onto Eric. If she got out of this alive, she swore she'd never be without a rifle. Eric had said they were guests here. Well, maybe guests don't kill the hosts, but this particular hostess was intent on killing them.

In a fury of teeth and claws, the lion charged. A deafening roar. Clare screamed. Then suddenly the sky lit up. It was Fourth of July—fireworks—flames shooting through the ink-black night. And then quiet. The only sound a shrill buzz in Clare's ears.

"What? What happened?" Clare felt Eric's arms around her, her body shaking against his, tears pouring down her face.

"It's okay. It's okay," he murmured gently, rocking her as her sobs subsided. "Remember? They don't like fire."

Clare saw the upturned gas can in the sand. Eric had flung gas across their small fire, creating a momentary blaze, enough to dissuade the lion.

Between sobs, Clare stammered, "So you know. When I said I wanted to experience Africa? This is not what I meant." She held him closely, her arms wrapped around his chest.

"She's gone, tonight. Think we gave the old girl pause." He gave her a boyish grin and nudged her shoulder. "Get it? Paws?"

Clare was nearly hysterical. "Pause? Paws? You can joke?" Her body, now suddenly very cold, refused to release him. "You are a cool customer."

"Don't think we'll sleep well out here. Let's get in the truck. It'll be on the squished side of cozy, but we'll be safe." Eric peeled her arms away but kept hold of one hand and led her to the truck. "Let me boost you up."

"I don't need a boost." Clare put her foot on the underside of the truck and pulled herself through the window. Her dignity wouldn't endure any more assaults tonight.

"Righto." Eric waited for her to settle along the side of the truck, flung the blankets in, and clambered up. She had rolled toward the roof. He'd suffocate her if he got in front. "This may require some gymnastics, but if you can, let me squeeze to the down side. I make a good cushion."

Clare scooted aside as much as possible, and Eric slid over her. For one lovely moment, his body was on top of hers. He was graceful, athletic. Then his elbow caught her in the ribs.

"Oof!"

"Sorry! You okay?"

"For a cushion, you have very sharp corners. Know that?"

"This okay?" he asked as she settled beside him. "I'll keep my hands to myself. No funny business. Promise."

"There's been enough activity of any kind for tonight. And I'm freezing, so be my guest." Clare wiggled to give him a little room, but his warmth was delicious. He fit her perfectly, body and soul. "You don't happen to snore, do you?"

"Poke me in the ribs if I do." He pulled the blanket over their shoulders. "Good night, Clare.

"Good night, John Boy."

"Who?"

"Never mind. Forgot you're a Brit."

But Clare couldn't close her eyes without seeing that powerful golden head rocketing at them, teeth bared, stretched out nearly into her leap. She'd seen a lion bring down a springbok, cleverly tripping it, then pouncing. Clare was haunted by the vision, the lion's amber eyes surveying the area for competitors wishing to share its bloody feast. And if this lion had unleashed her full fury, Eric's fireworks would have been too late. She would not, could not have veered away as she did.

And the sound. Would Clare ever forget the almost fierce, guttural laughter emanating from their attacker, the supreme confidence it would feast tonight? Tears traced their way down her face. She tried to still the sobs, but then she felt Eric's arm reach around her shoulder to hold her.

"You won't forget, but the terror will subside," he said so quietly she could barely hear him. "Now you'll have a fine story to tell your children."

He had an uncanny way of reading her thoughts. Sleep still eluded her. What was she doing in an overturned truck in Namibia? Less than an hour ago, she might have been killed, and for what? Life seemed to be living her, making its choices with every shift of the wind. And yet, the arm gripping her shoulder felt right. Maybe she could start taking charge of how she would live her life. But first, she'd made a commitment to

Daniel. And she liked him, somewhat. He wouldn't have gotten her in this mess. These thoughts continued until, finally, the warmth from Eric and her exhaustion overwhelmed her, and despite the fear and confusion, she fell soundly asleep.

A rosy streak of sunlight woke Clare. Eric's arm still draped over her shoulder, his hand neatly cupping her breast. The sensual warmth of his body keeping away the morning chill. Beneath her hip, however, ran the sharp edge of what she presumed was the metal window frame, and she shifted her weight.

"You awake?" Eric jerked his arm away.

"Yeah," replied Clare sleepily. "However, thanks to our outer spring mattress, I don't have any circulation in my legs. We have to replace this thing."

"The mattress store's just over that hill. Right now, though, your body is obstructing our getting coffee, which I badly need."

"Okay, okay." Clare grabbed the seat back and pulled herself up. "Yikes! I'm stuck. No joke."

"Can I give you a push?" Without waiting for her answer, Eric put his hands on her bottom and shoved her until she got through the window.

"That was rather humiliating, effective but humiliating," said Clare when she'd jumped to the ground.

"Sorry. Oh, just in case you need it, the loo is yonder, just at those trees." He handed her a roll of paper and a trowel, grateful she was experienced enough not to ask its purpose. "I'll get the coffee started."

She quickly returned to camp and, inhaling deeply, observed, "Coffee smells good." He filled her tin cup. "The fried eggs and ham come later?"

"Much later. Never, in fact." Eric topped off their cups. "Of course, that's not true for you. You'll be back at the Lodge. To-day, God willing. Tomorrow you can have your eggs. Rumor has it that Daniel spares no cost on food."

Clare studied him. "Eric—" She wanted to tell him what it was she valued more than eggs, more than comfort. That what he had to offer her and the planet far exceeded what Daniel offered, ease and entertainment. She took a deep breath and gathered her courage. "Pieter's not here yet, and if he does res-cue us before we die, I take back everything I'm about to say. But this adventure, this time with you. Well, it tops my list."

Eric beamed at her, then turned his gaze on the early dawn light as it gave shape to the landscape.

"But," continued Clare, "you do yourself no favors compar-ing who you are, what you want, what you love to Daniel."

They sat in companionable silence, watching the sun over-take the dawn. "It's a gift, being okay with silence," said Eric.

"It's beautiful out here, something so serene, like I can truly breathe." Clare looked out at the waves of sand, as endless as the ocean. "My last shoot was in Costa Rica. And that was gorgeous. But at times, I felt that the green would suffocate me, that one night I'd wake up with vines wrapped around my throat."

"Most people can't wait to get out of here. The animals, yes, magnificent. The land, not so much. Which is good for both the land and the animals." Eric had moved the gas cans again for seating, setting his as close to hers as he dared. "But the land and the animals are so fierce *because* they are so vul-nerable. I've seen equipment left by the Germans almost a cen-tury ago, perfectly preserved. Anywhere else, that stuff would rust, vegetation would cover it. Here, every injury man inflicts scars forever."

"Stop! I dropped out of school to come here to Namibia. I'll sign up for your lectures next term."

"Sorry. Pieter's heard them all, and Hosea and Zahara run when I start in."

"What about your lovely new assistant? Is she a good listener?"

"Not much interested. Growing distinctly less interested by the day." Eric replied.

"Cute, however. Spiffy clothes. Great hair," said Clare.

"You're the one with great hair!" Eric moaned.

Clare usually had breakfast, and like the hobbits in *The Lord of the Rings*, she had second breakfast and elevenses. Black coffee made her stomach rumble loudly. She shivered, the sound so similar to the lion last night.

At last they heard an engine.

"Hurray! The cavalry!" Clare jumped up.

"Fantastic," muttered Eric. "The cavalry is that bloody circus wagon. And with Daniel driving. Just gets better every minute."

Daniel maneuvered the large truck beside them and leaned out the window. Tourists gawked as if a bull elephant had materialized before them. "Clare! We've been worried. Sorry, Eric, we don't have a winch to right this thing. I'll detour to Rhino Camp and get you some help." Then he smirked. "How in God's name did you manage that?"

Eric stood as silent and prickly as the nearby camelthorn tree.

"Hop in, Clare," Daniel commanded, flinging the passenger door open. "Need water, Eric?"

"No."

Clare waved weakly. She'd never seen such abject misery.

⁂

AFTER DANIEL SPED off, Eric sat back down on the gas can, took a sip of cold coffee, then flung the rest. "No, Daniel," he said to sand, "I do not want your help. I'd vastly prefer hanging naked with hyenas chomping my toes off one at a time."

He was pretty sure Clare would never venture out with him again, and there was so much he wanted to say to her. To tell her that he didn't compare himself to Daniel, didn't envy Daniel one damn thing, except that Daniel had her, and she was what he himself wanted badly. But he was out of practice, totally unused to expressing emotion, except outrage. He'd gotten very good at outrage lately. Last night, when she'd curled up against him, that could easily have been for warmth. Any warm body would do. He couldn't read her feeling for him. The risk of exposing his vulnerability and his desire was too great.

He noticed a lone baboon staring back at him.

"Bugger off! You're alone too. Don't look so superior."

But at that exact moment, three females sauntered over from a thicket to sit beside the ape and began to groom him attentively.

18.

Clare glanced back to see Eric still slumped on the gas can, as forlorn and ridiculous as the truck with its wheels in the air. A part of her wanted to jump out and run back to him. Another part saw him as one of those hyper-political crazies on the college green, ranting some version of Chicken Little's *The sky is falling! The sky is falling!*

She'd also attached herself to hopeless causes. The float in high school that she and her classmates were building. When the rain came, they ran. Not Clare. She stayed true, stuffing sodden streamers back into the chicken wire and ending up a joke. Blue and yellow dye streaming down her face and arms. In college, she'd protested for myriad causes, and never, ever had her efforts effected a meaningful change. In fact, often she and her friends lost money or time or both. And usually they looked as idealistic and foolish as Eric.

True to his word, Daniel detoured from their scheduled outing to stop at Rhino Camp. A far cry from the luxury of Lodge at Damara, Eric's headquarters comprised what Clare guessed were a dozen tents raised on wooden decks. At the center squatted a two-story cinderblock building, presumably dining, housing, and gathering areas. Offices probably too. Daniel and Clare climbed down and were greeted by two clearly agitated staff members, as well as two yapping dogs. Clare offered her hand for the required pleased-to-make-your-acquaintance sniff and then stooped to receive her dog-kiss welcome. Hosea informed them curtly that Pieter had left early in search of Eric. The direction he'd headed confirmed that he would intersect with Eric before too long.

"I figured he'd be out. Not many people know this desert as well as Pieter," said Daniel. But as he and Hosea were studying a map, Daniel's group jumped ship.

"Hey! Stop! Get back here!" Daniel turned to head them off. "We're not staying here. Just making sure that fellow gets help. Everybody in the truck or we won't make it to our destination." Arms wide, he attempted to herd them, but these people were rule makers, not rule followers. To add to the chaos, Stacey emerged just then, a handmade Tour Guide badge pinned to her blouse. Soon, she was chattering and leading them through the dining room and lounge area and then back to the research lab.

Daniel shook his head and shrugged. "Might as well join 'em. They sure as hell aren't under my control any longer." He put his hand on the middle of Clare's shoulders. His touch was proprietary, very like Timothy's. What about her inspired men to treat her as a possession? Short of slugging him, she didn't know what to do but be guided along with the rest.

Clare could hear Stacey's nasal voice droning on and dreaded being held captive to her lecture. Until she entered the building. Staring at her from shelves ceiling to floor were rhino skulls. Hundreds of them. Bullet ridden, mutilated faces from poachers slicing off their horns. Her legs threatened to buckle under her, and Daniel's arm tightened to hold her steady. Stacey's speech was apparently scripted, as she rarely stopped even to breathe and had no intonation. But the information was gut-wrenching. Statistics, rhino population collapse from hundreds of thousands before 1970 to twelve hundred total. From poaching; from the military funding their wars by selling rhino horns to Yemen for sword handles or China for medicine; from poverty-stricken Africans armed with .303 automatic rifles left over from these constant wars; from machine guns mounted on tanks, soldiers chasing the rhinos down. All slaughtering these majestic beasts for their twelve-pound horns, leaving the mighty lords of Namibia to rot in the sun.

Glancing periodically at the 3x5 cards she clutched, Stacey went on about rescue attempts, about conservation, about education, about hiring former poachers and villagers to protect the rhino, thus making the rhino more valuable alive than dead. About the population having fallen to such disastrous numbers that authorities had considered hiring one guard for each rhino. About dehorning the animals, thus eliminating their value to poachers. About dying the horns or poisoning the horns. About the increase, though slight, in the population and the hope for the future. Suddenly, Clare didn't think Eric quite so foolish. He'd been doing this work for years, and in doing so, had given the rhino—and the planet—a spark of hope.

Beside her, Daniel checked his watch and paced impatiently behind the group. But they were mesmerized as Stacey went on reciting specific rhinos who were now pregnant and soon to give birth. How Eric and his group were tracking them to keep them safe. She told of Flora, who had just delivered a baby, and who'd produced a healthy calf five years ago. But she told also of another baby found dead, killed by villagers for no discernible reason. How Eric's organization hoped tourist revenue would help ensure the rhinos were safe.

Daniel saw his opening and shouldered his way to the front. "And that's where we come in," he said, his voice ricocheting in the cement room as he moved beside Stacey, who smiled nervously up at him. "Our tours are all about saving the rhino. About contributing to the success of conservation efforts. Lodge at Damara is the most successful tour company on the continent, certainly in Namibia." He looked at his watch. "But if we don't leave pronto, we won't see any rhinos except these dead ones. Ready?"

This time he was successful. The group, too stunned, Clare presumed, to resist, and too disturbed by those massive heads indicting them all, slunk out of the building.

Daniel shook Stacey's hand, "Come visit the Lodge. We'll give you a tour." He took a few steps toward the truck. "Clare? You coming?"

She was sitting on a folding chair in the corner. "I think I'll stay. I'm exhausted." The cloud of displeasure that darkened Daniel's face made her uncomfortable, but she held firm. And as the bus zoomed away, she felt a tremendous relief that she wasn't listening to him hold forth, nor was she on another spine-jarring ride across the hot desert.

Zahara moved to Clare's side. "You'd think this desert had enough hot air without him." Clare looked into her wise brown eyes, and the two women chuckled. "I'm the housekeeper here. Let me make you some lunch and show you where you can rest. With Eric cooking, I imagine you're starving." Clare gratefully accepted and was soon lying on a cot staring at the canvas ceiling. Within seconds, she was asleep, her dreams filled with ghastly images of rhino skulls.

What seemed like immediately, someone was gently shaking her awake. "Clare?" said Eric quietly. "Zahara said you were in here. You okay? Dinner is being served. Feel like getting up?"

"How long have you been watching me?" She sat up. "I hope I wasn't sleeping with my mouth open. You've obviously showered." She looked up into his face. He'd showered and shaved since she last saw him, and had combed his glistening wet hair back. What a vision to wake up to. A handsome man, with such a tender look on his face. Would he bend near enough for a kiss? Clare warmed to the thought. But no.

"Both your mouth and eyes were closed," chuckled Eric. "We're pretty busy, so it may be a couple days before Pieter can get you back to the Lodge. Think you may have had enough of my driving."

The mention of Daniel's compound broke the spell. Eric probably didn't want her here. He was busy. She was busy too.

She watched his fingers clench and unclench. "That's fine. Sorry to impose on your staff. I just couldn't—well, I just really needed this rest." She fretted with the sheet hem.

"I'm glad you stayed. Will you come back? I mean, when you're finished with Daniel's project. Maybe we, that is Pieter and I, can show you some of what we do. Maybe you'd be willing to go out again. If Pieter drove, that is." He picked up the empty water glass by her cot. "In all fairness, you can't complain I didn't show you any animals. Though maybe next time we can see them a bit more on our terms. A bit farther off."

"I'd love it."

"Seriously?" He broke into a wide smile. "Lack of judgment is a valued trait around here. Meet you at dinner?"

After Eric left, Clare found two containers of water in the bathroom, one hot, one cold, and washed her face. Zahara had told her they would heat water for a shower, but Clare had declined. Bad enough she was putting a strain on a camp that ran on a restricted budget. The comparison to Lodge at Damara was stark. Water there ran freely. For God's sake, each villa had an infinity pool. The evaporation off the main pool was more than all the water used for a week here. Growing up in what was basically a commune in northern California, Clare was actually more accustomed to life at Rhino Camp than at Lodge at Damara. *Gotta fly under the radar!* That was her parents' motto. *Because the Man can't see you.* She'd argued that her friends led lives easily detected by radar, and they seemed to have survived unscathed. But Clare had quickly learned debating with Trip and Rainbow was pointless.

Pulling her hair into a ponytail improved things. Never a fan of makeup, she applied a touch of gloss, pursed her lips in the mirror, decided this was as good as it'd get, and set off.

The dozen or so staff and students were gathered in the dining hall. Feeling self-conscious, she sidled along the concrete wall, grateful to see one seat available at the long wooden table. The young man and woman across from her were engrossed in a heated debate and either hadn't noticed her arrival or didn't care. Finally, Eric caught sight of her, and whacking a knife against his tin cup, introduced her to the group as a wildlife photographer. She noticed he didn't mention Daniel. The group smiled. Obviously they considered a photographer a mere bit of fluff. Not like them, serious scientists. But at least those near her now passed food. She was ravenous. Zahara and Hosea worked miracles in the kitchen, surpassing even Lodge at Damara's impressive cuisine. A rich stew, buttery rolls that melted in her mouth, and dense spice cake. Real food.

She had barely finished when everyone shifted their chairs to face a screen at the front. The young man beside her got up to present a paper on the kori bustard. Clare was fascinated by his study and impressed by his dedication, his long stretches in the desert to observe these birds. Full and rested, she enjoyed the intellectual stimulation. Lodge at Damara by its nature was home to service personnel and transient tourists. After-dinner talk there was largely fueled by alcohol, and about funny incidents or close encounters. Amusing but not stimulating.

In the darkened room, she hadn't noticed that Eric had moved beside her. She started when he whispered, "Get enough to eat?"

"Yes. The last roll got snatched before reaching me, but yes, I got enough."

"This is a rough group. You'd best watch out." He held up his hand, making it appear he had only three fingers. "This happened when I reached for the last piece of cake."

"Goofball." Clare turned back. Having finished his presentation, the speaker now stood, his back to the wall, fending off challenges from the group. If they had been hyenas at the table, snapping off a finger, devouring a foot, they were now full-fledged leopards going for the jugular. Clare was taken aback by the ferocity of their cross-examination. She realized how coddled she'd been by parents who adored her; by teachers grateful for her obedience; by lovers simply because she was blonde and beautiful. Never had she had been in a position that this man occupied, required to defend her ideas so forcibly—and in public.

Although she would have been reduced to a puddle of tears by the relentless inquiry, the presenter looked only crestfallen and a bit defiant.

She turned to Eric. "Hopefully, you have therapists on staff. That was vicious."

"Nah. He tried to slip by a rather dubious hypothesis and got busted. Or, rather, bustard." Eric winked. "Hurts the cause. We've got to get this right. There's too much at stake. Look, collegiality in action."

At the front of the room, the group had gathered with the speaker, and there was laughter and a general slapping of backs.

"Out here," began Eric, "we have been entrusted to assist creatures in a fight for which they are massively overmatched. If we apply for grants using shoddy science, we do the creatures a disservice. That fellow will live to battle another day." He gathered her plate and utensils and deposited them in a nearby tub. "Care for a stroll before bed? If you're not too tired."

And how could Clare refuse.

Outside, an indigo sky overflowed with stars. When her eyes adjusted, Clare could see the mountains outlined against the crimson sky. Cool air from the Skeleton Coast had rolled up over the dunes and spread a chill across Damaraland, and across Clare. Eric wrapped his fleece jacket around her shoulders, his hands lingering a bit longer than necessary.

"Too bad we can't store this." She clutched the collar tighter around her neck, breathing in the distinctive smell she remembered when lying next to him, a heady mix of sun and canvas and Old Spice.

"Only termites have found a construction method to accomplish that. Amazing creatures, those termites."

"You think all creatures are amazing."

"Not true. I detest flies. Hate them. Loathe them."

"Everyone hates flies. They don't count."

"Okay. You can't tell anyone, but I'm not crazy about hyenas either. I admit, the world needs garbage collectors, but those ugly bastards, they scare me. They're so sneaky, slinking around with their shrunken butts and massive shoulders, up to no good and looking it. Perfectly content to eat a fellow while he's still alive, gnawing off pieces, stopping to pick their teeth with his femur. Give me the jimjams."

"Just between you and me. You ever shoot one with your pop gun?"

"No. Legend says they don't really die. They come back and invade your dreams until you go mad. Then *you* die a horrible, miserable, suffering death."

"As a scientist, you fell for that!?"

"Never know." He stopped and turned to her. "Are you liking it here at Rhino Camp? I mean, I know you've only been here hours, but what do you think? Honestly."

"This will sound almost as strange as your hyena dream story. I come from northern California, a place so green and bountiful it's unimaginable." He gave her a questioning look. "Okay, here's how good life is there. When the original coastal inhabitants had a war, the rule was, first side to draw blood won. War over. Feasting begins. Not blood like killing. Blood like a pinprick. There was almost nothing to fight over. Land, fish, deer, water, berries, bears—more than enough for all." They resumed walking.

"But for whatever bizarre reason, this place feels like home. The wall around the compound helps, of course, but I feel so calm and peaceful. The quiet, the way objects, animals, everything exists solely because it has a crucial function. No excess. No waste."

Eric said nothing for a while. "Not just anyone can see this place as a whole. The students are fine, but mostly they break off a piece of Namibia and put it under a microscope. You're a rare exception."

19.

Walking the compound at Rhino Camp under the glimmering stars, Clare recalled a distant photo shoot on an English estate. After dinner, the host would always suggest a stroll. Clare, the others on the shoot, and the family dutifully trooped out to walk the garden with its man-made creek murmuring quietly on its straight path, along precise hedge rows, everything permanently caught in history. Perhaps clothing changed, certainly footwear had, but neither the hedges nor the path upon which those feet trod changed. At the time, she'd imagined gardeners who sprung young from the earth, madly trimmed the hedges until they were old and returned to the earth, their bones nourishing the garden. She couldn't wait to leave England. The tidiness was crazy making. Clare's mind, like a disobedient child, insisted on returning to Timothy. He was very like those English gardens, comfortable and wealthy, static and orderly. Her inability to fold clothes at all "properly" had made him livid. *Try to be present*, she scolded herself.

No verdant meadows, no bubbling brooks, no hedges here in Damaraland: only the dry creek bed and the chain-link fence fortified by thorn bushes stacked to protect the exposed perimeter. Shoulder to shoulder, she and Eric strolled this barren African estate. Oddly, Eric *was* English but belonged here, with his sharp edges, his passion, his stripped-down personality, and even his humor. Namibia for all its starkness had much humor. Baboons constantly eyeballing the goings-on.

The impossible construction of Eric's precious rhino. Majestic but also ridiculous with two horns, a body like a traveling propane tank, and sawed-off stumps for legs.

Timothy had a sense of humor, but mostly he laughed in derision. The stupidity of his students, his staff, his fellow faculty. Of politicians and protestors. Of environmentalists and whackos, which encompassed any group holding opinions contrary to his own. He would find much to smirk at in Eric. A man with a PhD and credentials to teach at Oxford or Cambridge choosing to spend his productive years in a tent on this lunar surface, living from one grant to the next. And Daniel? Would he smirk at Daniel? Perhaps not. Timothy admired wealth and its trappings.

Lost in thought, Clare instinctively jerked her hand away when Eric brushed it.

"Sorry!" He sounded offended.

"No, I'd put my body on auto-pilot and gone back to California." She wanted to grab his hand, hold it tight, show him that not only was she not repulsed by his touch, she longed for it. But now he seemed distant.

"There. On the mountaintop." He pointed.

A cheetah in silhouette, standing in stark relief against the night sky, just enough moon to outline him. "God, and I don't have a camera. Rats!"

"You have eyes, Clare. Just look. Print him on your memory."

"You're right. I forget. Looking through a lens isn't always seeing." They stood, arms touching, and watched the beast until he suddenly disappeared, dissolving into the black hillside.

Others had obviously walked the perimeter as the path was worn, the rut a deeper red than the baked surface. Probably less than two city blocks, the path followed the thorn brush barricade, which at night took on the appearance of an abstract metal sculpture. Piled six feet high against the chain-link fence, it was full of lacy holes. The path meandered where the compound was guarded by a high desert mountain, then back to the corrugated metal gate. Tents on raised platforms for Eric, Pieter, and Hosea and Zahara, and the researchers were scattered near the main building. Pieter's was the farthest. From her brief encounter, Clare recognized that Pieter was a man who required a lot of solitude.

"One more turn around the block?"

"Really?" Eric gazed at her for a long moment. "Fine by me."

"What sights were you visiting in California just now? Or maybe it wasn't a sight. Maybe a person. None of my business."

In a way, Clare didn't want Timothy to pollute this pristine land, not even in spirit. That if she named him, he would be here. And he would never leave. Not only would he be in Clare's mind, he would be in Eric's. But an awkward silence crept in, cold as the Skeleton Coast fog.

"Of course it's a fellow," said Eric eventually. "You're beautiful. Intelligent. Of course you'd have a fellow. Or at the very least, a string of broken-hearted fellows."

"Well, I have to say, that turban and crystal ball of yours are quite impressive."

"Doesn't take much of a crystal ball, Clare." He ruffled her ponytail and chuckled. "I went through the possibilities and kind of reduced the options to blokes. Probably a lot in your past—or the present?"

"Yes, in fact, there are approximately 432,678. Wait! I forgot Cuthbert. Make that 79. Abandoned men, all probably still crowded in the San Francisco airport waiting, hoping, praying

I'll return soon. Several may even have died by now of broken hearts."

"So what's he like?" Eric stopped then turned away.

"Hey! Wait up." Clare trotted to catch up with him. "You asked me a question. Don't you want an answer?"

"No, I don't." Eric kept up his dogged march.

"Fabulous! He's fabulous," Clare called out, and the distance between them grew until he had to stop, too. "Owns a Rolls-Royce Silver Cloud, a beach house in Malibu, one in Phuket. A chateau in the Alps, in St. Moritz. But hang on, he also runs orphanages in Asia and flies wounded coffee farmers in Peru to his hospital where he himself operates on them for free."

"All right! Stop! I said it was none of my business." Eric walked back to her. "You're joking, right?"

"Guess you'll never know." He looked so unhappy, so clearly fond of her that this time she followed her impulse, grabbed him by the shirtfront and kissed him, hard. Then she turned.

"You mean that?" He stood where she left him.

"Wouldn't you like to know," she called over her shoulder teasingly.

"I would. I would like to know," she heard him whisper back.

CLARE AWOKE BEFORE daybreak and snuggled deeper under the covers, the chill of the night still gripping the land. She thought of Eric, asleep in his cabin nearby. What distrust still existed that kept them apart? Or was it more than that? They were perhaps too old or too serious to hop into bed with no consideration of the consequences. Or maybe they had too much respect for one another, too much hope for their future to risk a casual night of lust. None of that, however, kept her from imagining what it would be like to lie beside him, her legs entwined with his. Their hands exploring the wondrous landscapes of each other's body. She felt certain he'd be a good lover, slow and patient and tender. A surge of pleasure pulsed through her.

Just then, a clanging, loud as a fire alarm, brought her bolt upright in bed. Soon the two dogs added to the ruckus, and then yelling. Clare threw on her clothes and rushed out just as Eric ran by.

"What? What's happening?" Her heart kicked painfully against her ribs. Africa, so many bad possibilities, she couldn't sort through them.

"Poachers!" Eric kept shouting, racing toward the main building.

Ashamed to feel some relief that at least she herself was not the target, she dashed back into her tent, pulled on her boots, and collected her camera and pack. They'd try to leave her, she was certain. But that was not going to happen. Better men than Eric and Pieter had tried to ditch her on perilous shoots and failed.

She was out of her tent and standing by the nearest truck when Eric and Pieter appeared, followed by a tracker and an intern. A second group of anxious researchers followed them. Eric looked shocked to see her.

"Where do you think you're going?" he demanded.

"I'm going with you."

"No, not another damn female!" Pieter brushed by her and threw gear into the back of the truck.

"There's room for five. You have four. I'll ride in the jump

seat, but I *am* going." She turned on Pieter. "And you, you blus-
tering puff adder, you need me. I've got a camera, and you're
going to need photos. So tell me which truck, which seat. Stop
wasting time."

Pieter raised his eyebrows. "Well, if you're that important,
you'd best ride in our truck." He flipped the seat forward, and
Clare, Chuck the intern, and the Himba tracker, Ezra, hopped in.

"We're not carting extra gear for you, so better have what
you need," Pieter said to her back.

"Eh, you'll be begging granola bars off me halfway there."
Clare wished it weren't just an idle threat. Namibia suffered
from a serious dearth of granola bars.

Pieter tilted his head back and roared with laughter. Eric
looked relieved he wouldn't have to intercede. As they backed
the truck out, they saw Stacey standing in the doorway in a
hot-pink nightie, her eye mask on her forehead. She looked
baffled by being up before daybreak.

"So what's happening?" Clare leaned forward between the
front seats to hear over the roar of the engine.

"A radio report came in from one of the villages that
poachers were spotted." Pieter spoke loudly. "Bastards are near
where Flora and the calf were last seen."

"What will you do?"

"Shoot 'em. Seriously, we'll shoot 'em." Pieter patted the
gun on his hip. "We won't kill them, though, because then we
can stake them naked to an anthill."

Eric turned to her. "Pieter's got an excitable side."

"Really? Hadn't noticed." Clare smiled.

20.

Clare sat back, wishing the poachers had had the courtesy to pay their visit after coffee and breakfast. Her stomach rumbled. And the ride was brutal, the truck clearly not intended for this speed on this terrain. She felt like a doll being slammed against the sidewalk by an angry child. Chuck was positively green with motion sickness.

"Try this." She rummaged in her pack and gave him a ginger chew. "Really, money-back guarantee you'll feel better."

"Couldn't feel worse."

He was a child, twenty-two tops.

"You the new den mum?" Pieter grinned.

Clare turned to the boy. "If you do throw up, aim for the back of his neck."

Eric glanced in the rearview mirror and smiled at Clare. He pushed the Land Rover fast over a dirt and stone road. Scars left from early explorers or German military, these roads cut across impossible terrain. And like every incursion by man here, they were scars that never faded. A good thing in this instance.

Clare pulled her hat firmly down and began sorting through her camera equipment. To get usable shots, she'd need every lens and every trick in her bag. Her career had taken off once she perfected the ability to capture animals in motion. Most photographers could snap the photo of a bear or moose or mountain lion, but Clare's genius, her signature, was that same lion slipping down a tree. One paw on a lower branch, three midair. What was below him? What was he after? She left that to the viewer to decide. Her clients loved the quality of suspense and mystery. And for that, they paid a great deal of money.

This mission was like none that Clare had experienced before. She would need to capture these murderers, and they would be astute enough to try to avoid that. *Dear God, don't let my photos be of their kill,* she prayed. The ghosts of those skulls at Rhino Camp had haunted her dreams that night. At least she had light and would not need a tripod to steady her camera. That would allow her to move and to shoot much more quickly. She'd won the skirmish with Pieter. She had not won the war. He would brook no fumbling, no delay, no failure on her part. Nor should he.

Thanks to the ginger chew, Chuck's face had turned from bilious green to a relatively normal pink. The dust billowed up around them, forcing them to close the windows. Any ocean chill had long been beaten back by the desert sun. The back seat seemed to Clare much like the mechanical bull she once rode on a dare in Jackson Hole, Wyoming—bucking, twisting, pounding her tailbone into the seat and jolting her internal organs.

Like Clare, Eric seemed utterly absorbed, his eyes intent, his hands gripping the steering wheel, his arms straining at the seams in his shirt. His Tilley hat shaded his eyes. She admired his sharp features, maybe more because she had seen them soften and change when he was embarrassed or miserable or joking. In an arrogant man, his features would be almost ridiculously handsome.

Eric slowed and spoke to her reflection in the rearview mirror. "We're getting close. The dust might give us away."

"You *want* to catch them? I thought we just wanted to chase them off."

Pieter turned in his seat. "We'd like to know which particular vermin are out there. The poor beasts have a lot of enemies, and the bloody government's not willing to do much. If we can bring them evidence, it's possible we can muster enough international attention to force them to act."

"Photos?" Clare asked.

"Bodies would be better."

Eric looked back quickly. "They have guns, Clare, and they won't hesitate to shoot the rhinos. Or us."

"You didn't sign up for one of Daniel's picnics, girlie," Pieter shouted above the roar of the engine.

"Maybe *Time* will publish my photo of you tying poachers to anthills. Make me a lot of money."

Eric ground the gears to low as they approached a rise, creeping to full stop just before the crest. The five of them piled out of the truck, the older three stiffly, a still queasy Chuck weakly, and Ezra like a gazelle. "Keep low." Eric motioned with his hands. "There's a wide valley below. Our other truck should be farther down the ridge."

They walked across the blazing hot terrain in a crouch to the top and then lay on their bellies. Clare felt a sharp rock jab her hip as she swung her camera bag around. But when she held up her camera with its telescopic lens, Pieter slapped his hat over it.

"What?" She was furious.

"They'll catch the reflection off that. Hold on a minute until we see what's down there." He spoke with surprising kindness.

"Of course, sorry."

"You probably don't hunt this species often."

"Not in the wild." Clare dug in her bag. "I've got a lens hood. That'll stop any reflection."

But the valley below was empty, stretching like the surface of Mars. Not even an antelope "God, Pieter, where are they? I thought surely they'd come this way. The villager said north-west of the water hole. If we've guessed wrong, it could cost Flora her life, and without her, the baby is dead too." He rolled onto his back.

"It's a bloody, big bastard of a desert," offered Pieter. Again, Clare was surprised by Pieter's kindness, though she'd never had any doubt he loved Eric as much as a brother.

"Look!" Ezra had scuttled beyond the top of the hill and off to their left. He was pointing excitedly at a miniature spiral of dust—without, Clare noticed, the benefit of either binoculars or her telescopic lens.

"Stunning eyes, Ezra." Eric stifled a sob.

"Flora." Eric rolled back onto his belly and looked at Clare. "She's strolling in all ignorance and innocence, the baby hopefully mucking around being a pest behind her."

"Go! Go!" yelled Pieter, jumping up. "Truck behind her. And it's not ours."

They scrambled into the Land Rover, Eric speeding off before the doors slammed shut. "We've got to get between the poachers and Flora. Fast!"

Startling Flora was a concern. They did not want her running into a trap but rather to distance herself from it. And how could the baby keep up? But the bigger risk now was the truck. Eric had to get between the poachers and Flora.

Clare clutched the seat back as Eric roared down the mountainside, moving south to end up behind Flora, who couldn't maintain enough speed to provide a buffer between her and a spray of bullets. Eric maneuvered crazily around a pile of sharp rocks. A punctured radiator would be the ruin of them all.

Chuck and Clare clung to the roll bars as the truck careened wildly to the valley floor, over ruts and sand swells. Ezra sat in the jump seat behind her, placidly smiling as if on a carnival ride. Clare admired him more with every encounter. Unlike the rest of them in the truck, so serious, so certain the fate of all the animal kingdom rested on their shoulders, Ezra just observed.

"There!" shouted Pieter. "Go left! I see them. Oh, Christ, they have machine guns mounted on the damn truck."

Eric swerved, steering a course directly toward the poachers.

Clare managed to get her camera out the window, the motor drive firing fifty frames a second. Mercifully, the road was smoother on the valley floor. Her heart beat wildly. Eric appeared to be on a suicide mission, aiming straight for the poachers. Through her lens, she could now see the poachers' faces, though they wore sunglasses. But with this lens, she could capture a mole on a cheek.

Pieter shot a startled look at Eric. Clare believed Pieter unflappable. But he was decidedly worried, which added greatly to her own fright.

A head-on collision in the middle of the Namib Desert was not how she imagined her life ending. At this speed, at least it would be over quickly, though. Flora would live, she thought. She would glance with her beady little eyes at the heap of burning vehicles and charred bodies. Then lumber on in search of shade. Maybe wondering what all that fuss was about. Clare actually kind of hated Flora right now.

Looking through the viewfinder, Clare made fine adjustments. But there was nothing. Only sand stretching forever. She pulled away from her camera. Gone.

The poachers had wheeled around and fled.

Pieter and Chuck were yelling and laughing jubilantly. Eric slowed the truck to a stop and rested his head on the steering wheel, exhausted. Clare simultaneously wanted to slap him and take him in her arms.

"Did you see the look on their faces?" Chuck asked. "Thought we were going to kill them."

Pieter looked at Eric and said softly, "That exact thought occurred to me."

"No anthills today, eh?" Clare put her hand on Pieter's shoulder. She'd had close encounters, but roaring down the barrel of a mounted machine gun was new.

Pieter covered her hand with his own. "Sorry to disappoint. One day I'm buying me one of those rocket launchers." He patted her hand.

The second truck finally pulled alongside, and the driver craned his head out, his face flushed with alarm. "You guys are insane! You realize how close you were to a crash? Man, I've never seen anything like it."

"So, who were they?" asked Clare. "I got twelve hundred photos, but they were pretty disguised."

"Ex-military, probably. If their bloody civil wars aren't devastating enough, they also leave vehicles and weapons scattered across Namibia for any asshole to pick up and use." Pieter turned to her. "We'll give your photos to the regional governor. Even so, he'll probably just tut-tut over them and do nothing."

"Let's go see if our girl got her feathers ruffled." Eric stepped unsteadily out of the truck. "Pieter, you drive. I'm done for today." He climbed in beside Clare, leaving a delighted Chuck to ride up front with Pieter.

They drove slowly for several miles. Ezra perched on the

fender looking for tracks. Now and then, he'd jump down and run in graceful zigzags, using hand gestures to communicate with Pieter.

Clare had the window down, the air still a blast furnace. But she felt calm. Her life had been handed back to her. Again. This was the second time she'd nearly been killed while with Eric. The thought dawned on her, he might not be all that good for her health.

Once again he seemed to read her thoughts. "You okay? You can ride up front. Chuck will trade with you."

"No. Survivors are always found in the back."

"I wouldn't have rammed them, you know."

Pieter turned, and he and Clare looked at Eric, their eyebrows raised.

"Well, I wouldn't have!" Eric insisted.

"You had us fooled," said Clare, putting her hand on his knee.

Pieter suddenly braked and pointed. In the distance stood Flora and Flossie. Clare used canned air to blow the dust from her lens and began shooting. Mom had obligingly, and most photogenically, tipped a euphorbia tree over into a hammock, allowing air flow below and above. Flossie appeared to be fighting sleep as any infant does, butting her beer-barrel nose into her mom's ribs, finally giving up and settling down. Clare conceded if their suicide mission had insured Flora's safety for now, maybe it was worth it.

"Flora's got a good idea," said Eric, lowering his binoculars. "Let's go home. I could use a beer. And a nap."

21.

After the excitement and this long, long day, Clare sat alone at the end of the huge communal dining table. She'd finished her dinner of greens and lentils and was drinking rooibos tea when Stacey sat down beside her. "How can you drink that stuff? Wouldn't you just kill for a coconut latte? Seriously, I'd pay fifty dollars." She stared wistfully at the cinderblock wall as if a Starbuck's barista might appear. "It'd have to be a venti, though."

"Make mine a caramel macchiato. And yes, I do want whip. Mounds of the stuff," added Clare.

Stacey looked delighted to find a kindred spirit. "With those caramel swirls on the top. And ice. God, how I miss ice! Zahara doles out ice cubes like they're gold nuggets."

"I want a burrito too, with cheese and sour cream and guac. And chips with salsa."

"Fries on the side for me. With real ketchup. And a beer not made from elephant piss." Stacey bumped against Clare's shoulder.

"And COLD!" They both shrieked with laughter.

Clare leaned back into Stacey and said dreamily, "In a frosted mug." Somehow that caused them to dissolve into hiccupping, snorting giggles, tears running down their faces. A release, Clare thought, from the intensity and seriousness of Rhino Camp.

When they straightened up, Clare noticed the disapproving glances of researchers. The scene from their eyes—two

American airheads, giggling like teenagers, a little secret society of women who shouldn't be in Africa, much less Namibia, much less Rhino Camp. In high school, she'd been teased for inappropriate friendships, though Stacey would probably never become a close friend.

But the young researchers here were so serious, so self-righteous. So judgmental. Clare had sympathy for Stacey. The scientists made it abundantly clear Stacey did not measure up. So involved in their work, they'd judged her quickly, found her wanting, and circled the wagons against her.

"I heard about what happened today," said Stacey. "Sounded scary."

"It was. I have to say, I thought we were all going to die."

"Glad I didn't go." Stacey fussed with her cuticles, then looked up at the clusters of researchers by the tea urn. "Not that anyone would ever think of asking me."

"Stacey, it's not personal. They didn't want me either. All they ever consider is the animals, and generally, only whichever one is their particular specialty."

"They did let you go, though."

"I can be really pushy when I have to be. And I'm used to being the only woman." Close up, Clare realized how remarkably pretty Stacey was. "How do you keep your face looking fresh in the hideous heat? Usually, I look like I've been bobbing for french fries."

"Hardly." Stacey pulled out her Evian spritzer. "They smirk at this," she said, holding up the can, "but try it. Amazing stuff."

With the late afternoon breeze kicking up, the cooling mist felt wonderful. Clare noticed a few researchers regarding them with disdain. "One more time." Stacey giggled and spritzed them both, looking like she'd found a lifeboat in these shark-infested waters.

Clare looked into Stacey's beautiful eyes, outlined in blue. "I'm not sure Rhino Camp seems like a very good fit for you. Are you liking it here?" Clare pretty much knew the answer. And after being the oldest student in her recent classes, she also knew what it was like to be alone in a group, and how much she'd appreciated anyone's kindness: the cafeteria lady, the janitor, a professor or two (*not* Timothy). Clare didn't believe the researchers here were deliberately cruel, but deliberate or not, they were unkind.

"Africa. It sounded so much better than it is. And I love animals. We have two cats and three bunnies and some parakeets. So my father talked to one of his university friends, and voilà! I was on my way to the land of *Lion King*." Her face clouded. "Only it isn't. And the animals aren't the only vicious creatures. And they aren't even clean!" Stacey's little girl voice carried, and that last line was heard. She rolled her eyes and then whispered. "I mean, I know water's in short supply. But these people don't even *try!*"

She seemed on the verge of tears, and Clare was too exhausted to offer solace. "Can you leave Rhino Camp? Go back home early?"

"No. This is my third try at an internship, and they'll kick me out of graduate school if I don't finish."

Clare shifted away a bit. "I need to get some rest."

Suddenly Stacey adjusted her face and posture. Like someone clicking together the last piece of a puzzle, she regained her composure. "Thanks for the chat," she said, almost dismissing Clare.

"Maybe we can talk tomorrow."

"Sure. If you want." Her shoulders ramrod straight, her eyes ahead, she marched through the enemy encamped around the tea urn.

22.

S tacey groggily awoke, then stiffened as she realized exactly where she was—on an uncomfortable bed, a cot really, in an uncomfortably bare room. Namibia. Sounded like some dismal intestinal disease. The symptoms of which pretty much paralleled the awful reality of her "study abroad" indentureship at Rhino Camp.

Daddy (Pierpont Winship III) had bribed her school's department of zoology—as well as the Rhino Camp research facility—with his usual largesse, ensuring three months of utter misery for his only daughter at this godforsaken outpost. He had mentioned "academic enrichment" in a terse email, but she knew her banishment had more to do with a series of less than socially acceptable romantic escapades. What was college for, if not to expand her horizons beyond the suffocating confines of Park Avenue? She had to admit the caddy might have shown a certain lack of judgment. And the bartender. And the—but this catalog of indiscretions wouldn't change one single bit of her current plight. Stacey sighed. Daddy's email announcing her fate still stung: "My dearest Anastasia [always trouble when he used her birth name], Since you have demonstrated such a keen interest in wildlife, I have taken the liberty of..."

Rhino conservation. What a joke. She had yet to see a single one of the ridiculous, clumsy beasts. The only wildlife so far involved the two yapping furies that inhabited the research headquarters, Rhett and Scarlet. Obnoxious, hyper little monsters. Oh, yes—and baboons. Stacey shuddered at the memory.

Was it her fault she had been abandoned in the truck trashed by those dreadful apes? She could have died there for all anyone cared. She sniffed, then lifted her sleeping mask from her face and blearily checked off another date on the calendar hanging near her pillow. Forty-six more to go.

She flopped back onto the bed with a huff.

As if noisy fleabags and mortal danger from monkeys weren't enough, there was the utter lack of sympathy that she received from Eric and Pieter. Eric, though decidedly handsome, in a dark, brooding manner, was positively obsessed with his studies. And with the poaching crisis the area was experiencing. (She had to assume the poachers experienced better luck with rhino sightings than she had, if they were going to make a go of it.) Eric struck her as a living version of that weird captain—what's his name—the one with the white whale. And Pieter made no disguise of his contempt for her. For everything about her: her coiffed hair, her stylish clothing, her nasal voice, her utter lack of wilderness experience. Who did they think they were getting, Crocodile F-ing Dundee?

Well, there was no getting around it. She glanced at the calendar again. Yup. Forty-six more days of this crap.

Stacey rose, rubbing the sleep from her eyes and giving her face a little spritz of Evian. She reached cautiously for her fuzzy pink Ralph Lauren slippers. She hadn't needed to be told twice to always knock any footwear before putting them on. To always shake her clothes out. To always pull a drawer fully open before reaching into it. That was the drill. Such a perfect hiding place for so many deadly creatures, this stinking country's primary claim to fame. Essentially the drill was to exist on red alert, constantly on the lookout for menace and mayhem. This perpetual vigilance was exhausting. Even ants could be deadly here. Not to mention just about every snake.

She stood, flapping her matching pink Ralph Lauren robe listlessly, then shivered, remembering a Facebook post. Before her banishment to hellhole on a stick. It was of an outdoor latrine in some other hellhole in southern Africa. In the photo's dim light, at first she could barely make out a dark, tubular shape looming against the small canvas room's wall. The tube descended from open darkness into the toilet below. A huge, horrifyingly perpendicular python. Anaconda. Whatever. Slowly, her eyes reconciled the nightmarish image of her projected fears and the picture's reality: wildly humorous, obviously, to someone. An elephant had discovered a convenient drinking fountain, that was all. Siphoning all that delicious fresh water in the cool night. Still, she could not overcome her initial, primal response. The photo struck her as being very much like those stupid pictures, the ones with dueling images: a vase or two faces, a beautiful woman or a death's head. An elephant's trunk—or a gigantic snake.

She gave her slippers another vigorous whack, slipped them on, and tightened the sash to her robe before fluffing out the luxurious bath towel she had brought all the way from Bloomingdale's. The curt orientation message had indicated that accommodations here at the research base in Damaraland were "Spartan," a decided understatement. Dumbaraland was more like it.

As she padded down the long hall toward the bathroom, the familiar late morning sounds of the compound greeted her. Zahara washing dishes. Scarlet and Rhett barking furiously, as usual, at goodness knew what. Pieter shouting a series of dire commands that they quiet down. She could smell the delicious fragrance of freshly brewed coffee, one of the camp's few concessions to civilization. These were the welcome, almost homely, moments when all felt comfortable, secure. As if she weren't in stomach-churning Namibia after all.

She cradled her treasured black soap, her loofah, her whitening strips. Now for her morning ritual. Having secured the bathroom door, she gazed into the mirror as she ruffled her rich brown curls. Ugh. Were those crow's feet? Damn climate. Like living in a furnace. She lifted her chin and scanned her throat. Definitely would have to step up the spritzing. And ration her arsenal of moisturizing creams and lotions. If she wasn't careful, she'd be reduced to whatever she could find in Zahara's kitchen. Mayonnaise? Goat lard? Heavens! She knew the response she'd get from Eric, not to mention the predictable tirade from Pieter, if she so much suggested a drive to the elegant shops at the Lodge for supplies. Stacey frowned and shrugged. Men.

She reached into the shower and turned on the faucet, slid out of her robe and nightie, and kicked off her slippers. Then she piled them all on the closed toilet seat. Just as she began to draw back the waxed canvas shower curtain, she heard a heavy thump. Some inconsiderate dope must have left a shampoo bottle or something, and it had fallen off a shelf. Annoyed, she tugged the curtain aside.

An icy wave shot up her spine. She gulped. Then stumbled back. There, coiled in the steaming shower stall, lay an enormous, steel-gray snake. It raised its coffin-shaped head and hissed, its jaws wide. Dripping fangs protruded from its white-lipped, inky-black mouth.

Stacey felt her heart bruising her ribs, its pumping deafening her. Paralyzed, she stared at the snake, which slowly began to uncoil.

She blinked. Not a drill. Red alert.

Whimpering in horror, she whipped the curtain closed and hurled herself against the locked door, fumbling hysterically with the latch. She could scarcely breathe for the choking sobs that convulsed her as she clawed the door open and, spinning into the hallway, slammed it shut.

She screamed—a shrill, suffocating wave of misery and fear.

Footsteps thundered in the stairwell. First to answer the hysterical summons were the two dogs, who raced up the stairs, barking frantically at this unfamiliar, unearthly sound. Once they had inspected Stacey and determined she wasn't in any immediate danger, their ears cocked at some different, more subtle sound. From the bathroom. They approached the closed door, then stiffened, hackles up, tails erect.

"Scarlet! Rhett! Damn you!" Pieter bounded up the stairs and turned into the hall, then skidded to a stop. "Stacey?"

In his haste, he had nearly collided with a very naked Stacey. Shrinking against the far wall, he covered his eyes and reddened.

"What the—what's the matter?" he stammered then lowered his hands slightly, keeping his eyes locked on her face. "Get a hold of yourself, girl. What is it? A mouse? A beetle?"

Stacey took a deep breath, her mouth gaping like a goldfish, but she couldn't speak. Her eyes bulged, and her face was drained of all color.

The dogs, as if on cue, began to bark and scrabble furiously at the bathroom door.

Pieter, desperately averting his gaze from Stacey, bellowed at them, "Easy! Leave it!" He gave a mock kick in their direction. Then he reached for the doorknob.

"No!" Stacey shrieked. "No! Suh … suh … snake!"

Pieter's hand jerked back.

Zahara had just joined the group and was trying to assess the chaos. Shaking her head, she draped a dish towel across Stacey's chest, then reconsidering, lowered it.

"Something's in there," Pieter growled. "Keep the door closed, hear?"

Zahara nodded, clearly alarmed. Still holding the strategically inadequate towel, she began to console the quivering girl. "Oh, Miss Stacey. You all right? Let's get you to your room. Get you dressed." At this gesture of kindness, Stacey began to sob even more violently, collapsed into Zahara's capable arms, and allowed herself to be led down the hall. "There, there. Everything's all right. You'll see." Just to be certain of the truth of her words, Zahara called out over her shoulder, "Mr. Pieter, what do you—"

But he had disappeared. And so had the dogs.

LATER THAT EVENING, at the dinner table, a now fully clothed but still wan Stacey forked anxiously at her salad as Pieter recounted the morning's excitement for the benefit of the mesmerized research students, as well as for Zahara, who hovered nearby. And for Eric, who seemed less than entertained by the narrative. Yet another distraction from his work.

Pieter had just diplomatically condensed the towel scene when he leaned back in his chair, cradled his hands behind his head, and surveyed his rapt audience with a rakish smile.

"You see, first I had to get the dogs locked up. No telling what was in there. Stacey was in no condition to describe the 'Suh … suh … snake.' Could have been anything." He chuckled. "Didn't think Zahara would approve much of my shooting up the bathroom, but thought I should carry my pistol—just in case." Relishing the building tension, he paused, then resumed. "Went around to the tool shed. Got a hoe—and an ax. But when I went back to open the door, something was wedged against it. Something heavy. Something alive." He paused again. "No choice but to give that damn door the biggest shove of my life. So I jumped back and waited. Soon enough, the head appears, fast. Making a run for it—mamba, for sure! Then, BOOM! Down goes the hoe. Then the ax."

The room went quiet. Mamba. Swift. And deadly. Their bite, known widely as "the kiss of death."

Eventually, one of the researchers ventured a breathless, "How long do you think it was?"

"Difficult to say." Pieter stroked his chin thoughtfully. "Too many pieces."

Stacey chimed in shrilly. "Not enough pieces, if you ask me." She shivered, then sniffed. "Pureed would have been fine. Just fine."

Pieter laughed. "Ah, Stacey, you have a sense of humor after all."

She shot him a kiss-of-death look, threw her fork down, shoved her chair back, and called, "Here, Rhett, Scarlet! Come." Then in a trembling singsong, "Let's go to bed, okay? Check out the upstairs, okay? Good doggies. Come." They followed her obligingly, tails wagging, as she left the room.

Eric smiled. "Looks as if she's got some new friends. Thought she was frightened of dogs. Snakes more, it appears." The group responded with a collective, if somewhat tentative laugh. "Naked, you say?"

"Well, I—"

Eric couldn't help grinning at his friend's obvious discomfort. Even so, he refrained from any further discussion regarding dish towels. Then his mood turned serious. "Can't imagine how a snake that large got into the second-floor shower. Pipes?"

Pieter shook his head. "No idea. We'll have to be more careful, that's all. Glad Stacey found it before the dogs did." He bit his lower lip and gave it a long suck. "Now, that would have been bad."

Eric nodded. Everyone was silent. Clearly, both the story and the meal were over. One by one, they slowly rose to help Zahara clear the table and headed off to inspect their tents. Very carefully.

Even so, no one slept particularly well.

This was especially true for Scarlet and Rhett, who couldn't understand why they were locked in a room with this peculiar human, who all night long flailed about in her sleep, crying with plaintive urgency, "Suh . . . suh!"

23

Clare was walking back toward her tent, head down, thinking about her conversation with Stacey the previous day, when Eric caught up with her.

He smiled bashfully. "I was wondering if you'd like to go for a swim. Before you go back to the lodge tomorrow. There's a water hole, pretty close. Complete with a waterfall, a small miracle in the desert. An ancient spring, if you can imagine. Or the rest are watching a movie if you'd prefer that."

"A swim sounds wonderful. And knowing your staff they'll be watching *Born Free* for the 853rd time."

"Saw you talking to Stacey."

"She's kind of lonely. People here aren't very nice to her. And I don't think she has much to do."

"You mean after she gets up at ten o'clock? After she puts on her makeup?" Eric's face turned red. "I know. It's a problem. I tried making her the official camp tour guide. That only generated more ridicule."

"She belongs at the Lodge. She'd love it. They'd love her. She has people skills, not animal skills."

"You jest! People skills? Have you seen how she gets along with my researchers? That's not possible."

"They haven't given her much of a chance." They'd reached Clare's tent. Zahara or Hosea had put down the mosquito netting and lit a small lantern for her.

"Suits are optional," Eric started, reddening, "but do grab a towel. I'll be right back."

Optional? Hmm. That was unexpected, Clare thought. She dug through her pack and found her bathing suit.

When Eric returned, she asked, "Got your Nerf gun?"

"It's not far, but you'd better stay close. Really close." He held out his hand, and she took it.

Being outside the compound felt exciting, a bit dangerous. "You've done this before, right? I mean, people go here? At night? Not just the lions and tigers and bears, oh my." Clare quickened her step to keep up, his long stride equaling two of hers.

"Lions are like Parisians. They rarely think of eating until dark. Most unfashionable. There'd be talk." He pulled her closer, tucking her arm under his. "We have a good hour before dark."

"Before the bistros open?" She laughed. "I feel like we're sneaking out our bedroom windows, meeting high school buddies to smoke in the park. Except the worst consequence of that is we'd get grounded for a week. Rarely did anyone in high school get eaten alive, though my friend Sarah's parents were seriously mean." Being nervous had always made her chatty, not a trait she liked in herself.

Eric simply shrugged and grinned.

As they walked down the dry creek bed, a dust devil spiraled and caught the light like a rose curtain fluttering in the breeze. Eric seemed in his element: confident, composed, happy. But she noticed he did have his pistol and was grateful.

"What was that?" Clare stopped, listening.

"What?"

"That noise. Didn't you hear it?" She held his arm more tightly and walked on, but kept a close watch on the scattered bushes.

"Probably just lizards. I think we could take 'em." When

they reached the pool, which really did have a little waterfall, she was entranced. Two crested porcupines glanced resentfully at them, then waddled off into the brush. A box turtle scuttled down the mud bank and slid into the water.

"Turtles? In the desert? This place never ceases to amaze me." Clare put her towel on a rock and stripped down to her bathing suit

Eric stared at the ground. "I'll deliver my very thrilling turtle lecture later. Better we get a swim in." He undid his belt and stepped out of his pants. Clare was relieved he was wearing trunks. She admired his muscled chest and legs. She caught him blushing. "Watch the mud. It's slippery." He held her hand as they waded into the cool water.

"Thank you for bringing me here! I *love* this place. I've never been swimming anywhere more beautiful. Not Hawaii. Not Costa Rica. You expect that there. But here in the desert, it's just miraculous." She put her hands on his shoulders and kissed him lightly on the cheek. Eric stood motionless as he watched her glide into the pool and under the waterfall.

Day was ebbing, the horizon an artist's palette, bleeding blue to purple to rose. A few stars twinkled in the deepening sky. And the mountains, sharp, red, and foreboding in day, were softening into charcoal. The desert heat radiated off the rocks and sand, and the water felt delicious. Clare dipped under. Much life must depend, and had depended for eons, on this little pool.

ERIC PADDLED ABOUT and floated on his back, but he kept a careful watch. Clare might not appreciate another close call, and it was possible a particularly ambitious lioness might cut her nap short to go hunting. He also watched Clare, letting the waterfall pour over her head, her shoulders, her breasts shining wet.

Despite Clare's delight at the oasis, Eric wasn't sure she belonged here. In Namibia. And if she wouldn't or couldn't live here with him, he didn't think he could make love to her, not like he wanted to. His heart was nearly lost now, but if his body had its way, the memory of any embrace would haunt him forever, destroying his peace and ability to live this life he felt was his destiny. Better to let her go before surrendering body and soul. Eric was jolted from his reverie by the airy sound of bellows. He prayed that Clare could see him motion to her and quietly leave the pool.

Clare, still treading water, looked to where Eric was pointing and gasped. An elephant was ambling toward their swimming pool, seemingly unperturbed to find two humans floating in his water bowl. She backed up the mud bank as the elephant approached on the other side, his forehead now furrowed in disapproval. Slowly, he lowered his trunk, slurping some water, blowing some over his back.

"That's quite a sight," Clare whispered, after they put some distance between them and their unanticipated guest

"Yeah. Don't be taken in by his I'm-just-a-regular-guy shtick. He'd be perfectly happy to put down one of his big feet and squish us like jelly between his toes. Or swing that trunk and knock us halfway to your California. I've seen one send a full-grown cow flying."

Eric recognized this elephant from a large notch in his ear —an old guy, probably ousted from the herd by a youngster. No good to anthropomorphize him, but difficult to avoid. He looked lonely, used up. He swung his trunk and flapped his ears like huge, moth-eaten blankets. An attempt, Eric surmised, to assert dominance over another male, even a puny human. The sight of him discomforted Eric. Was he a reflection? A warning? *This is what you'll become if you don't hold fast to that woman. I, too, thought I'd be young forever, useful forever. Virile forever. I wasn't. Nor will you be. Just because you stay busy doesn't mean time isn't relentlessly washing over you.*

They stood watching in awe. Clare moved to face him, put her arms around his waist, and pressed herself to his chest. He looked down, swept a strand of wet hair off her cheek. Without consulting his doctoral brain, for once, he kissed her, crushing her wet body against his own, his hand slipping just inside the band of her bikini.

The elephant gave a thunderous snort.

Eric whispered into Clare's ear. "I'm not sure our visitor approves. Let's go back." Clare groaned but pulled gently away.

Eric wasn't sure how he ever found the will to let her go.

"Take care of yourself," he said quietly to the elephant, who'd resumed drinking. And the two walked in silence back to camp.

24.

Clare hadn't left the confines of Lodge at Damara for over a week since her return, and the constant requests for reshoots of preening guests had begun to wear on her. She knew it was strictly against lodge rules—and her contract—to use one of the smaller Jeeps without a guide and prior authorization. But she rankled under the restrictions. It seemed to her that Daniel was simply being overprotective. Or possessive, wanting her continuously at his beck and call.

When she crept into the garage well before dawn, she wasn't surprised to find the watchman there.

"Good morning, Missy Rainbow. You are up early."

"Good morning." Clare hoped her smile didn't betray her nervousness. "Yes, I know. Very early, but I need to get an important shot. A series, actually. And I understood that all the guides were reserved for game treks today. Thought I'd use a small Jeep. Won't be gone long. Not going far at all."

"Sorry, Missy Rainbow, but I can't let you have the keys without permission."

"Didn't Mr. Sypher or someone from the office call yesterday? I understood it was all arranged." Clare felt guilty about the lie but exhilarated by the impulse to gain even a few hours of freedom.

"No one called. That I know of. Sorry. Let me just phone—"

"Oh, no, I wouldn't trouble anyone at this hour. Really. I'm sure they just forgot. I'll be back before anyone realizes I'm missing."

The watchman's eyes widened with concern and confusion.

"Your job is important. I know that. And I will take responsibility. Scout's honor." She vowed that if caught she'd protect the man.

In truth, Clare had never been a scout. Her parents objected to the "militarization" of most youth groups, particularly their unhealthy "capitalistic" indulgences, selling such toxic commodities as cardboard cookies and lead-based holiday wrapping paper.

"Look," she urged, "the kitchen even packed my breakfast." Beaming, she waved a rather sodden doggy bag containing a sizable chunk of New York steak and grilled potatoes from dinner the night before. Clare could never finish any meal at the Lodge. No wonder the gym operated 24/7.

"Well . . . if you say so, Missy Rainbow. But Mr. Daniel, he get—" The guard had probably never seen a doggy bag. Or such a radiant smile. Reluctantly, he handed her the keys. "The tank is full, the radio charged. You drive safely now." He paused, his face a mask of worry. "I would be more comfortable if you would just let me phone—"

"Thank you. No need. Please, don't worry."

Clare felt a rush of adrenaline just turning on the ignition. She put the stick into first and slowly left the basement parking area, coasting down the winding hill toward the gate. Fortunately, the main gate could be opened using the Jeep's automated device. And the entry station wasn't manned until dawn. Clare had planned her little excursion perfectly.

Freedom. She marveled as she gazed through the rearview mirror, watching the massive gates swing closed behind her. She knew exactly where she was heading. Just thirty miles down the road, then off-road for a few miles. The terrain was difficult but not impossible. She had been to this water hole with a tour group. Unfortunately, the visit had been marred as most of the game had been scared off by the busload of clamoring guests. The excursion had been further dampened in that Eric and Daniel had had a considerable altercation about that very fact. Eric had seemed particularly concerned that the tourists were becoming a nuisance, especially to Flora and her calf, who were known to frequent this particular water hole. Eric worried that the presence of humans in such persistent numbers would habituate the animals, making them more vulnerable to poachers. Daniel insisted in no uncertain terms that Lodge at Damara and their game tours actually protected the rhino with their constant presence. It was as if each arrogant man felt he owned the rhinos and the vast desert they ranged.

Clare felt a sudden thrill. Perhaps she might see the elusive pair, mother and calf. A small chance. Certainly not the primary reason for her private expedition. She had, on that prior occasion, noticed a number of bowerbird nests in the nearby trees and since then had hoped to get some pictures of the fabulous birds themselves. Like most creatures in this harsh landscape, they would be active in the very early morning.

She loved the crisp air rushing over her as she drove into the darkness fading to gray. She even loved the Jeep's lurching as she turned carefully onto what was little more than a gravel path off the main road. The engine's hum seemed like music to her. So perfectly alone. Not a single person to worry about. Not Daniel, with his incessant demands and intrusions. Not Eric, with his penetrating eyes, his sensuous smile. His passion for the rhino, and thus, his constant judgment of her affiliation with Lodge at Damara. She sighed. Men—how they seemed to weigh her down with their ambition and desire. Now she could be truly herself in the purest solitude of nature. In the serenity of a new day being born.

She took a deep breath, as if to cleanse her mind of everything but the glorious morning blossoming into color around her. There. The small grove of scrappy trees was in sight. Just beyond lay the water hole. She cut the engine. No sense ruining any potential shots today. Clare looked at her watch and took a relaxed breath. She easily had an hour or so before she needed to return or before any tour groups might invade the area.

Clare checked her camera gear and placed a couple of lenses into the pockets of her vest. Just as she was about to open the door and begin the short hike to the trees, a series of ghastly whoops and shrieks cut through the crystalline morning air.

Hyenas!

They usually hunted at night, but possibly they had come upon a lion's kill and were engaged in their usual savage histrionics.

Clare's curiosity got the better of her. If the bowerbird shots weren't meant to be, she might get some of a substantially more dramatic nature. She turned the engine back on and cautiously edged toward the din issuing from just beyond the trees. With any luck, she could shoot from the safety of the cab.

Just as she rounded the scrim of foliage, she gasped.

There was Flora, standing helpless, her head lowered, thrusting wildly at the attacking beasts. Flossie, so vulnerable, kept clinging to her mother, trying desperately to crawl beneath her, to hide behind her forelegs. Mirroring her mother's parries, she swung her little head in helpless self-defense, but her tiny nubbed horns posed little threat to the shrilling, snarling horde.

In numb horror, Clare groped for the radio. If she could just reach Eric, Daniel, anyone, help would come. If she could just—Clare looked at the recharge button in disbelief. It flashed a hostile, admonishing red. The two-way radio was dead. Hadn't the watchman expressly told her it was charged? Of course, he had. Clare shuddered. She knew better: never trust anyone else with your safety. Not here. This was an oversight worthy of Stacey Winship, not Clare Rainbow-Dashell. She had been in such a rush to escape the Lodge, she hadn't even thought to check. Her heart plummeting, she glanced at the fuel gauge. At least that read accurately. But a full gas tank would be of little help to the besieged rhinos.

Clare could only watch in horror as the hyena pack worked systematically, some taking turns distracting Flora, while others lunged at Flossie, trying to grab the baby by her neck, tearing into her backside, snapping at her stumpy little legs. Anything to injure her, to separate her from her mother. Still others would rush Flora's flanks, bite at her, then retreat. Clare could sense the brave pair's welling fatigue. The attack must have been going on for some while. It suddenly struck Clare as odd that Flora never circled, challenging her attackers, establishing a wider defensive perimeter. Instead, she just stood there, her massive head churning the air, scimitar horns flashing while the predators mobbed her and her helpless calf.

As she drove the Jeep nearer, Clare recognized the cause of their peril and gasped in anguish. Flora couldn't swing her great bulk around. She couldn't walk. She couldn't even move. A poacher's wire snare had gouged her right foreleg inches deep just above her ankle. An agonizing injury, Clare realized, terror and panic welling inside her. The rhino was trapped there. And so was her baby.

Clare didn't have a gun. She had nothing. Slowly she edged the Jeep toward the melee, then blasted the horn a few times. A few slathering faces turned, but that was all. Immediately, they resumed their ferocious assault. They were bent on a warm meal. And they wanted it now.

It occurred to Clare in a sickening wave that Eric was right about the potential damage of tourism to the animals' instincts. Less so, for the ancient and reactive rhino. It was, however, cruelly apparent that the hyenas had become habituated and were unafraid. Her small vehicle, to them, presented about as much menace as a large rock.

Clare edged the vehicle even closer. She couldn't risk injuring the rhino by driving into the fray. She could bump a few of the marauding clan with the Jeep's fenders or wheels, but little more. She looked about in desperation. If she got out, she would risk becoming prey herself. It was a sacrifice she was unwilling to make. Tears filled her eyes. What would Eric think of her, standing by and watching this terrible scene unfold, doing nothing. A miserable, unfeeling coward. Unworthy of Namibia. Of the rhino. Of him.

But something deep inside Clare wouldn't permit that. She swung the door open, and clinging to the frame, began to shout. "Get OUT! You hear me? GET OUT!"

The hyenas seemed deaf. Their grunting and squealing and growling drowned out her voice. Above the demonic cacophony, she could hear Flora's great gusts of breath, like giant bellows. The baby stumbled, obviously weakening. The hyenas grew increasingly bold.

Clare grabbed her tripod and hurled it into the nearest cluster of beasts. They broke, then scampered a short distance, yelping hysterically. Her aim was good. Encouraged, she drove even closer. She could see the tufts of hair on Flora's ears, the blood covering Flossie's haunches and neck.

"STOP IT! GET OUT!" she screamed.

Without thinking, she reached into her camera bag for her heaviest telephoto lens and threw it at the closest, a huge male. Another direct hit. The animal howled, then loped off.

That left only a few animals still in the fight. And their attention divided between their prey and this newly distracting presence. Clare felt a chill when they turned their ravenous eyes on her. She emptied the contents of her camera bag at them, but to no avail. The creatures only dodged the increasingly smaller pieces of equipment hurled in their direction, as if they were all playing some freakish game.

In desperation, Clare looked about for any remaining projectile. She honked the horn. To no avail. Just then, she remembered her doggie bag. She tore it open, ripping the meat into chunks.

"LOOK!" she cried eagerly. "Look what I have! MEAT! TAKE IT!" She lobbed a few pieces in their direction, but as far from the trapped victims as possible.

The largest of the remaining hyenas stopped. It sniffed, then raced toward the meat and gulped it down. The others followed. Clare flung more meat, each time farther from the rhino pair. The hyenas charged the treats, snarling and snapping, their tails erect, their manes bristling. Clare threw the last pieces of potato as far as she could. Immediately a battle broke out among the hyenas. They became one great roiling ball of fur and fangs. And during those precious moments, oblivious of Flora and Flossie. Clare slowly pulled the Jeep between the battle and the weakened rhino pair. A temporary barrier, nothing more.

"Hold on, girls," she wept, choking. "This is it. I have no plan B." Clare laid her head on the steering wheel. It was all over. She could only stand witness for the doomed mother and baby.

Just then, a loud booming—a bear blaster—sounded nearby. Through the ferocious din, she could hear the rumble of an approaching engine.

Clare hammered the horn. "Over here! Please! Please help us," she cried, tears coursing down her face.

Another blast. Closer. Then another. The hyenas scattered, cackling and shrieking.

Clare gasped as a familiar vehicle rolled up.

"Clare! What in the name of God—are you all right?"

25.

Clare could scarcely believe her eyes. "Eric? How?" She began to sob anew. "It's Flora. She's terribly injured. Flossie too. I got here. The hyenas—" She began to sob anew.

"Stay put. I'll take a look." He stepped out of the cab. Then he stopped, startled.

"Clare, there's camera equipment all over the place." He held up a shattered flash attachment. "And not in very good shape. You sure you're all right?"

"It was all I had. No gun. Nothing. I'm fine." Clare sounded as if she was trying to convince herself as much as Eric. "Really. Not a scratch."

He edged around Clare's Jeep to get a better look. During his years working with wildlife he had seen quite a bit—but nothing had prepared him for what he now beheld.

Flora, her tremendous head bowed, her nose almost touching the ground, was gasping huge breaths of fierce surrender. Eric flinched. The gash that encircled her leg was almost certainly bone-deep. The little calf clung to her mother's side. She was wild-eyed, panting, and covered in blood. He crept around them, giving them plenty of space.

"There, there, girls," he whispered. "You've seen enough trouble, haven't you? So bloody unfair."

Flora snorted but didn't lift her head. All fight had ebbed from her.

Eric moved completely behind her. She had suffered massive injuries to her hindquarters. Chunks of flesh were missing from her legs, and her tail was mangled, hanging by a mere tendon. Eric finished the circle, coming to a stop at Clare's window.

"It's bad, Clare." He choked, then swallowed. "Very bad."

"I know!" The look on Eric's face cut her heart. "I tried."

"If she has any chance, she needs immediate veterinary care. And constant protection until it arrives. Poor, brave girl." Eric shook his head. "I'll radio Sypher. He's closer. Maybe he could spare some guides. Pieter will help, but it will take longer. The students—well, they're fine with databases and field samples, but I'd hate to pit them against poachers or hyenas. Or—"

"Don't say it," Clare pleaded. A pride of lion would eagerly avail themselves of such an easy meal. Rhino or student. It wouldn't matter.

Eric reached for his radio and called Lodge at Damara.

"This is Eric Bolton. I need to speak to Mr. Sypher. Right away. That's right, Bolton. Thank you." Eric forced a smile in Clare's direction, then glanced around the Jeep. The rhino seemed frozen. Only their ears twitched. Flora's great sides heaved. Eric scanned the area. No sign of the hyenas returning. "Yes, Daniel. It's Eric. I'm out at the Zebra Pan water hole with Clare. Need the coordinates? Yes. With Clare. I don't know. Stop yelling. I had nothing to do—"

Clare's eyes widened.

He took a deep breath, then continued. "Look, Daniel, I need your help. A couple of rhino are seriously injured. Hyena. They wouldn't have made it without Clare. I don't know, Daniel! For God's sake! Look—we need your vehicles and guides. To form a barricade, guard them until we get some medical help here." Eric looked up at Clare. At first, there was hope in his eyes, and he almost smiled. Then his eyes blazed dark. "You what? Repeat that. Are you bloody serious? Yes. I'll tell her. And Daniel, you'd best tell your people that I will shoot any of them on sight if they want to make a show out of this. You hear me—any of them!"

Eric smashed the radio into its holder.

"Son of a bitch!" he shouted. "Claims that all his guides and vehicles are reserved for the rest of the week. Wanted to know if they could arrange a special party to come take a look." He spat into the dust and then looked up angrily. "Oh, and you. He wants you back at the Lodge immediately."

Clare was silent, appalled at Daniel's lack of concern for the rhinos. Then she calmly asked, "What can we do now? We need to do something."

"I'll call Pieter. There's a rhino specialist in Windhoek. Sheldrake. But it's a long drive. Don't know how quickly he could make it. Or whether she'd survive transport." He peered around the Jeep at the exhausted pair. "I can't believe this happened. And for what? One day, the only evidence of these beasts will be their horns made into sword handles hanging in some museum? Or worse, ground into useless powder for useless cures?"

"And what about Flossie?"

"Clare, they will almost certainly have to be separated. She will need intensive husbandry while her mum heals." Eric's voice sounded distant, almost disembodied. "If she heals. Feeding every three hours. Dressings. Medication."

Clare could sense Eric was close to tears. She touched his shoulder.

"I'll stay. With you. With them. No matter what."

Eric laid his hand over hers.

"Okay. So, you are telling me that Flora must get help, but that she probably wouldn't survive crating and the long road trip. Correct?" Clare felt strangely lucid. As if she were a candle glowing in some dark, mysterious space.

Eric nodded.

"I've heard of animals being sling-transported by helicopters in dire emergencies." She remembered the dramatic rescue of a horse that had slid down a huge slice of mountain one Tevis Cup endurance race, held in the Sierra Nevada. She had been on assignment. The incident was terrible, but the horse survived. "If Flora hasn't sustained any injuries to her back or midsection, it might work."

"She doesn't seem to." Eric paused, then shook his head. "Impossible, Clare. I can't even begin to think of the expense."

"Surely your conservation trust has some discretionary provisions. For emergencies?"

"Nothing that would cover a helicopter medevac to Windhoek."

"Well then," Clare said quietly, "I will cover it."

"You'll what?"

"I'll cover it." Clare was warm with hope.

"I've heard Daniel pays well, but he isn't paying you that kind of money, Clare."

"I have money. Of my own." She looked away from Eric, toward the trees, and mumbled. "From photo prizes. And lectures . . . and stuff."

Clare realized this lying business was perhaps coming too easily. Still her pride and modesty wouldn't allow her to reveal her vast inherited wealth. Her own parents had dedicated their lives to avoiding its oppressive immensity. And Clare had inherited much of the same reticence. In that moment, though, she knew she would give it all away for the chance to save Flora. But Eric mustn't know. She couldn't bear the thought of his judgment.

She turned back to him, her eyes shining with resolve. "Please, let me help. Now. We haven't time. Get someone at camp to make the call. Here. Use my card." She fumbled in her back pocket. "Fly the vet out—and whatever assistants are needed. They can make the necessary evaluations then. We haven't much time, Eric. Please!"

Eric grabbed the radio, enlivened by Clare's urgency, and radioed Rhino Camp. Fortunately, Pieter was still around to make the arrangements. He would then drive to their position with provisions and some of the more stalwart graduate students.

After hanging up, Eric began, "With any luck—" But Clare had taken him by the shoulders and kissed him.

"Everything will be all right. I feel it, Eric."

Eric seemed to have returned to his senses. "Right. Let's get to work. They have enough shade, for now. We've got to get some water close enough. They must be terribly thirsty. And let's cut some branches off these thorn trees. We'll make a partial kraal. Discourage any more unwanted visitors. We can secure most of the area using the trucks." He surveyed the area, calculating distances. "The rest we can patrol."

"Did Pieter say when we should expect the transport?"

Eric looked at her blankly. "There is a lot to organize, Clare. I doubt we'll have any idea until later. Let's see what we have of use in my truck." Eric smiled at the scattered carnage of cameras and accessories. "Appears you've already emptied yours."

She looked around her. The sun had reached its zenith, and heat shimmered everywhere. Off the sandy ground. Off the trees. Off the still, shallow water. She wiped her brow with her forearm as she watched Eric unload items from the truck.

"This rescue may take some time, Clare."

"As long as it takes," she whispered to herself. Then she strode toward him. "How can I help?"

26.

After hours of hacking and wrestling branches into a makeshift barricade, Eric and Clare stepped back to admire their handiwork.

"Amazing what one can achieve with an ax and a couple of Land Rovers, isn't it?"

"Not to mention a small forest of thorn and acacia."

Eric couldn't help but notice how her laughter sparkled, despite her obvious weariness. Just like her dazzling emerald eyes.

"Pieter should be arriving soon. We'll be able to keep them safe until the chopper gets here, at any rate."

They had filled a cooler with water and nudged it toward Flora using a long branch. She huffed a bit when it got close but otherwise ignored it. She took only a long, deep sigh, her head drooping even lower. The calf nuzzled her mother's face and whined, sounding more like a puppy than anything. Flora's ears twitched, but that was all. Flossie turned, puzzled by the new smells of cut wood and petrol and humans. Assuming no immediate peril, she staggered under her mother's teats and began to suckle noisily.

"Good sign?" Clare asked.

"Yes. For Flossie."

Clare used her shirt tail to wipe away her tears.

"Extraordinary how persistent, how strong life is. Even in the face of such, such monstrous injury," he whispered.

They listened to the baby's sloshy sucking, which filled the otherwise soundless air. Flora could have been hewn from granite. The only motions that betrayed her as a living thing were the occasional swivel of an ear or a shudder that rippled across her massive frame.

Before long, Eric and Clare were jolted from their reverie by the roar of an engine. As the vehicle neared, they could recognize Pieter accompanied by two of the researchers, Chuck and Greg—and, to their amazement, Stacey, who was clinging frantically to the roll bar with one hand, an oversized sun hat clamped to her head with the other.

Pieter leapt from the driver's side and, with a jerk of his chin in Stacey's direction, snarled, "Don't even ask." He strode past Eric and Clare toward the rhinos. About twenty feet away from them, he squatted, stroking his chin with one hand, taking it all in. Then he rose to join Eric and Clare.

"Sheldrake promised me they'd get here before sundown. Quite a bit to organize. He'll be flying up with the pilot and two assistants. The rest, we'll have to manage." He paused. "Can't imagine the cost. Not in any budget I've seen. I didn't think we had—" He raised an eyebrow and looked at Eric. "Just gave them the card number, as you said. Right?"

"Thanks, Pieter." Eric scanned the shrubby enclosure and frowned. "I suppose we'll have to clear all this away to make room for the evacuation. Poor Clare. What a day she's had." He nodded toward Clare, who was rubbing scratched, weary arms while attempting to answer an onslaught of questions by Stacey. He noticed that Clare kept shaking her head, but with less insistence. Her weariness was palpable. Then she cast her eyes imploringly his way.

Pieter noted the exchange as well and scowled. "Nothing I could do. Insisted on coming. Insisted on getting dressed. Like that. A bloody garden party." Eric grinned at the way Pieter made the words sound like growls. "I gave her five minutes. Damned if she didn't pull it off."

The men looked askance at Stacey's attire: elaborate hat, huge sunglasses, beflowered sundress, and low-heeled white sandals. Sandals.

Eric grinned. "Maybe we could ask the kind doctor to deposit her at Lodge at Damara on the way back. Or perhaps there's a Disneyworld in Johannesburg?"

"She'd certainly be her own attraction." Pieter offered a mirthless smile in return.

"She'll be of little use to us dressed like that." Eric studied her a minute. "Hyena bait, perhaps."

Pieter chuckled.

"You think I'm kidding," Eric said.

"No, my friend. I believe you. So we have a few hours. Has Flora taken any water?"

"No. Nothing. Flossie's been feeding. Barely. That's about all. They're both awfully weak. And I can't imagine the pain and stress. The blood loss." Flies buzzed about on the wounds and the dark, wet sand beneath the two.

"Chuck! Greg!" yelled Pieter. "Step lively. You're not on a family vacation. We've got to clear this brush to make room. The chopper should be here before long. If it isn't, well, there are enough of us—we can guard them ourselves. But we have to be ready for the doctor and his team."

Eric approached Clare and Stacey. "Sorry. We'll have to take it all down." He waved at the brush enclosure. "Without knowing when—"

"Don't worry," said Clare. "We had to protect them. You didn't know."

Stacey stared at them both quizzically. Then they were all distracted by the wrenching snaps and crackling as the men began to pry limbs and branches loose and drag them away. Flora snorted but quieted immediately. She appeared on the verge of collapsing.

"Easy there," Eric cautioned. "I don't want to stress them any more than necessary." He handed Stacey a pair of binoculars. "Take these, Stacey. Make yourself useful. You are now officially designated our Hyena-Early-Warning System. You might have a better view from the truck than the ground." But Stacey had anticipated the value of relative altitude. At the very mention of hyena, she had clambered into the Jeep.

When Eric joined the men, he noticed Clare tugging at a particularly stubborn branch. She looked pale. It was obvious she had overextended herself. Eric felt a wave of tenderness wash over him. "Clare, you don't have to work anymore. You've already done enough. Please, rest."

She gazed into his eyes, hesitated, then resumed yanking at the branch.

"Please. For me. We'll need you fresh when Dr. Sheldrake arrives." He unwrapped her hands from the branch and led her toward the shade of a nearby Jeep, where he grabbed a blanket from the back and laid it on the ground. He leaned Clare against the cab, then filled a canteen with some cool water. "Here. Drink." He marveled at her lovely long throat as she gulped the water. "Not so fast. I'm afraid you're a little dehydrated. Easy does it." He gently lowered the canteen from her mouth. Then he took off his shirt. "I'm sorry I haven't anything more, more elegant." He poured water over his shirt, wrung it slightly, then began to daub and stroke her face.

After Eric washed her face, he moved down her throat,

swabbing it ever so carefully. He drenched the shirt again and placed it on the nape of her neck, squeezing the refreshing liquid down her back. She sighed at the welcome chill. Eric continued, cleaning the thorn scratches lining her arms He could feel her trembling.

Eric asked his patient, "Better?"

Clare could only nod.

"Have another swallow. You need to rest. I promise to wake you."

After she finished, he cupped the back of her head into one broad palm and, his other arm firmly around her waist, lowered her onto the blanket. Their eyes locked, but Clare turned away, faint.

A high-pitched squeal caught Eric's attention. He rose, buttoning his comfortably damp and now sweetly Clare-scented shirt.

"Hey, HEY!" Stacey was waving one free arm frantically while gazing through the binoculars, gesturing toward the ridge of a nearby plateau.

Was it possible that the pilot had gotten the wrong coordinates? No. Pieter had confirmed them twice. Eric had also been careful to describe the setting: the water hole, the trees. Surely, the vehicles would have been visible, even from a distance.

Could it be some other danger? Hyenas, returning to their purloined meal? Lions?

He scrambled into the Jeep and snatched the binoculars from Stacey. Peering intently through them, he took a sharp breath, then set his jaw.

27.

"**I** don't frigging believe my eyes. Those bastards!"

Eric felt uncontrollable rage boiling up in him. A Lodge at Damara tour bus and assorted support vehicles had lurched up onto a nearby ridge and were currently disgorging their contents of guests, guides, and staff. Eric scanned the small crowd. Yes, he could see Sypher among them, pointing here, giving an order there. Some employees were setting up telescopes while others assembled a large green pop-up canopy and began to lay what appeared to be a sumptuous buffet beneath it.

"Get out, Stacey!" Eric choked on his words as he glared toward the ridge.

"What about my lookout duties? What about the hyenas?" She caught herself, snatching her Evian and her hat as she tumbled from the Jeep.

"Find another truck. A tree. A goddamn boulder. Just get out. Out!"

As he spoke, he fumbled with the ignition. His grip was so fierce that he feared he might snap the key. He took his pistol from the glove compartment and laid it on the seat next to him. He then thrust the Jeep into reverse and wheeled it savagely toward the ridge.

Suddenly, he skidded to a halt. Pieter had dashed into his path, waving his arms. "Christ, Pieter, what do you think you're doing? Can't you see that those bastards are making a carnival of this? When I begged them for assistance?" His voice lowered darkly. "When I told him I would shoot any of them on sight if they tried to make a show of this."

Pieter leaned over the front fender. "Eric! Come to your senses. They're not interfering with anything up there. We need you here. We can't risk losing you. Not for a minute. You can finish this Sypher business later."

He pleaded, "This thing between you and Daniel—what does it have to do with Flora? With any of this?" He waved back toward the rhinos, the growing jumble of brush. "Eric, you've got to see reason."

Eric stiffened. He could imagine Daniel staring down at him, laughing. His stomach churned at the thought. Another wave of fury raged through him. Perhaps this had all been planned. Some sinister "drama" for the guests. Eric realized this thought was too far-fetched, even by Lodge at Damara standards. Surely, the rhino hadn't been targeted. That would be criminal. The snare must have been intended for a lesser animal—a wildebeest or gazelle. Some lucky photos of a lion pride's feast to post on Facebook. Not Flora.

Eric drew his hand across his brow. Lesser animal? What was he thinking? A snare was the cruelest form of capture. It condemned any animal to death by starvation, thirst, predation. Poachers. Not even Sypher would stoop. But what about his head guide? Didn't he work off bonus "commissions" for photo hunts?

No. Eric shook off the vile possibilities. Pieter was right. The heat was making him irrational. Maybe he should just lie down in the shade next to Clare until his senses returned. He rubbed fiercely at his temples.

A reassuring voice brought him back. "Calm down, old friend. We need you." Pieter had come around to the side and gripped Eric's shoulder. "Move aside. Let me drive. And put that gun back where it belongs."

Eric obeyed, almost automatically.

It was true. He was needed for the rescue operation. Flora needed him. Flossie, too. He sat rigid as Pieter negotiated the turn and rejoined the incredulous group. Eric noted that Clare had risen on one elbow and was rubbing her eyes against the sunlight.

"Everybody, back to work. Professor Bolton here thought there might be trouble, but it appears our friends from the Lodge are keeping their distance." The group slowly resumed their demolition efforts.

As Pieter and Eric sat together, the radio suddenly squawked to life.

"Baby Huey to Rhino Man."

Eric grabbed the receiver. "Rhino Man here. When can we expect you?"

"About forty minutes. That's four zero. All clear for landing?"

"All clear."

"Baby Huey out."

Eric hung up. He had helped with a helicopter rhino transport a few years earlier at Etosha. A male. Horribly mutilated. Poachers had wounded the animal, then hacked its horns from its living face, leaving the animal to die in agony. Dr. Sheldrake had been summoned to tranquilize the bull. Then they had tied each of its enormous legs to a winch. It was the most amazing sight Eric had ever seen. A rhino, being lofted into the air, upside down, swathed in brightly colored blankets, like some impossible, ponderous pendant. Yet despite all their efforts, that rhino didn't make it. After tens of millions of years of evolutionary success, it had come to this. The world had never been a kind place for rhinos. But they had endured. It was man. Modern man. Eric dragged at the brush with frantic energy, Pieter laboring at his side.

Soon, they heard a distant purring, which transformed into a rattle, then a deafening *THWOP THWOP TWHOP* as the helicopter hove into view. It landed about fifty feet from the rhinos. Dr. Sheldrake jumped from the cabin and hunkered out from under the craft's slowing blades, clutching a large satchel to his breast. When the engine stopped, the pilot and two veterinary assistants emerged.

Eric greeted the doctor with an outstretched hand. "A sight for sore eyes, Doctor."

"Good to see you as well, Bolton. How's our patient?" The veterinarian assessed the situation with professional alacrity. "We've got to work quickly once this rescue gets going." He turned to Eric. "Bolton, you're going to take the calf, correct? I'm afraid we'll have to dart her too. Can't risk any further injuries." Sheldrake gave some quiet commands to his assistants, who swiftly began to retrieve equipment from the helicopter.

"As I remember, Bolton, you're a bit of a hand with a lasso. You be in charge of the calf. We must keep her away from the mother once she starts to go down. We've got extra rope if you need it."

Eric bounded toward his Jeep. Clare was waiting there, looking anxious.

"I didn't want to get in the way."

"We'll let you know when we need you."

He found a coil of thick rope buried in the back and rushed toward the circle of men surrounding the rhinos.

Dr. Sheldrake was loading a metal dart with a bright pink

nylon tuft into his gun. "M99. Etorphine. Almost three thousand times more potent than morphine. Step back. Everyone. Anyone gets stuck with this is a dead man."

A wry smile drifted across Eric's face. He couldn't help but think of Sypher with a pink-tufted dart in him.

"I think three milligrams should do it for the mother," Sheldrake explained. "I've added some tranquilizers as well. She'll go down in about three to five minutes. Fraction of that dose for the baby, but she'll go down more quickly, so we need to get her to safety. Listen up. Once I shoot, there is no margin for error. Not a second, not a single movement. At the end of minute one, get the calf away from its mother. Cover her face and plug her ears with cotton wool." An assistant started to hand a large package to Eric. Clare, who had silently joined them, gently took it from him.

"Minute two, we place the stretcher and net on the mother's near side. Benjamin, you cover her face with the wet sheet and fasten it. Jason, you cut the wire snare. Minute three, everybody to her far side. We'll try to keep her sternal, kneeling, until we've got the transport sledge and net right next to her. Do not let her fall. I want cotton stuffed in her ears too. I will give her an antibiotic injection. Then we'll roll her. Secure her. After that, Pilot McKenzie, you will work your magic. Any questions?"

The atmosphere was electric with anticipation.

"Oh, and in case I forgot to mention, mind the horns." Sheldrake chuckled. "One. Two. Three. Clear! Fire!"

The dart hit Flora in the neck with a soft thump. She didn't react. He loaded another dart, this one with a green nylon feather.

"Clear. Fire!"

Clare flinched as it hit Flossie, who squealed in discomfort. She clutched Eric's arm.

It all unfolded just as the doctor said it would.

Pieter and Eric looped the end around the Jeep's trailer hitch for leverage and pulled the unsteady baby toward them. Clare rushed to Flossie's side, then placed a wet towel over her nubbly face. She laid a blanket nearby and watched as the two men eased the baby onto it. As they returned to help with Flora, Clare gently stuffed Flossie's ears with cotton and stood watch over her

Flora had wobbled onto her knees soon after Jason had freed her from the snare. The men gave a collective heave-ho as they rolled her onto the sledge.

As his assistants strapped Flora securely, Doctor Sheldrake stepped onto the stretcher, wielding a hypodermic the size of a turkey baster, and inserted it into a large vein in her ear.

Everyone's focus was shattered by a shriek followed by a thud. All heads turned.

Stacey had fainted. Out cold.

The graduate students retrieved her sun hat and glasses, then took her by foot and arm and half carried, half dragged her back toward the now deepening shade of a vehicle.

"What's the matter with that woman?" Sheldrake asked, clearly perplexed.

"Just about everything. Truly," Eric replied. He shook the veterinarian's hand. "I—we can't thank you enough for this."

"Thank me when she pulls through, Bolton. We ready?" he asked the pilot. "Good. Call you with any developments."

As the helicopter engine roared to life, the doctor and his team sprang into the cabin. The blades created a thunderous whirring, and dust and debris flew. The craft hovered above

Flora, slowly, slowly winching her up, then began to rise into the air, Flora's stretcher rocking like a cradle in the luminous violet sky. High above the anxious group, the chopper swung toward the south, its thwopping growing more faint until it disappeared altogether.

The assembled rescue team stood silent, in disbelief of what they had just witnessed. One of the researchers was ministering to Stacey, still in shock from the hypodermic horror. Eric realized he and Clare were standing side by side, his arm around her waist. Somewhat awkwardly he released her, then turned his attention to the ridge. Deserted, just as he'd thought. Apparently the show was over, the revelers departed. Enough entertainment for one afternoon.

"Let's get Flossie back to camp before dark. Greg, you drive Clare's Jeep. They can bloody well come fetch it themselves. First, we dig out the rest of this goddamn snare." Eric kicked at the dirt. "We're taking it with us. Evidence. Some bastard will pay."

28.

Meanwhile, Stacey lay in the sand like a wilted tropical flower. Eric watched the young researchers gaze down at her, helpless and puzzled. A two-thousand-pound rhino? No problem. This porcelain doll? Problem.

"Should we leave her?" asked Pieter. "She's sleeping peacefully." But as if she heard, Stacey wobbled to her feet and was helped into the truck. "Oh, well, just a thought."

"Hey!" Eric hollered. "Now that you chaps have assisted that damsel in distress, help us load this baby."

After a great deal of heaving and grunting, the group wrested the inert mass of baby rhino into the Land Rover. Clare hovered close by and climbed in beside Flossie. Eric cleaned and bandaged Flossie's wounds where the hyenas had slashed at her, nearly ripping off her tail.

"Okay, Pieter, think we're set. See you in camp. We'll be a bit slow. I don't want to jostle the rhino or Clare too much." When the others left, he returned to Clare. She'd braced herself against the back of the seat with her long legs stretched beside Flossie. Her canvas hat lay beside her, and she'd caught her hair into a ponytail

"You'll be okay back here? I'll take it easy, but it's still going to be bumpy."

"I'll be fine." She smiled weakly. "You were pretty impressive with that lasso. Could have been a rodeo champ. Will Flossie be okay?"

"There's a good chance. But if she is okay, it will be because of you." He paused for a moment. "It's good you're close to her. She's dehydrated and cold. You'll be like her mom."

"You think Flora and I look alike?"

"In oh so many ways." Eric smiled. "And keep a blanket over yourself as well." He had the gate of the truck halfway down and stopped. "I hate to tell you, but we're going to need you for a while."

Eric watched Clare rest her head against the seat and tuck the blanket closer over Flossie. From her pocket, she pulled out some lip balm and eye drops. Eric thought, right now, those might be more valuable than her expensive Nikon lenses.

Eric drove carefully around rocks, through dry creek beds, and over sand swells. In the rearview mirror, he could just see the top of Clare's head. This day seemed already forty-eight hours long, and it wasn't over yet. His life was often like that. Days filled with heart-pounding panic or excitement, interspersed with days of nothing. Writing grants, writing research papers, mentoring young scientists, playing referee between staff and researchers.

Clare had demonstrated she could endure the stress. She had grit, no doubt about that. But could she endure the boredom after Flossie recovered, if she recovered?

Sypher would soon demand that she return to her job at the Lodge. Just the thought of the man set Eric's blood boiling. For the thousandth time, he cursed the fates who sent Stacey to him and Clare to that bastard.

Eric had seen Clare's work online. It wouldn't be right—giving that up to be with him. She had talent. He didn't feel proud of the thought, but without her cameras she was of little use to Daniel and of great use to him. Maybe she would stay, at least until her cameras were replaced. Flossie would be a welcome ally in his hope to keep Clare at Rhino Camp.

Flossie's arrival caused much excitement back at camp. Though still groggy, she was recovering from the sedative, and once the men carried her into the animal pen, she showed some curiosity about her new digs. The staff had cobbled together a nursery for her next to Elvis, the resident goat, who was instantly enraptured with his new roomie. Eric mixed a batch of Nestlé's Rhino Milk. Clare tested the formula on her wrist and offered the bottle to the baby, who found it acceptable and sucked noisily.

"Good baby," cooed Clare. "But that overbite. Eric, we may be in for some orthodontic bills."

Eric and Clare settled down on the straw, Flossie fast asleep as soon as the bottle left her lips. Elvis with his yellow eyes kept close guard over them.

Later that evening, Pieter stood in the doorway. "You two know that baby's got one of her fat feet on a banana peel and the other in the grave, right? You know that." Clare was leaning against the wall, her blonde hair cascading over her shoulders. Beside her leg, now covered with Clare's sweatshirt, lay Flossie, her eyes closed, her breathing shallow, a little stub-nosed bullet, so ugly she was irresistible "Mother Nature's cruel. Often vengeful."

Pieter reached down and tugged gently at Flossie's leathery skin. "Least you got her hydrated." He watched Clare gently caressing behind the nubbins of one bandaged ear. Eric rose to stand beside him, leaning on a pitchfork full of straw. "You made a first-class bed here. Might be more comfortable than mine."

"That's a pretty scene," said Pieter when he and Eric were

out of earshot. "Clare looking adoringly at Flossie. You looking adoringly at Clare." He sighed. "You know, old friend, that baby's too hurt. Bastard hyenas made mincemeat of her rear. If she doesn't die of blood loss, she could still die of infection. Will and optimism won't likely beat the odds here."

"Maybe you're right, Pieter, but what the hell do you suggest I do?"

Pieter walked a few yards away, put his hands in his pockets, and looked at the night sky. "There's the Southern Cross. I love this country. Everything that walks or crawls or slithers across it. But I'm not fool enough not to see there is little mercy here for man or beast."

From a distance, he added, "Those wounds are bad. I don't know if we can keep her here. She needs to be moved to a clinic."

"Not yet. I can't do that yet. You know those places. They're good but sterile. And they don't have the staff to be as attentive as we can."

"You mean as attentive as you and Clare can," clarified Pieter.

"I know, I know. She's going to leave. And we've got jobs to do here." He walked over to Pieter. "It's a shame we got there after the show. Clare, trying to bean the hyenas with lenses. Camera gear worth tens of thousands of dollars strewn across the sand. And when she ran out of projectiles, she remembered her lunch. Fortunately, she's got a healthy appetite and had a big hunk of steak. When I got there, the hyenas were savaging her leftovers and each other. But that wouldn't have lasted long. She'd run out of options, and she'd used herself and her Jeep as a blockade. Those hyenas would have devoured her had she stepped out. They certainly would have gotten Flora and Flossie." Eric's broad shoulders slumped. He could feel the weight of all this. "After that, I can't send the baby off. Let's see how she does tonight. She's a tough little tank. Put up a good fight for the hyenas and hopefully will for us."

"I guess." Pieter shook his head. "Wait here. I'll bring some whiskey back. Need anything else?"

"No, thanks."

"'I've got my love to keep me warm,'" he whistled as he walked away.

When Pieter returned to the nursery, he handed Eric a bottle of whiskey and two glasses, winked, and left. Clare was still stroking the calf and cooing gently. Eric feared Pieter's assessment was correct. The situation had all the earmarks of a runaway train. And though he would throw his body on any tracks to protect Clare, the crash here might be inevitable.

Eric poured two rather full glasses and handed one to Clare. A dim bulb cast a pale yellow glow, accentuating the honey highlights of Clare's hair.

She looked up at him, then accepted the glass. "I've made up my mind. I'm taking Flossie home to California. My parents would adore her. They're always adopting pitiful creatures, but they don't have a rhino. Yet."

"Oh, grand idea. As she grows, she'll play well with the others and be a constant comfort to your parents in their old age."

Eric knelt and clinked his glass against hers. "A toast to our heroine! Stacey probably drinks from Waterford, but with the heft of your credit card, I'm guessing you drink from Baccarat." He smiled over at her. "You one of those billionaires who fly under the radar?"

"No. And this glass is clean; it's full of whiskey. And that makes it just about as perfect as it gets."

"Okay, maybe one day you'll tell me the story of Clare, woman of substance and mystery."

"Let me know one night when you can't sleep. I'll tell you my life story."

"I'd like that, and I have a lot of those nights." Eric nudged her shoulder playfully, and she returned the pressure. "We make a fair team. Don't you think?"

"Yes, but let's not repeat today. Okay?"

"No, God willing, this one will never be repeated." He looked over at her. "You came here to take Daniel's photos. Just another job, or did you choose Africa?"

"Honestly?" Clare sipped at her whiskey and slumped against the wooden slat. "It wasn't so much about coming to Africa as it was about leaving California."

"I'd like to hear more, one day. But now you need sleep. You don't need to stay. Go get some sleep. I'll be here. Tomorrow she'll need you."

"I'm not leaving, so you can forget about it." Clare looked up, a stubborn little tilt to her chin. "You go sleep."

"No, we'll stay together." He sat down on the other side of Flossie and stroked her back. Her breathing was still ragged. "Sleeping in the straw with the world's ugliest baby between us, plus the Peeping Tom neighbor." He glanced toward Elvis, wide-eyed, his head poking between the slats. "It isn't exactly what I dreamed of. But I'll take what I can get."

Clare smiled sleepily at him, her head lolling against the wood wall. "She may be an ugly baby, but she's our ugly baby."

"For a little while, Clare. Be careful."

"That's all right. You and Pieter think I don't understand, but I do. It's a miracle she's alive. It'll truly be a miracle if she survives this night." Tears dropped from her chin, and she wiped them with her sleeve. "I just feel like I've lost a lot lately. Like the ground keeps shifting out from under me. And I just can't lose Flossie too. And God only knows if Flora will survive."

Eric moved to comfort her, but she shook her head. "Don't. Any tenderness right now and I'll never stop crying. I'm just tired. What a nightmare."

"Not true! Because of you, it *wasn't* a nightmare." Eric chuckled softly. "Camera gear everywhere. Hyenas ripping into your doggie bag and each other. And you, sitting in the Jeep like John Wayne. No, it wasn't a nightmare."

She reached for his hand and pressed it to her lips. "Let's get some sleep."

"Mind if I move by you? This baby's breath is lethal."

Eric stretched out beside her as close as he dared, his hands behind his head. When he finally turned to ask her about life in California, she was asleep. He pulled the blanket over her shoulders and looked at her face. Smudges of dirt stood out against her pallor, though the places where he'd wiped her throat with his shirt were clean. Long eyelashes fringed her cheek. And despite the sun and heat, her lips were soft and sensuous. The temptation to kiss her was strong, but he would await an invitation. "Night, Clare," he whispered.

Flossie's snoring awoke Eric sometime after midnight. Though Pieter might think straw was a great mattress, Eric's right leg disagreed. But Clare's arm was around his waist, and he'd risk amputation before losing this unintentional embrace. Her breasts were pressed against his back, and he just lay there soaking in the closeness, wanting to wake up every day for the rest of his life with this woman beside him. Soon, he fell back to sleep.

Pieter brought them coffee the next morning. "Hey, sleepy heads. Your baby's awake."

Clare pulled her arm quickly away from Eric and sat up to check on Flossie. Then she grasped the cup of coffee in both hands and took a long sip. "Thank you. I don't know if I've ever needed coffee more."

Pieter thrust the other cup at Eric, "That's quite a scene."

By now Flossie was up on her stubby legs. "Think the child better go outside or you'll have to change the bed. Come with Uncle Pieter." Flossie looked back at Clare and Eric. But weak and wobbly, she eagerly followed Pieter who held a bottle. She nosed around outside and peed a little, horizontally, a challenge for unwary caregivers. It was a good sign that she could and would suck from the bottle.

After Flossie drank her milk, she flopped down in the deep straw as if someone had kicked her legs out from under her, promptly fell asleep, and began snoring like a brass band. Eric taught Clare to change her bandages. The wounds were deep and beginning to fester. "They're bad, Clare. It's good she's walking. Very good. Amazing. But she's so little."

"Well, we'll just keep her as clean as we can and keep the antibiotics going. That's all we can do."

"We'll turn you into a wildlife nurse yet."

29.

The next morning, Eric saw Hosea approach. "Doctor Eric," he began, his eyes averted. "It's Lodge at Damara calling. Again. Mr. Sypher's assistant. Says they want the Jeep returned immediately. And Miss Clare."

Eric scowled at the garish optic-yellow-and-lime-striped vehicle like some hallucinogenic zebra, parked alongside his drab Jeep.

"Tell them they can pick up that circus wagon anytime. We'll leave it parked just outside the gate, keys in. I doubt it will be in any danger. I don't want any of those bastards on camp property. As for Miss Rainbow-Dashell, that's her decision. Will you tell her, or shall I?"

"Professor Eric, I . . . I . . . ." Hosea stammered.

Eric blew a short breath of resignation. "Of course, I'll let her know about the call. I believe she's out performing whatever miracles she seems to be having with that rhino calf. Never seen anything like it."

Hosea smiled. "Yes, indeed, that baby surely took to her. I'll move the Jeep right away."

Eric sighed as he watched Hosea negotiate the long, sandy drive toward the gate. Everything had been so much simpler before Lodge at Damara befell the area. Pristine serenity. Just Eric and the rhino. Well, of course, the others. Pieter. Zahara and Hosea. The rotating bands of graduate students with their refreshing idealism. Their limited experience. Before the poachers' intensified invasion of this blasted Eden. Before Clare.

It was only fitting that he tell her about Daniel's order. Perhaps then he could read something in her eyes, in her face. Something that would communicate an entire world to him. A future together. Or not. Eric strode toward the boma.

Inside, munching away at fresh hay, stood the goat, who *maaa*'d at him sociably.

"Hello there, Elvis, old boy. Enjoying breakfast?" He patted the goat absently. "Where are your girlfriends? Out for a stroll?"

The goat blinked his strange yellow eyes and continued tearing mechanically at the hay.

"Not telling, eh? Well then."

Eric emerged from the shadowed structure into the bright light of a clear morning and lifted his hand to his brow, scanning the compound. No sign of them. Perhaps they had gone behind the central area. It was obvious they couldn't venture too far due to the extent of Flossie's injuries. Eric was just rounding one of the tent cabins when he heard a delighted chirping.

"That's it, baby. Come on, now. You can do it!"

Clare was urging the calf along, in little surges. She would trot ahead and then coo blandishments at Flossie, who would hobble after her. The baby rhino was a model of determination. And affection. At every few steps, Clare would reward her with gentle strokes and scratches. And effusive baby talk.

Eric stood transfixed by the scene.

Clare looked up from nuzzling her charge and shot Eric a dazzling smile. "Look at our patient, Doctor! See how well she's doing. Isn't she? Isn't she the best baby in the whole wide world? Yes, she is!"

"Well, whatever you are doing, Clare, it seems to be working. Looks to be some combination of physical therapy and child psychology. Got your hands on a spare copy of Dr. Spock?"

Flossie butted her head into Clare's outstretched hands, clearly wanting her undivided attention.

"You two are becoming quite the pair. Inseparable. Who'd have imagined?"

"She's such a delight. Such a strong life force, Eric. I never allowed myself to think—" Clare stopped and turned pale.

"None of us thought she'd pull through, Clare. But I'll admit, just this once, I couldn't be happier to have been proved wrong."

He watched as Clare's slender hands lovingly followed the lumpy contours of Flossie's wrinkled gray face. Was it his imagination, or had something blossomed inside of Clare? She seemed radiant, as if mighty suns flowered within her. He could almost feel the fire of Namibia coursing through the delicate veins on her temple, her wrists. He could see the elemental geography in the fine planes of her cheekbones. Was it an illusion? Eric himself felt heated and dazed. And confused. None of these emotions pleased him.

Clare turned to him and asked, "Everything all right? Flora?"

"Yes. Well, and no. I've got a call out to Sheldrake. Should hear something later today." He exhaled and shook his head. "No. It's Sypher. Apparently, you are to leave. At once. He doesn't seem to trust you with the purloined vehicle—or to be on your own again after your hyena encounter."

"But I'm not ready to leave. Flossie needs me." She patted the calf's broad head.

"Won't argue with that, Clare." Eric felt a pang. "This is between you and Sypher. I'm out. I don't want anything to do with the man. Pieter and I are going on patrol." Then he spun on his heels and walked quickly away.

"Eric, wait!" she called.

But he just kept walking.

30.

The following day, Zahara arrived at the boma. "Miss, here's your shirt. Dr. Eric said to wash it." Zahara handed Clare the blue sweatshirt emblazoned with the California university logo in fuzzy yellow letters that had been Flossie's security blanket the last few nights. As with everything Zahara did, it was spotless and folded perfectly.

"Thank you." Clare stood immobile holding the garment in front of her, staring at the logo as if it were a foreign thing, tinged with danger. Her mind whirled with emotion. The memory of that delicate pink rose that unraveled her life with Timothy came unbidden. Odd, she thought, how small, everyday items can bring down worlds.

She was awakened from her reverie by Eric's presence at her side. They must, she thought, have a psychic connection.

"Zahara washed my sweatshirt. She said you asked her. Flossie likes it. It's fine here."

"Clare." Eric hesitated.

"What?"

"Flossie's terrifically loyal." He hesitated again, scuffing at the dirt like a schoolboy.

"Oh, for heaven's sake, Eric, spit it out!" Clare instinctively shoved her shirt under her arm.

He blurted, "I can't risk Flossie getting more attached to you because I don't think you're going to stay." Silence hung between them. "So? Are you going to stay? For three months? Three years? Maybe longer?"

Clare looked away. It was a fair question. "You're right. I don't know." She gazed out the door, threw the shirt into the straw, and strode out of the boma toward her tent.

"Clare!" he called to her back. "It's not as if you can't be with her. It's just, we need her to bond to a couple of us." But when she didn't turn or respond, he added softly, "You could stay here, you know. I'd love you to stay."

Nothing was said the next day. Clare noticed Eric's shirt was now Flossie's security blanket. And Clare took turns with others caring for Flossie, as Eric had asked, but still she often fed her and scratched behind her ears, which Flossie adored. Elvis, demanded equal treatment, insistently shoved his pointy snout between Clare's hand and Flossie's ear at every opportunity.

Clare had dug out the camp's antiquated camera gear, cleaned it up, and was now spending too much time taking photos. Flossie sleeping. Flossie rolling in the mud. Flossie attempting to get her two hundred pounds airborne into a joyous bounce just like Elvis. Flossie smiling with her overbite. Flossie sitting, one hind leg posed coquettishly behind her. Soon, Pieter and Eric were asking her to join them out scouting and asking if she would allow them to use her photograph for their fundraising website.

After a particularly productive day–gemsbok, ostriches, zebra—Clare was headed back to her tent when Eric caught up with her. They walked to the nursery to check on the kids, who were curled up together.

"Apparently Elvis is immune to her snoring and snorting and gut-wrenching gas attacks," said Clare, leaning over the enclosure.

"Love conquers all." As if to test that theory, Flossie let rip a big, juicy fart and then a soft sigh of relief. Eric pulled his shirt over his nose and mumbled, "Lord God, that's a foul stench. What does Nestlé put in that stuff?"

"Let's get out of here. Go back to the camp. Let the children sleep. Poor Elvis."

Everyone had disappeared into the big room for movie night, except Pieter who only watched movies involving car chases or outdoor adventures. And when Eric discovered tonight's feature was *Sleepless in Seattle,* he bowed out. Clare loved this romance. All warm and cozy and sweet. But she'd seen it many times, so she followed Eric outside.

Although Eric walked her to her tent most evenings, she wasn't sure why he never made any attempt to linger. At first, she'd been relieved. After all, she'd come to this vast emptiness to find who she was, what she wanted. Her disastrous time with Timothy had knocked her off her bearings, romantically speaking. And, except for the moon, it wasn't possible to find a place with fewer distractions than the Namib Desert. She'd resolved not to bring her mental clutter here or to add emotional clutter by initiating another romance fraught with difficulties, though the difficulty with Eric was geography. Namibia, the exact middle of nowhere. What she sought was the mental version of closet cleaning. Take everything out, give the closet a good scrub. Sort through the mess. Keep items that fit the life she wanted. Discard the rest. Simple.

Tonight, however, her body resolutely ignored that agenda, and her mind thrust aside Daniel's summons. Tonight she wanted what Meg Ryan had with Tom Hanks.

"Good night," said Eric, bending down and kissing her lightly on the cheek. "See you in the morning."

"Yes. Good night." Her lips formed the appropriate okay-we're-done-for-today words, but her body, without warning or permission, leaned into his, her hand grasping his shoulder. She could feel her hips pressing his, and his belt digging into her belly. But he pulled away, his eyes wide, and she gained control of herself. Nonetheless, those few seconds lingered with searing intensity. The pressure and heat were still there after she'd stretched out on her bed. The smell of him, like sun and toast and spice.

Lying there staring at the hexagonal canvas ceiling where the lantern flickered Rorschach patterns, she thought what a dreadful nun she was turning out to be. Every configuration looked to her to be people making love, different positions, each Rorschach flashing raw intimacies. What had it been? Nearly two weeks at Rhino Camp. And how long had she been in Namibia? A month or so, and her mind was already consumed with lust. Admittedly, this man was gorgeous enough to derail the vows of all but the most resolute acolyte.

But apparently, it was only in her mind. Either he was not interested in women or he wasn't interested in her—because any sentient male could pick up the signals she was broadcasting despite her best efforts. At times she'd felt a flash of passion from him, but oddly, it was in the beginning, and as they'd grown into better friends, he seemed to pull back.

She blew out the small oil lamp Hosea lit for her each evening and crawled under the sheets. Somewhere in the dark, lions roared their hunting song, chortling and grumbling. Hyenas added their shrieking to the chorus as they slunk behind, wary of those ferocious claws and teeth, but ever hopeful for leftovers. The desert was rather like New York or any big city where workers and shoppers went busily about all day, and at night the killers and fighters came out.

Sleep eluded her completely. The screens and tent flaps were down against the mosquitoes, but she could see Eric's light was still on. *Really,* she thought, *we should talk. Days are so busy, so many people around. Night is the only time for a serious conversation.* Her mind wasn't buying any of this, but her mind wasn't running the show right now. She jumped out of bed and into her jeans and sweater before good sense had an opportunity to interfere.

"Eric?" She climbed the three steps and knocked lightly on the wood support. Inside there was a rustling of paper, and then he appeared, still in his work clothes. Why that surprised her, she didn't know. Did she expect he'd change into a velvet smoking jacket and embroidered slippers? Or English schoolboy striped pajamas? Or he'd be naked, with a leopard skin around his loins? It was clear she'd interrupted him, and if she could have aborted this hormone-driven insanity, she would have. But at this point, it was too late to ask to borrow a cup of sugar.

"Anything wrong?" Mercifully, he didn't talk to her through the screen but pulled it aside to let her in.

"Can I borrow a cup of sugar? Not really. Trouble sleeping."

He chuckled and looked at his watch. "You couldn't have counted very many sheep."

"No. Blessings. I was counting blessings, and I ran out."

"That I find hard to believe. Come in. Sit. Let me read from this paper I'm writing. Put you out straight away."

"I was thinking we could talk about Flossie."

"Oh, I see." He held the door open for her. "Well, that's going to need some whiskey." Clare felt immediately at ease. She noted that every flat surface of his canvas room bristled with papers and books. After a brief, frantic search, he found two glasses behind a stack of journals and poured the whiskey. "Sorry, no ice. You Americans like your ice."

"It's alcohol. That's all that counts." Clare looked for a place to sit other than his bed, which was also littered with academic debris.

"This wood torture rack they call a chair is about it, unless you're okay sitting on the floor, the carpet." He put down two kilims as cushions, and they stretched out their long legs side by side.

"Nice," she said, and clinked her glass to his.

"So? What's this about Flossie? We've talked about braces. And I fear the odor problem's just a permanent part of her charm."

"No. It's the future." She saw his eyebrows furrow.

31.

He took a deep breath and a sip of whiskey. "Okay, let's hear it." He'd guarded himself against this moment, pulling back as much as possible, resisting taking her hand when it brushed his. Resisting moving his lips just a bit west of her cheek to meet her sumptuous mouth. There wasn't much more he could do to protect himself from certain heartbreak when she left. And he was quite certain she was about to announce just that. It hurt him that she was so cavalier. But in all fairness, how could she know his feelings when he hid them so zealously?

"Well, this is serious." Clare frowned deeply. "I really think we should apply for a slot in a prestigious preschool. London or New York. I know it's expensive."

He leaned his head back, and releasing his breath, roared with laughter, "What?"

"Seriously. If Flossie's to have any chance at Harvard or Cambridge, it's not too early to plan."

He drained his glass and set it on the side table. "Drink that. Put your glass down."

Surprisingly, his authoritative tone worked, and she obeyed, leaning over to set her glass on the floor. As she turned back, he grabbed her and scooped her against him, kissing the top of her head. She tilted her face up, offering her lips, offering her mouth, her soul.

And finally, *finally,* he kissed her.

Not the little sister kiss he'd given her before, but a full, long, passionate kiss. Then he held her.

"You think we could discuss tuition in the morning?" He stroked her hair, and it slipped like liquid satin through his fingers. How long he'd looked at this golden hair and wanted to touch it, feel it spread across his chest. She seemed to have no idea of its power to arouse. Stuffing it under hats, yanking it into ponytails or whipping it into some Celtic knot. He could hear her now talking, but the words seemed a distant murmur. Until . . .

"Is it all right if I stay?"

At that, he took her by the shoulders and said firmly, "Not with those boots on. Zahara'd have my scalp."

"You're a hard man." She laughed and tugged at her boots.

"You have no idea," he whispered.

"I heard that." She kicked off her boots and slipped down her jeans. As she bent over, Eric drank in the sight of her outrageous pink panties. All this time, under all that khaki rode this do-me pink silk. When she slipped in bed, he pulled her to straddle him, and that mass of golden hair flowed down her shoulders. Kneeling on top of him, she moved her hips ever so slightly. His hands cupped her breasts hard. She leaned over, her fingers tugging his hair, and kissed him, gently biting his full lips and meeting his insistent tongue. His hands slipped under the elastic and gripped her bottom, forcing her forward and back. She moaned with pleasure.

"Stop! Wait." He fought for breath, and she moved off him. "Before we go further—I know, I know, we're pretty far—but—I can't do this."

"What? For the love of God, what game are you playing?" She flung herself back on the pillow.

"I'm not playing games!" He studied the ceiling, afraid to look at her, much less touch her. "That's exactly the point, Clare. This isn't a game to me. I think I love you. And I don't think I can make love to you. Not now. Not unless—"

"Not unless what?" She propped herself on her elbow and looked into his eyes. "It certainly isn't mechanical difficulties because, sorry to tell you, your equipment seems fully operational."

"No, my equipment hasn't been this—operational—for a very long time."

"What's all this torment? What *is* the problem? Your folks won't approve? You're gay? Married? A priest?"

"Are you staying, Clare? I want the whole package. I want tonight, more than I can say. But I want every night. And I want children. And I want to grow old with you. Right now if you left, I'd be—" He fought for words, shaking his head in frustration. "I'd be sad. But if I make love to you, if I feel what it's like to have you, to caress you, touch you, be a part of you, and then you left—it would destroy me."

Tears rolled down her cheeks, and she lay back down.

"I could lie, but you don't deserve that. The truth is I don't know. I know I want you. Right now, I *really* want you. But I don't yet know if I want this life." She managed a small smile. "And what about you? Would you leave? Come to California with me? Give up your entire life's purpose?" She shuddered.

He wiped her tears and took her hand. "We'll be okay. Despite our best efforts, we have yet to get ourselves killed. Chances are, we have time. Time to decide. Time to consummate this love when it's right."

Gently, he rolled her on her side and slid his body close behind her. His right hand wrapped around her ribs, and she clutched it just below her breast. He sighed: she fit perfectly against him. Was she the key that could unlock the life he'd always imagined?

32.

Things had been tense for some time at Rhino Camp, but Eric had noticed that recently the atmosphere had gotten positively electric. Poachers were evident everywhere but nowhere to be found. He and Pieter continually came across snares (some unsprung, many tragically not) and burgeoning garbage middens latticed by meat-drying racks. Dr. Sheldrake had called to express concerns about Flora's prospects, as she seemed depressed and, perhaps as a consequence, her wounds were not healing as had been hoped. Sheldrake proposed that the mother might benefit from the company of her calf, even though both he and Eric realized that the window of reintroduction had probably passed. Flossie loved her bottle, her humans, and more than all else her partner in crime, Elvis. The pair's depredations in camp were notable for their creative variety: no place—or person—was exempt. They had pillaged Zahara's kitchen, rampaged the chicken pen, and raided the researchers' bath area, where they devoured soap, tipped shampoo bottles, gnawed on towels, and festooned the area with massive webs of trampled toilet tissue.

But all this was nothing compared to the tension that radiated between Clare and Eric. Stacey would glance at them across the table during meals and roll her eyes in disbelief as they sat, their eyes averted, silent, pecking at their food. Pieter just looked worried and annoyed. Zahara would sigh, then assume whatever task awaited with furious gusto. Even the researchers, normally raucous and posturing, seemed oddly subdued in their presence.

During one dinner, the quiet was rattling everyone's nerves. Even the lanterns whispered and hissed, like ghostly adders.

Eric could stand it no more and suddenly blurted, "Sheldrake called today. Said we need to think about driving Flossie to the rehab center. To be with Flora."

"No!" Clare cried. "She still needs us. Her bottles. She would try to nurse. How would that possibly help? She could be killed. And Elvis? He would be—"

"Left to his own devices," Pieter chuckled, relieved to break the tension. "Frankly, I've been considering electric wire for the boma. Those two are a force of nature—and not a particularly welcome one. More like a tsunami. Or an earthquake." He grabbed a roll from the basket with an emphatic flourish.

"I agree," Eric replied. "Floss is becoming more huge and powerful by the day. At some point, we have to consider her prospects in the wild. It may be too late as it is."

"But she's still a baby," Clare urged, pushing away her plate with her fingertips.

"Maybe she could learn to be a real rhino," Eric added quietly. "From her mother. She can't stay here forever."

Clare's face had reddened and her lip quivered. "Why not?"

Pieter burst out, "Because this is a research station, not a petting zoo. A couple thousand pounds she'll get to! Think of it. And certainly not a rehearsal zone for would-be parents." He glared around the table. Everyone's head was down, studying the remains of the meal.

Clare's chair gave a resounding screech, and she fled the room.

"Pieter." Eric cast a pleading look at his friend, who had leaned back in his chair, his arms folded defiantly across his chest. His expression, unyielding.

"You need to go to her," Stacey whispered to Eric. "Now."

"Bloody hell!" Eric pushed away from the table. He glanced longingly at the stairs to his study, then to the large open porch, shook his head, and left the glum tableau, stomping in the direction of Clare's tent.

When he got there, he rapped tentatively on the door-frame, then more insistently. No one answered. "Clare?" he called. He opened the door slightly and peered into the cool darkness. "Clare?" She wasn't there.

Eric next strode to the boma, where Clare lay nestled in the hay, one arm thrown across Flossie's broad neck. Clare was weeping. Flossie lay stoically beside her, the world's largest, least absorbent handkerchief. Elvis strained his neck across the rails of his stall then bleated at Eric.

Eric knelt beside Clare and caressed her shoulder. She didn't turn. If anything, her sobs became more wrenching.

"Please, Clare. You've—we've—got to talk about this. It's not going away."

"I offer myself to you, and you reject me—and now you say we need to talk." She met his eyes and wiped a soggy sleeve across her face. "You've got nerve."

It was obvious that Clare was overwrought and that tonight any further discussion would be less than ideal. Perhaps in the clear light of morning. The last thing Eric wished was to escalate any misunderstanding. There was too much at risk. He recognized that.

"I know you're hurting, Clare. And that's the last thing in the world that I want. What Pieter said was out of line—I don't know. He can be so blunt at times. But I think we would both benefit from a good night's sleep. That night, with you—I couldn't. I'm not thinking very well. Can we just postpone this until we're a bit more, more ourselves?"

Clare had quieted. She seemed limp, wrung out. Flossie heaved a great sigh.

"And just when or where do you propose . . . that we be a bit more ourselves?"

Eric wilted under her tone, then rallied. "Let's go for a drive tomorrow. Bring a camera or two. Hopefully not the disposable kind." He noted Clare didn't so much as smile, and proceeded, "There's a marvelous site I don't think you've seen. Birds. Termite mounds all about. Very picturesque."

Clare nodded.

"We'll leave by dawn. Zahara will pack something. You should get some excellent photos."

"And we'll talk?"

"Yes. We'll talk."

When Eric returned to the main building, he was relieved to see that the dining hall was deserted. There was the familiar clatter of post-prandial cleanup emanating from the kitchen. Eric peeked through the door.

"Zahara, I know it's a lot to ask at this hour, but could you put together something for tomorrow, early? I'm taking Clare birding."

Zahara's eyebrows rose. "Of course, Dr. Eric. I'll pack something nice for you. Leave it in the fridge."

"Thank you."

"Oh, and Dr. Eric, Hosea said you had some calls. Note's by the phone."

Eric skimmed the list. Grant, wanting to know how Stacey

was working out. Eric could scarcely suppress a guffaw. Sheldrake, saying Flora had taken a turn for the better. Sypher—Eric sucked in an acid breath—demanding that Clare return to Lodge at Damara. Immediately. Or be held in breach of contract.

Eric crumpled the paper and stuffed it into his pocket.

Tomorrow. Every blasted thing would have to be taken care of tomorrow. No getting around it. Damn.

AS THE NIGHT sky gave way to early glow, Eric saw Clare sitting motionless on the veranda's bleached wooden bench, her hands folded in her lap, gazing into the distance. He paused in the shadows, struck by her beauty, as always, but her utter serenity in the soft light moved him to his core. He waited for the wave of confusion to pass, then forced a smile and nodded in the direction of the truck. "Think we'll get lucky today."

"Hope so."

Her response troubled him, it was so hollow. "Well then, let's be off." He passed her a thermos of coffee. "I've loaded some sandwiches in the back—and there's fruit if you're hungry."

Clare shook her head and climbed into the passenger seat, arranging her camera bag by her side. Eric took the gesture symbolically. Her work would come between them. That much was for certain. Eric groaned inwardly. Fitting. After all, didn't his as well?

Racing the rising sun, the miles passed uneventfully and Clare's mood seemed to brighten. When they left the main road, the truck lumbered and lurched along a dry creek bed for miles before ascending onto a hilly plain. Eric pointed to a copse of thorn trees.

"There! That's our destination."

The rolling hills, punctuated by termite mounds and skeletal shrubs and trees. A slight tinge of verdure promised water just beyond the scrubby grove. It was an altogether lovely scene. As they pulled up, a cloud of raucous, iridescent blue-green parakeets billowed and swirled before settling back into the canopy.

"Oh," she cried, "this is perfect. Thank you for bringing me here." She sprang from the truck and trotted toward the thicket of thorn and acacia.

Eric watched her lithe figure in admiration. *Don't mind me,* he thought, securing the vehicle's doors. *I'll be along. Any minute now.*

When he caught up with her, she was crouched low, her camera clicking away as she aimed it here, there, everywhere. He leaned against a tree and watched her, rapt. At one point, she spun and focused her whirring apparatus on him, a puckish smile crossing her face. *Oh, Clare, if you weren't so beautiful, and talented, and passionate, this whole mess wouldn't be happening.* He hadn't returned her smile. She pointed the lens back toward the sparse foliage.

At last, Clare lowered the camera. "How about I stash the camera and we take a walk? It's still cool. We can have lunch a bit later."

Eric cringed. A walk? Hardly. The talk? Inescapably. "Sure. Let's take a look at some of those termite mounds. They're not too far."

The two strode along in brittle silence. At last, Clare could bear it no longer and burst out, "Eric, why would you bring me here today? Why invest any more of your time and energy when you don't want me? It's clear. You didn't even defend me

—us—against Pieter last night. I don't get it." She looked deep into him, her green eyes flashing.

"I do want you, Clare. That's not in question. Would never be." He hesitated, frowning. "I brought you—" he stammered. "It's just that, well, Sypher called. He wants you back. Pronto. As if he owns you or something."

Clare balked. "No one owns me. I do have a contract, you know."

"Break it. I don't know. I don't see why you have to go back to that obscene lodge with its obscene occupants, its obscene pretense—"

"You mean ecotourists and ecotourism?"

"Greenwashed exploitation. It's a ruse, Clare."

As they picked up their pace, both became flushed from the exertion.

"I don't see how it's exploitative at all. It brings tourist dollars here. It enhances global awareness of an endangered environment. It's sustainable." She faced him. "Are you jealous of Daniel? Because there's no attraction for me there."

"No, but he has to be attracted to you. Any man would be."

"Well then, what is it? That he's made something out of nothing here?" Clare challenged.

"Oh, I can see you've been properly indoctrinated," he growled, and whacked his hat against his thigh. "Do you have any idea of the impact these tourists—and their dollars—have on this fragile ecosystem? On the Himba and Herero cultures that get caught up in this sham? Why, they've all become nothing more than curiosities. Might as well be in a zoo. This whole country might as well be a zoo."

"Those are pretty righteous opinions. How can you say that?"

"Because there is no wilderness when you careen about in garish vehicles, impinging on the lives of iconic, vestigial creatures. Lands. And it's not just the animals, the land, but the sky, Clare. Did you notice the stars at Rhino Camp? Surely you did. No stars like that anywhere near Sypher's theme park."

"Eric," Clare countered, "people don't come here for stars."

"Well then, how about pollution? Do you think all those buses charging about use clean energy? And noise. Do you know that in many of the big game parks, the predators are starving because all the bloody traffic drives away prey? Morning, evening. Key hunting opportunity is key viewing opportunity. Game over."

"So you think that only world-renowned researchers like yourself should have access to wilderness?" She raised her chin.

"Possibly. Yes. If there is to be wilderness. Yes." He paused. "But it can't be wilderness with boreholes and dams and roads and people."

"Get real. Compromise is essential when progress is inevitable."

"Think what you like, Clare." There was a bitter edge to his concession.

"Let me offer you a quote: *There are universal values, and they happen to be mine.*"

"Fine, you'll go back to the Lodge and continue your eco-, eco-whoring for a couple of weeks. Then what? Back to California? Maybe set up a wild animal park? You can afford it. Show your dedication to 'wilderness.'" Eric was shocked by his impulsive cruelty. Not the talk he had planned at all. He wished he could take his words back. The whole conversation.

They stumbled on. Eric realized Clare's eyes were glazed

with tears. He wanted to take her in his arms, to kiss her and hold her and promise himself to her, body and soul. Instead, he lifted his head, gripped her arm fiercely, then jerked to a halt.

With sudden ferocity, he hurled her to the ground, crushing her body with his.

She strained to turn her face. Gravel dug into her cheek. "Eric—stop! You're hurting me."

"Shhh!"

A rhino. Sixty yards, max. So distracted by their quarrel, Eric had committed the gravest of errors out in the bush—being unaware of his surroundings. He only hoped that they were downwind and that the huge rhino had neither seen nor heard their oblivious approach. He glanced about desperately. Nothing but termite mounds and scraggly foliage passing as trees. How could he have put her in such danger?

As he lay atop her, he pressed his cheek to hers and drew a deep breath.

A few blasting snorts. Then a thundering.

"Find cover! A tree—anything!" he shouted as he pulled her to her feet. "Run, Clare! Now!"

Clare's eyes widened. He gave her a brutal shove in the direction of the truck, and she staggered off, slowly gaining momentum until reaching a full, panicked run.

Eric paused. There was only one hope—and that was to give her enough of a head start. He had to distract the bull. Yanking his hat from his head, he dashed toward a cluster of termite mounds. "Hey!" he screamed as he waved the hat about. The rhino, confused by all this darting and waving and shouting, skidded to a halt. He lifted his nose, his beady eyes scanning the vicinity for mortal foes. "Hey!" Eric called out again. The rhino wheeled and renewed his charge. Eric now sprinted for his life. He cast his hat to the ground and sped for the relative safety of a mound, where he hid, gasping. The rhino, clearly enraged, stabbed the hat, tossing it about, snorting furiously. Then the beast looked up.

He plowed into the nearest mound, scything his horn into its side. Nothing. He rammed it again, then made a series of brief defensive charges at the air.

Finally, tail aloft, an erect flag of triumph, the massive bull turned and trotted off.

Eric wasn't going to take any more chances. He waited, his heart pounding, until he felt secure enough to leave the protecting shield, then scanned the tracks near the gutted mound. The bull had retreated in the same direction he had come. That would mean Clare should be safe. Should be. How could he have done this? And how could he have even contemplated someone joining him in this perilous, deadly place? Absurd.

He raced toward the truck. It seemed impossibly far, but at last he reached it. And there she stood, her face streaked with tears and dust. Her arms, trembling, reaching out for him.

33.

The next morning at Flossie's pen, Clare was startled to see Stacey enter the boma. Flossie was greedily guzzling the bottle Clare held.

"She's so cute. Her little horn looks like a first tooth breaking through," said Stacey. "Can I try feeding her?"

"Sure, but watch your feet." Clare looked with misgivings at Stacey. It was as if her childhood Barbie had come to life. In Africa. Her lush brunette ponytail exploded from the very top of her head, and a few carefully extricated corkscrews sprung down her rouged cheeks. She wore a pink striped cotton shirt, red capris, and perky red tennis shoes with candy cane laces. "Actually, watch your entire body. She just can't grasp the concept that she weighs two hundred pounds."

Clare maneuvered out of the way, carefully transferring the gigantic bottle to Stacey, as taking it out of Flossie's mouth often resulted in painful nudges. But Stacey wasn't prepared for the force Flossie put on the nipple. When it popped out of her mouth, Flossie lunged at it, causing Stacey to squeal and jerk back, causing Flossie to lunge again, causing Stacey to squeal louder and retreat farther, causing a chain reaction of hysteria. They were a merry-go-round, and Clare couldn't find a way to hop on. Both creatures were increasingly frantic until, finally, Stacey flung the bottle and scrabbled onto the top rail of the enclosure, stunned and near tears.

"I'm so sorry, Stacey. I forget how rambunctious our baby is," said Clare, climbing up beside her.

"Baby? That thing tried to trample me." Stacey's ponytail had slipped and now cascaded out her left ear.

Flossie mewed. She rolled the bottle with her nose, but her overbite that would one day prove useful in stripping thorny branches foiled any attempt to stanch the milky sweetness dribbling onto the straw.

Clare put her arm around Stacey. "You okay now? Wanna go get some tea?"

"I'm not cut out for this place," Stacey wailed, swiping at the tears with her sleeve. "I'm just not cut out for this. Even the babies are—"

Clare hopped down, helped Flossie suck the last few drops, then closed the gate on her pitiful squeaks. "You'll eat again, greedy guts. See what you've done? No one's going to play with you if you don't behave. Now go to sleep."

As if on cue, Flossie dropped onto the straw, asleep nearly before she landed.

"She's cute when she's sleeping," said Stacey. "You're right. Maybe that bush shit they call tea might help."

As they walked across the compound, Clare glanced to see who was around. She wasn't exactly proud of it, but for the most part she avoided Stacey, a bottomless pit of neediness, an emotional tar baby. Get one hand stuck, and soon both feet are stuck as well. Clare didn't feel up to the task. And Stacey's position at Rhino Camp was problematic, both politically and personally. Pieter made no secret of his feelings about her. The other researchers pointedly ignored her. And Eric was too much the gentleman to say anything, though it was clear he felt Stacey had been foisted off on him.

But as the only other non-science person, Clare felt a kinship with Stacey. She missed the camaraderie of women, and whatever her other shortcomings, Stacey had a PhD in girl talk.

The two women settled on the thatch-covered veranda with mugs of steaming tea and looked out at the stark mountain, watch guard of the compound. The blazing sun overhead bleached the landscape.

"How anybody can think this place is beautiful totally beats me," said Stacey. "It's like every rock, every bush, every tree is screaming, 'Fuck off! Go home!'"

"That's a bit harsh," Clare said, chuckling.

"Maybe, but it's true. I can't believe I ended up in this hell-hole. It was that stupid propaganda my father saw online: *Volunteer in Africa! You'll Never Be the Same!* Yeah, you'll be dead— or wish you were."

"You've got to admit, we won't be the same after this. Africa has changed us, or me at least." Clare thought the mountain majestic, its sparseness beautiful. And she loved the mystery of this place, even knowing danger lurked deep in the caves, behind the bushes, under the rocks. And Clare was growing increasingly fascinated by all of it. A rhino? Who decided to build a walking tank—with two ridiculous horns? Why did oryx have swirly stripes around their muzzles? Giraffes? Elephants? Too preposterous for words. She was spending long hours reading about Namibia and its flora and fauna. Eric was an encyclopedia, but she wanted to learn some of this on her own, admittedly in part because she wanted to impress him. She'd always loathed the female tendency to take up whatever hobby, interest, or sport the boyfriend had, but she truly felt as if her heart needed to know everything about this place.

Stacey interrupted her thoughts. "You remember that

suh . . . suh . . . snake?" She shivered. "The one in the shower? Deadly. All the researchers said was, 'Be careful. With cobras, cover your eyes.' Oh, right, thank you so very much. That really helps. Everybody always brings a snake identification book into the bathroom." She took a sip of tea, crinkling her nose. "Now I don't take a shower without poking a stick in first. A really long stick."

"Stacey, for the love of God, leave! It isn't good for you here."

"I already told you, this is my only chance at an internship. I can't go back. Daddy would—You at least have a sweetie."

"What do you mean?" Clare stiffened.

"Um. Well, for starters, you two aren't very subtle, you know." Stacey jostled Clare's shoulder. "He's cute. What's the problem, except he totally loves it here? Guess you could just enjoy the moment."

"Yeah, well, he's kind of a more serious type. Not really into *enjoying the moment*." Clare had to admit, it felt good to talk with someone, a woman, though Clare also felt as if she were somehow betraying Eric. Stacey might not be the most trustworthy confidant.

"You mean he's serious? Like marriage? Oh my God, you'd have to stay. No way would *he* leave." Stacey squinted at Clare. "Aren't you from California? That's a great place. Malibu, surfing, Saks Fifth Avenue, food. Oh, God, and cocktails. Seriously, are you nuts? Love can totally mess with your brain, you know. Then one day you wake up, and it's like, what? Namibia? Really?" She flung her rooibos, and they watched as it arced into the sunlight, splashing in a mini eruption of mud. "Yuck! Awful stuff. My mom is sending me some decent tea. As if it'll get here this century."

A Jeep rolled through the gate, kicking up a billow of red dust that hung suspended in the still air. Three young researchers jumped out. "Snotty bastards. Like they're so important. Like the continent would sink without them. And you know what? Half of them spend their time inspecting shit. I mean, for real shit. Oh, yeah, that's totally important. Someday I'm gonna give them some. See what great discovery they can make from mine." Despite herself, Clare giggled like a sixth grader over poop jokes.

But her thoughts were getting jumbled by this conversation. When she was with Eric, she felt such desire for him. But Stacey, as goofy as she appeared, had touched a chord. Malibu was fantastic. Mexican food? Fantastic. Zinfandel? Fantastic. California? Fantastic. A surge of homesickness rose so sharply, she gasped.

"So? We've established why I'm still here," said Stacey. "But what about you? All you have to do, or so I hear, is take some photos for that gorgeous hunk at Lodge at Damara, and you can go home. Resume life as it's supposed to be." She paused. "Unless you're so in love you can't leave."

"I don't know," said Clare, suddenly evasive, uneasy with the reminder of her professional obligations. "I probably better get back to Flossie. Elvis is already thinking up ways to get her in trouble today."

"No, you don't need to get back. She's still sound asleep. You need to answer the question. Not for me. For you. For Eric. Guess if he loved me, I'd have trouble figuring out if living in hell was worth being with him. He's like *Gentlemen's Quarterly* cover material. Though seriously, he needs new clothes and oh, God, a haircut." She pushed back a cuticle. "Still, he could park his shoes under my bed any day."

"Stacey?"

"People do get divorced, you know. Sometimes, a girl just changes her mind because she didn't understand the deal. It's not like if you married him, you couldn't ever leave."

Clare adored Stacey's philosophy of life. *Try it. If you don't like it, you can bring it back for a full refund with a smile.* Pure Neiman Marcus. Eric acted like he'd die if she left him, but he wouldn't. And his happiness wasn't entirely her responsibility to ensure forever. No one could sign up for that even if they wanted to. But niggling doubt obscured her vision. He was the most honorable man she'd ever met. And yes, she could divorce him, if it came to that. But he was offering the best of himself and deserved the best of her in turn. Damn! It was like marrying a man with eighteen children, only he had Namibia and eighteen rhinos. *Marry me, marry Africa.*

Rooibos had no caffeine, certainly no alcohol, but whatever was happening, Clare felt inebriated. She looked over at Stacey, who had crossed her legs and was wagging one back and forth, her buttermilk skin moving in and out of the light. Clare tugged her pant leg down over the stubble on her own leg. But the compulsion to expose her soul to this walking, talking Barbie overcame her. The circular thinking about Eric was driving her nuts.

"You're right. Love, or maybe it's just infatuation, is messing with my brain. I feel so confused. If we were home, he'd ask me out for a beer. We'd talk, maybe go out a few times, then have sex. Maybe move in together." Clare thought about how successful that method had been with Timothy. "Maybe not." Yeah, that had worked out so well for her. "Or maybe I'm just too old."

"You're not old. My grandma got married last year, for God's sake."

"Stacey? Grandma?" Clare was feeling tired right now, but that hurt.

"No! I didn't mean you're like a grandma. Just saying." She reached for Clare's hand.

"Guess I have to admit that I really like him. He's in my dreams constantly, in my thoughts—always. And honestly, I don't feel old. I feel like a teenager, which by the way, doesn't feel all that great."

"So what's stopping you? Marry him." Stacey shrugged. "You're not like my girlfriends back home."

"I do think he loves me. Says he does. But Stacey, I think he loves this place more. I might have to settle for second best. And that doesn't feel good. He's such a zealot." Actually putting her thoughts into words was helping, even though the words were still a jumble in her head.

"Yeah, he's got that Ninja Warrior thing going. That's for sure. Like, lately, he's totally gone Ninja. The poachers. You notice?" Stacey rummaged through her pocket, extracted her mini Evian and spritzed them both. In a while, the hot stillness would be challenged by an afternoon wind and then the evening chill, but midday, the heat was thick. A wool blanket suffocating everything and everyone.

"If I do stay, will you promise to send me cases of that stuff? Boxcars," joked Clare.

"For sure. It's made me really popular. All the researchers think I'm one of them when I pull out my Evian." She spritzed them again. "Well, screw them."

"I have noticed Eric's been a bit crazy. Poachers are his nemesis. Actually, I may not even be in second place. It'd be rhinos, Namibia, poachers, and if there was time left over, maybe Clare."

"My dad buys and sells businesses. He's totally crazy about buying and selling businesses. Positively orgasmic. But my parents have a good marriage. They love one another. They love me. What? You think Eric should just follow you around all day like Flossie does? And you have your photography thing. Does that mean you can't love him?" Stacey scowled at the researchers headed in for lunch.

"You're right. I love photography. And this place is fantastic for that. But that's kind of my point. I came here after being so deceived by a man—by myself, actually—and what I wanted was to find myself and my independence." Clare grabbed hunks of her hair. "Yikes! I'm a mess."

"Not really. Let's see if I got this straight. You don't want to marry Eric because he has a life outside of adoring you. And you don't want to marry Eric because you want a life outside of adoring him. See? All you're saying is that the only acceptable marriage under your terms is you and Eric staying in bed twenty-four seven until they cart your bodies to the compost pile. That's totally logical." Stacey put her arm around Clare's shoulder and squeezed. "Love isn't logical. You're trying to get over a guy screwing around on you, but that wasn't Eric. He's a whole different set of problems, so you can't apply the lesson you learned from one jerk to another. The lessons are never repeated. Every man is an asshole unto himself. So to speak."

"Thanks, Stace. That makes everything crystal clear," said Clare, rolling her eyes. "Let's go eat."

34.

Eric was overjoyed that Flossie had gained strength and her wounds were healing. She slept all night alone now, snuggled up in both Clare's and Eric's shirts. During the day, she trotted enthusiastically after Clare or Eric but grew very displeased, mewing plaintively or squeaking like a rubber duck, if they abandoned her for their offices, or meals, or any activities that didn't involve indulging a rhino calf. If they weren't available, substitutes were tolerated. Stacey had become a favorite, though skittish, babysitter.

But if Flossie was confident her parents were close by, she loved being with just about everyone and everything. The two Jack Russell terriers, Scarlet and Rhett, amused her, but they weren't very interested in hanging out. Flossie's big feet had a tendency to come down randomly and without warning, which was worrisome given their tiny terrier feet. And the last time they allowed her to join a game of fetch, she'd flattened several balls. Mostly, they watched her warily from a distance.

Not Elvis. Elvis loved Flossie. And, oh, did she love him. She followed him everywhere and learned many new things and had many great adventures and a few mishaps. Elvis was never busy in his office. He never left her to have dinner or watch movies or listen to lectures. Elvis always had time for her.

As soon as it was clear Flossie would survive, and her wounds were sufficiently closed, the researchers spent several evenings digging a private mud hole for her. Elvis didn't like dirt between his toes, but he watched as Flossie lolled in the mud. Afterward, the two raced along the compound wall, Elvis lapping Flossie, bounding twenty yards ahead, and then returning to offer a bit of grunting encouragement. This diversion was repeated for hours in the cool mornings and evenings.

When the sun was overhead, they napped companionably on the cool concrete of a doorway. The residents who didn't trip over them and curse usually offered at least a welcome scratch behind the ear. At suppertime, Elvis was always at Flossie's stall, watching her nibble supplemental euphorbia leaves with her charming overbite. Later, the two strolled to Elvis's for his dinner. And at night, Elvis curled up in her nursery. They were Best Friends Forever.

Until trouble paid a call.

"Bloody hell!"

The shouting brought Eric bolting out of his office. In the compound stood Pieter, yelling, his face crimson.

"What's happened? What's wrong?" Eric whirled around, looking everywhere. But he saw nothing. No people, no animals. Nothing.

"You've got to do something with that little monster. Today. Right now."

"Monster?" Eric was confused. In all his years with Pieter, he had never seen him so agitated. Lions, hyenas, baboons—nothing fazed him. Well, except Stacey. "Pieter, stop. Tell me what's going on."

Clare joined them. "What's the matter?"

"They broke into my tent. That's what's the matter. The bloody little buggers, they mucked about. Turned over my dresser. Everything's all over the floor. Then she stomped all over my clothes. Bloody fat muddy footprints!"

"Flossie?" asked Clare.

"Yes, Flossie." Pieter glared at her. "And Elvis, I suppose."

"It's Elvis, Pieter. He's a bad influence. We shouldn't have let them get so close."

Pieter stared open-mouthed. "You don't appear insane. You look normal, like a normal person. This bloody rhino has turned you into a raving lunatic!"

Just then the two criminals peeked around the corner, Flossie's stumpy nose and Elvis's pointy one. They stood shoulder to shoulder, curious about the commotion but not quite sure it was prudent to investigate.

"There they are!" Pieter pointed. "Look! They're smirking. I'm shooting the both of them."

Clare looked at Flossie. "She's sorry, Pieter. See? She's scared."

"Oh, she doesn't bloody well know how scared she should be. And she *is* smiling, Clare. Elvis always has that evil grin on his face, but she's joined him. She's made a pact with the devil."

"Pact with the devil? Who's the lunatic now?" Clare stifled a giggle. "Just calm down. You're scaring her. Bit of mischief, that's all. I'll straighten your room."

The next morning Clare and Eric sat across from each other at breakfast when Eric announced, "The baby needs a field trip. Today we're going to the big kids' water hole."

"It's too soon." Clare pushed her plate away. "She's still scared. The water hole will traumatize her."

"We're not sending her alone." Eric was smiling at her. "We'll be right beside her. You can take your camera lenses in case we get attacked."

"Ha, ha. No. Let's let her get more comfortable. Next week. Maybe."

"She's *too* comfortable. That's the trouble. It's time she had some fun and adventure, *Mom*," he added. "Besides, it's the water hole. She'll love it. All the other kids will be there."

"That's exactly what I don't want! What if there are hyenas? What if she gets totally freaked out?"

Eric tried cajoling her. "We'll hire a psychiatrist, I don't know. Clare, remember your first day of kindergarten? Scary, right? But then fun."

Nonetheless, Clare was adamant. No water hole. Not for a while.

35.

Clare stood in the heat and watched as Flossie rocketed around the compound perimeter, her flat, fat feet kicking up in unison like a rocking horse. At two-hundred-plus pounds, Flossie could outrun anything at camp and turn on a dime. Full grown, she would weigh well over two thousand pounds, run up to thirty miles per hour, and maintain the turning radius of a Porsche. But like any child, she touched base often until mom patted her head, then tore off again. Elvis ran with her but kept a watchful eye on those lethal feet.

At nap time, Clare sat beside her on the straw. Flossie snuggled up, thumped her huge head next to Clare's leg, and was instantly asleep. No need to coax this baby to nap. Clare rubbed the rough skin and gently scratched the nubbin where one day would grow a three-foot horn worth an emperor's ransom.

"What's going to happen to you, Floss?" asked Clare. "Your mum's still in terrible shape. But they're doing what they can." Flossie sighed.

Clare rested her head against the kraal wall, and Elvis stuck his sandpaper tongue through to lick her ponytail.

Clare knew Eric was concerned she'd leave. But she was concerned she couldn't. What kind of life awaited her here?

Like all children, Flossie would leave home one day, hopefully reunited with Flora. And Eric had made it clear. Rhino Camp was not an orphanage. Would never be an orphanage.

What was she thinking? He was gone so much. Could he be a husband to her—to anyone? Or just a phantom who showed up in the night and was gone by morning? For all his faults, when Timothy wasn't cheating on her, he'd at least been attentive. If this were almost any place in the US, she could easily occupy herself. A board dug into her back, and she shifted her seat in the straw.

But what if she did stay in camp? What if she found work alongside Eric? Made his life hers? He'd already requested several of her photos for his publications and wanted more. Thoughts went round and round in her head like little cars on a crazy carnival ride, but each thought careened off the track and then crashed. She rubbed her stiff neck. This acute indecision was wreaking havoc on her body as well as her mind. How often she had made bad decisions, irrational leaps of faith that landed her in trouble. And each year she got older, the climb back to herself was steeper. The climb from Namibia, from Eric might be the one that killed her, at least her spirit. Or would it be the leaving that killed her?

Clare's ruminations were interrupted when Flossie emitted an eye-watering fart, and then smiled with sweet relief. "Oh, God, you're a stinky baby!" Elvis retreated to the far end of the shelter. And holding her breath, Clare wriggled away from the dozing rhino and fled the boma.

Her eyes focused only on the ground, Clare was startled to encounter an equally distracted Eric. "Oh, hi. Visiting Floss?"

"Yes, until the gas attack." She fell in beside him, and they began an aimless stroll around the compound perimeter. "Probably her ploy to get some privacy. I've often suspected men of using that same strategy."

"Women don't fart?" He smiled down at her.

"Never."

"Flossie's a female," he reminded her.

"Yes, well, and I fear she'll never be admitted to the better circles. Charm she's got in spades. But control of bodily functions? Impossible. We simply can't hope they'll overlook *that* at bridge club."

She was close enough that he occasionally brushed her shoulder with his.

"Guess your time is up. You'll have to go back to the Lodge. Soon."

"Yes, I got an impatient, an imperious, call from Daniel." Clare hesitated. "He does have reason to be impatient. After all, I'm supposed to be working for him, finishing the photo project." She glanced at Eric, she hoped not too pathetically. Why wouldn't he talk to her? Ask her to stay? She resented him at this moment, his stiff English bearing, his rigid outlook on life, his self-imposed martyrdom.

Eric walked on. "Flossie will miss you."

"I know. You were right about having other people tend to her." She stopped and turned to face him. "Of course you were right. This is your job. And my job is to take photos for Daniel to entice more people to come to Namibia to pester your rhino."

Eric looked into her green eyes, then shoved his fists into his pockets and responded hoarsely. "I can be a bit rigid on that. I do know money rules politicians, and tourists bring money." He turned away. "Any thought you might get back here? Visit, perhaps?"

She studied his profile, his eyes haunted by desire, his handsome face etched by the desert sun, and took pity on him. If only he knew the hold he had over her. "Couldn't leave Namibia without kissing Flossie goodbye."

"Clare," he stammered. "Flossie's not the only one who'll miss you. I think you know how I feel."

"I think I do. You being so eloquent and all. 'Silver-tongued devil' they call you around here." She did know he cared for her. *Oh, but Eric,* she thought, *feeling is not enough.*

"Pieter and I are leaving before dawn tomorrow."

"I know."

He brushed her cheek with his lips. "Well—all right then."

36.

After guzzling a gallon or two of formula, Flossie grunted and belched contentedly as Clare ladled bucket after bucket of water onto the baby. She rolled and wriggled, a muddy vision of rhino delight in the wallow the researchers had created. Now that her wounds were healing and she was spending more time outdoors, Flossie needed the protection of the dried mud, from the sun and from insects. That, and the fact that little is more deliriously sensual to a rhino, particularly a young one, than a mud bath.

"Look at you. Quite the young lady," Clare gently scolded.

Flossie rose to her knees and snorted, splattering Clare with a mist of reddish mud.

"No manners at all. And how does this reflect on me, on my rhino-rearing skills?"

Flossie, as always blissful in Clare's presence, flopped on her side and scissored her stumpy little legs.

"Why, if you weren't so cute, I'd—"

Hosea came running toward them, breathless, his eyes wide.

"Miss Clare, you must come at once. Mr. Sypher. He's here. Says he must speak to you."

"What?" Clare felt a surge of panic. "Yes. Of course." She looked at Hosea, who wouldn't meet her gaze. "Don't worry. I'll handle it." Then she started. "Eric's still out, isn't he? And Pieter? Do you know?" She realized she was trembling.

"Still—still out," Hosea spluttered, still looking down.

"Can't believe he would be so foolish—so insolent. I told him I'd be back," Clare muttered, then straightened. "Hosea, please stay with Flossie. She should be fine, but—oh, Hosea, she'll need her bottle in an hour, and I haven't . . . haven't had time—" Clare looked about despairingly.

Hosea nodded. "I'll stay. Ask Zahara to warm the bottle. I will watch our baby." He paused. "You can take care of yourself, yes?"

Clare felt her world collapsing. "Yes," she replied in a small voice. She didn't sound very convincing, even to herself.

As she neared the building, she could see the limousine parked next to the porch. The driver relaxed nearby in the shade. The limo. Obviously a scare tactic. The bald gesture indicated Daniel meant business.

Zahara rushed to greet Clare on the front steps. Clare could sense her indignation at this intrusion. "I told him, Miss Clare, that he is not welcome here. If Doctor Eric returns—oh, my. Terrible."

"It's all right, Zahara. Don't worry. Would you warm Flossie's bottle?" Clare felt as if she were sleepwalking. "You know how to mix the formula. She'll be hungry soon. You can take it down to her. Hosea's with her. I'll be fine."

Zahara retreated into the kitchen.

When Clare entered the great room, Daniel's back was to her. He was looking at a number of artifacts, including some impressive horns confiscated from a local poaching bust years ago.

"Daniel," Clare said softly but she hoped purposefully. "To what do we owe—"

He turned and flashed a disarmingly wide smile. "The

pleasure of my visit? You've been ignoring my calls. And I had begun to worry." Suddenly his face darkened. "Surely you know you are still under contract."

"That hasn't escaped my attention, Daniel. I just—there were more imperative needs here. I'll fulfill whatever obligations I have once my work here is finished. Please, try to understand."

"Actually, I have tried. And I don't. We are at the peak of tourist season. You appropriate a vehicle. You almost get killed. You disappear for weeks. And where does that leave me, huh?"

Clare squirmed inwardly.

"I fail to see the attraction here, Clare, when you could be at the Lodge." He motioned to the concrete walls, the rough wooden furniture. Then his gaze settled on Clare. "Don't they provide laundry service here?" Daniel sniffed at her rhino-splattered outfit.

Clare decided to try another gambit. "My equipment. I'm afraid it was all destroyed. The hyenas."

"They've been known to devour frying pans and tent poles, but cameras?"

Clare nodded emphatically.

"Clare, really. Do you have any idea how much insurance I carry?" he asked. "There's a reason. We can have them all replaced within a week. Down to the last flash attachment. Any other concerns?"

As Clare struggled with an answer, Stacey padded into the room, bleary-eyed. "Coffee, need more coffee." Without acknowledging either of them, she ambled on to the kitchen.

A moment later, Zahara poked her head through the door, shaking a gallon of rhino formula. "Anything I can get you, Miss Clare?"

"This place is a circus." He grabbed Clare by the wrist. "Look, I need to talk to you—in private—not in Grand Goddamn Central Station. There any place we won't be interrupted?"

Clare looked about wildly. "The office upstairs. Daniel, let go of me."

He released her, then stepped back. "After you, Clare."

37.

Clare could feel Daniel's eyes on her as they mounted the stairs. Why did she feel so powerless in his magnetic presence? Like a child. No, too much a woman. She opened the door to Eric's office, crowded with books and manuscripts. Rhino photos taped all over the walls. A lone window was open, but there was no breeze.

Clare shivered when Daniel closed the door behind them. Yet she felt a pang of relief that he did not lock it. Small favor. She took a deep breath and edged toward Eric's desk.

"Have a seat. I won't be long," Daniel commanded.

Clare felt like a puppet as she walked around the desk, attempting to put a barrier between them, and sank into Eric's swivel chair.

Leaning across the desk, Daniel glared at her. "Clare, I'm taking you back to Lodge at Damara. Today. No excuses. I want you there. I need you there. And I will have you there."

Clare murmured a barely audible protest.

"Again, you don't seem to understand. You are under contract. And what is more—" He had moved around the desk as he spoke. Now he stood behind her. He placed his hands on her shoulders, then let them slide down her arms and tightened them.

Clare shuddered. "Stop it."

He bent his head to her ear, grazing it with his lips. "Damn it, Clare! I've missed you. Your company. I have feelings—"

Trapped between the desk and Daniel's insistent grasp, Clare struggled to escape. This couldn't be happening.

Daniel swung the chair around, then pulled her up, arching her into him. He grabbed her hand. "Feel this. My passion. How much I want you." He kicked the chair aside.

Taking her chin roughly in his hand, he pressed his mouth onto hers, his tongue probing hungrily. Then he clutched her from behind and drew her fiercely against him. With one violent gesture, he swept the papers from the desk behind her and bent her backward onto it.

As his lips roved greedily down her neck, she called out, strangled and afraid. No one answered.

Daniel began to paw at her shirt, lowering himself onto her.

"Clare," he rumbled, his full weight upon her, "you know you want this too."

She couldn't breathe. His heaviness, his mouth drinking her cries. His paralyzing urgency.

As he fumbled with his belt, she tried to push him off, but he fought her back. He pulled her legs around his waist, and his hands groped her breasts, her belly, her buttocks. He moaned through relentless kisses. "Yes, Clare. Yes."

Clare thrashed frantically even as he pinned her arms behind her. He was too powerful. Her strength ebbed with every breath.

"You know you want this."

The snaky sound of a zipper. Clare groaned.

Just as she gave up all hope, a pounding on the stairs, and Eric burst through the unlocked door. "It's true! What the bloody hell!" he shouted. "Sypher, you're dead. Get off her! Right now! Save your fucking for fucking Lodge at Damara."

His face scarlet red, he watched them clumsily rearrange themselves. "Get out. Both of you. Now!"

Tears streamed down Clare's face. She tugged her shirt closed, shaking in mortified denial.

Eric turned toward Clare, his features contorted. "And you. Hosea'll send your things along later. Just leave." Then he sneered and gave a forced laugh. "Oh, that's right. I forgot. You have nothing here."

Clare's face crumpled at his cruelty, the shame of his assumption, and her eyes grew large with pleading. But although Eric was staring straight at her, it was evident he didn't see her at all. He had shuttered his heart against her. The heart she had hoped to win. Forever.

ERIC STOOD ASIDE, his fists clenched, glaring, as Daniel forcibly guided a disheveled, and weeping Clare past him and out the door. Footsteps retreated. From his office, Eric heard the muffled sounds of expensive car doors opening and closing. The hush of wheels receding along the gravel drive. Then silence.

His own labored breathing. Unbearable. With a wrenching sob, he grasped the chair and smashed it against the wall.

38.

aniel had clenched Clare's wrist, half dragging her, as he fled the building. Reaching the limo, he shouted to the dumbfounded chauffeur, "I'm driving. Get in back!" Then he pushed her into the passenger seat and sped down the driveway, his tires throwing up a cloud of dirt and gravel. A dusty wind whipped though Clare's open window until Daniel ordered her to close it. He drove wildly over the swales and ruts. Muddy tears smeared her face as she wiped them away with her sleeve. The image of Eric's own face, its pallor of utter devastation, haunted her. How could he believe her capable of such monstrous betrayal? And with Daniel? Silent sobs wracked her body.

She'd run to Africa, not to this job, but to escape Timothy, a man very like Daniel. Yet once again she had put herself in the position of slave to a master. At least in California, she'd had a haven to escape to. Here in Africa, Eric's fury had just shut all options but to stay at Lodge at Damara until her contract was completed.

"Your boyfriend gives up easily, doesn't he?" Daniel snarled over the hum of the engine. "Threw you to the lions fast enough. That should be a wake-up call."

Clare pulled herself up straight and attempted to dry her eyes. "He threw me to the hyenas. You're right about that."

"Hyenas?" Daniel looked over at her, his eyebrows raised. "Well, this hyena would have put up a fight. I'll tell you that.

He was about to bawl, like a baby. You need a man, Clare. Someone to watch over you."

"And that would be you, right? The man who just tried to rape me?" Clare massaged her bruised arms and stared out the window at the setting sun, praying they'd be back before dark. Daniel wasn't a threat to her out here, not with the chauffeur along. And clearly, he wanted the security of the Lodge as badly as she did. "Yeah, you're just what I need, a man brave enough to attack a woman he outweighs by a hundred pounds." Anger helped. Once she located it through the mix of terror and grief, she felt at least slightly more in control. Good sense told her to shut up. Until she fulfilled her contract, Daniel was her boss. He held her reputation as a photographer in his hands, and for now, she needed the structure of her work at the Lodge. As much as she detested him, they needed to coexist— she hoped as far away as possible.

The light was fading, and he sat forward hunched over the steering wheel, intent on the asphalt track and the two head- lights slicing the dusk in front of them. Exhausted, she leaned back in her seat and studied the flimsy clouds, ghostly fingers stretching across the sky seeming to point accusingly at her, at Daniel, at Eric. Cool ocean fog once again battled the desert heat as it did every evening. If she'd been with anyone else, it would be a magical time of day. That thought made her heart catch. *Oh, Eric, you fool. You've thrown us away.*

Daniel drove recklessly, pushing the powerful engine, rushing to get back to his kingdom. When they approached the Lodge, guards opened the ornate gates. He sped by, leav- ing them to choke in dust. After he skidded to a stop in the drive, he flung the Cadillac door open and bounded up the entrance stairs two at a time. Clare remained in the car, taking a few deep breaths, attempting to compose herself. To her surprise, Chioto opened her door and helped her out. "Your cameras, miss?"

"My cameras? Huh, no." She rubbed her lips. "Thank you." Mercifully, the African staff rarely probed for information, though she could see the confusion on Chioto's face. At the Lodge, only silent subservience was rewarded.

Clare went quickly to her room, avoiding eye contact with any staff or guests she encountered. Once inside, she shut and carefully locked the door. Peeling off her filthy clothes, she stuffed them in the hamper and stepped into the shower. Hot water ran over her head, down her shoulders, soothing the bruises from where Daniel had slammed her down on Eric's desk. Rivulets of red dirt ran over her breasts and stomach. How much water would it take to wash away the filth of Daniel's touch? She shuddered to think what would have happened if Eric had not burst in when he did. Sinking to the shower floor, her back against the cool tiles, she allowed herself to cry in great heaving sobs, the sound muffled by the water, the tears washed down the drain.

Wrapping a thick robe around her, she pulled a tiny bottle of scotch from the minibar. Back against the down pillows, she watched as the sun sank and the stars blinked on. Daniel's hearty voice rose from the patio, and she thought, *He is a hyena.* With all the cunning and cruelty of that devilish beast. She cringed at the memory of the attack. She would have to be very careful for the time remaining at the Lodge. None of the employees would dare defend her against him, if it came to that.

A knock at the door startled her. "Dinner, missy?"

It was Kakuve, the floor steward. Clare guessed she'd seen her come back. Or perhaps Chioto had indicated as much.

Clare unlocked the door, and Kakuve handed her a tray, delicious aromas rising from beneath the starched napkin. "Oh, Kakuve, thank you. I'm starving. I didn't realize it. You're so kind."

Kakuve smiled shyly and, bowing, backed away without a word.

Clare devoured the curry and rice. The simple, delicious food made her feel grounded and strong. When she finished, she poured another tiny bottle of scotch and regarded the festivities below her on the patio. Moroccan tin lights mimicked the stars, and candles flickered on the tables. Couples clustered around the narrow pool, the light from their cigarettes and glinting cocktails reflected in the water. And beyond them, the deep, dark desert with its mystery and danger.

Daniel reigned, slithering amongst the guests with his benevolent-ruler smile plastered on his face. He, too, must have showered, as he looked fresh, glowing tan, hair swept off his face, white dress shirt open at the neck, and fitted slacks. To have committed such an act of violence against her just hours ago and now show no sign of guilt or remorse—or of anything remotely human—was chilling. Business as usual. His heart was as icy as the ocean fog and centered solely on his power and appetites.

The next morning, Clare awoke with a headache and felt stiff and sore. She splashed water on her face and examined her reflection in the mirror. *Okay, you look a mess. What now? What fantastic plan do you have now? Everything has worked out swimmingly so far.* Sore eyes with purple smudges beneath them looked back, sad and lost. What next was fairly easy to answer: coffee, ibuprofen, eggs, and toast. She went down to the deserted patio and ordered breakfast.

She owed Daniel twenty or so photos of wildlife, both animals and tourists. With luck, she'd soon be on a plane home. In the meantime, she needed to stay clear of him except in public places. Daniel would requisition her camera gear carte blanche. For the time being, she had a couple of smaller cameras.

A solitary elephant was drinking at the water hole. She admired his mountainous brow, his glittering eyes amidst the dull gray wrinkles. Even at this distance, she could make out those long, long eyelashes. That would be some photo, if only she had her telephoto lens. An ancient, wise soul. Looking at him, she felt oddly at peace for the first time in what felt like a very long ordeal.

A deep voice jolted her from her thoughts. "You look like ten miles of bad road. No sleep? Thought you'd be tired. Big day yesterday."

Revulsion filled her when she felt his touch on her shoulders. His thumbs began to work at the knot of muscles down her neck.

"Get your hands off. Now," she hissed.

"What a tone!" Daniel sat down, his crisp white shirt replaced with an equally crisp khaki one. "Let bygones be bygones. I'm sorry. I, well, I do think I owe you an apology." He glanced around then leaned in. "You just, or rather, I just . . . I want you. Badly. Is that so wrong? But if it's not mutual, well, I can live with that."

Clare shuddered. "It is *not* mutual. I have never given you any indication I had any feelings for you." Forcing herself to look him in the eye, she added, "I *do* have feelings for you now, however."

He smiled, looking puzzled.

"Now I loathe you. However, I entered into a contract with you, and I will fulfill it. To the letter. When I finish, you will pay me, have a driver take me to Windhoek, and that's the last I hope ever to hear from you or about you again."

"Harsh." He stared out at the water hole. "If that's what you want, okay."

As he rose to leave, Clare said to his back, "I need my equipment. There'll be a list put on your desk today. And I want Chioto, and only Chioto, available to drive me on shoots."

Without turning, he said, "Fine."

She walked to the edge of the terrace, looking for the soulful elephant, for his spiritual consolation, but he'd gone.

39.

Clare left as soon after breakfast as possible, gathering her small camera and telling Chioto—and herself—that this was just exploration for future shoots. In truth, she'd face any wild beast just to get out of Lodge at Damara and away from Daniel. The kitchen staff had hastily packed a lunch basket for them, and the two drove out the gate. It wasn't as early as Clare would have liked, the warm sun already tipping the scale against the cool fog. In addition, Daniel had assigned her a Jeep with no air-conditioning, one of his evil little paybacks, she presumed. One of many before she finished this miserable job. But Clare actually liked the dry wind whipping around her. She looked over at Chioto, the picture of contentment, a peaceful companion. A rifle rested between them, one of the Lodge's many requirements, again not what Clare would have liked. She just hoped they would never have to use it.

The bouncing along, the going somewhere, anywhere, soothed Clare's frazzled nerves. She could leave behind Daniel *and* Eric, sick of them both for different reasons. Chioto downshifted, and they ascended a steep dirt track laid down by gemsbok or zebra to the crest of a hill. Once on top, they stopped and jumped out, scanning the horizon with their field glasses. Clare loved this, the air perfumed with scruffy brush, the vastness and emptiness of the desert. It thrilled her. But at that exact moment, a wave of sadness swept away her well-being. Eric's rush to judgment had deprived her of the possibility of his love and of a life in Africa beside him.

Chioto spotted the beast first, a big lioness padding along a sandy ravine with that characteristic feline swagger. Stopping randomly, the tawny cat swung her massive head, surveying the area, sniffing the air.

"Let's go see what she's up to," Clare said. Chioto grinned and hopped back into the Jeep. They headed straight over the edge, the Jeep's wheels slipping sideways.

They stayed downwind so the lioness wouldn't catch their scent but would still be clearly within view. When she stopped, they stopped. But mostly she just ambled along, confident and deadly. Clare focused her camera and fired off a couple shots, but she feared that nothing would work very well. They were too far away. Chioto took the Jeep up a low swell so they could be closer but not startle the big cat. She was out for a meal for herself and perhaps some family back home, a fact they respected. Prey had indeed grown more scarce, thanks to the constant presence of clamorous tourists.

Ahead and to the left, still out of view of the lioness, Clare spotted a small baboon, a young teenager at best, judging from his size. And typical of teenagers, he was not paying attention to his surroundings, just toying with a termite mound, poking at it with a twig, totally absorbed. Chattering quietly at his find, he sat on his bald bottom, studying the mound, tilting his head quizzically at this new problem, alternately scratching his chin and his rear end. But the lioness soon sighted him, and unlike the baboon, she was fully focused on her surroundings—and on this oblivious little morsel. Her gaze swept across the landscape to make sure the rest of the clan was not near. A pack of baboons was more danger than a single lion could handle.

Clare looked at the baboon through the glasses, his rascally golden eyes intent on the termite mound. Probably, he was out for all the adventure he could muster before his parents came looking for him. But as Clare moved the camera lens to the right, the lioness came into view, now crouched low to the ground, taut, ready to spring, the only movement a twitch in her tail. Clare looked over at Chioto. This was Mother Nature's call, not theirs.

Clare took a few more shots of the scene, predator and prey. The lioness coiled tight, ready to attack. Clare's stomach knotted. The lioness appeared momentarily distracted. Had she scented them? Clare's hopes soared. If only the little baboon would look up! *Turn, little guy! Turn!* But the cat quickly returned her attention to what she hoped would be an easy meal. She sprang, catching the baboon by one rear leg. The baboon, shrieking in terror, whirled around, sinking his fangs into the lion's paw. Free for an instant, he raced for a nearby mopane tree and madly scrambled to the very top. Clinging to a slender branch, he continued screaming as he swung wildly back and forth on his precarious perch. Clare could see blood on his flank. But he was so terrified the adrenaline probably kept him from feeling pain, for now.

The lioness put her front paws on the tree, shaking the trunk, but the thick umbrella of leaves and small branches prohibited her climbing. She glared up at the chattering baboon and then lay down in the shade, crossing her front paws, presumably to wait. Clare longed for her motor drive, for the ability to shoot thirty frames per second, to have captured the chase. However, she'd done her best with the point and shoot. Perhaps luck might be on her side.

She and Chioto looked at the little baboon, as high in the

tree as he could get, still shaking with fear and rage. Well, he'd lived to learn a lesson. Hopefully, his kin would hear the racket and come to his rescue.

Chioto grinned. "Lucky fellow. Today."

"It's too much for my nerves." Clare looked at her watch and saw it was only eleven o'clock. "Let's get out of here."

After driving half an hour, Chioto found a beautiful picnic spot. They ate their lunch in the shade of a tree, leaning against the trunk. He made them a cup of tea with his small gas stove. He rarely spoke and seemed to have no moods but good ones. Plus he always gave her his chips. The perfect man.

They scouted a couple more water holes for another outing and took their time getting back. Dinner would be served on the patio tonight, as it was calm and warm. The stars would be glorious, the food delicious, and the wine flowing freely. And there would be many, many people to occupy Daniel's attention.

In her room, she showered, dressed, and went down to dinner, starving despite the rather large lunch. Servers dressed in colorful Herero clothing glided around the tables with trays of roasted springbok and vegetables. The wine was a South African pinotage, smoky and earthy, with delicious notes of tropical fruit. Daniel did not stint, nor should he at the prices he charged.

Quickly finishing her dessert, a berry compote, Clare made her way back to her room and changed into pajamas. She'd sacrifice the pleasure of a starry and balmy evening of watching animals parade to the water hole rather than risk another encounter with Daniel. He'd nodded in her direction, a decidedly unfriendly look, when she'd joined a table far from his. Mercifully, however, he hadn't come over.

Settling at her laptop, she inserted the memory card, anxious to see if she'd caught anything worthwhile today, though it was unlikely without either her telephoto or the motor drive. If her camera gear was not delivered soon, she would be forced to talk to Daniel. The computer whirred as it downloaded the images. She sat back with a glass of scotch, waiting. Up from the blank screen, like a modern miracle, popped the little baboon, staring right down the barrel of her camera lens. Naughty yellow eyes, insolent smirk, near-human fingers scratching at a punk rock hairdo. A stunning portrait of a simian delinquent.

She wished she could keep it from being wasted on a Lodge at Damara advertisement. That, of course, was impossible.

40.

The midday heat was oppressive, even within the thick concrete walls of Rhino Camp's main building. Eric and Chuck had left before daylight to scour a hundred-mile tract to the southwest, and Pieter had summoned the other researchers for a reconnaissance expedition to the north. All because reports had come in of increased poaching activity in the area. Everyone in camp was tense, anxious: ivory-bearing wildlife weren't the only victims of the poachers' malice.

Even Hosea was gone for a few days gathering provisions in Windhoek, leaving Zahara and Stacey in charge. He was due to return that afternoon. Stacey had spent the morning with Rhett and Scarlet, who now accompanied her everywhere. She was taking no chances of being caught unawares after the mamba incident.

"That's Stacey's sweet babies," she'd squeal enthusiastically, tossing them bits of leftover egg and sausage from the breakfast table. She also carried a plastic bag filled with dried strips of kudu steak, which she dispensed regularly as an unabashed incentive for their loyalty. Pieter had grumbled that they now more resembled chubby rock hyraxes than sleek Jack Russells.

Stacey had spent the morning, dogs at her heels, doing her low-impact calisthenics and beauty regimen. After a brief lunch of greens and vegetable soup with Zahara, she and the dogs retired upstairs for a nap. But Stacey was feeling restless. The news of recent poaching was unsettling, especially this close to camp.

She wondered whether extra police or game wardens were being assigned to the vicinity to protect the animals. People as well. Too agitated to rest, she decided to visit Eric's office to see if she could log into his computer and do a little sleuthing about any new developments. Suspecting Zahara might disapprove, Stacey shut her bedroom door quietly and whispered for the dogs to follow her as she tiptoed down the hall.

The door was unlocked. After the dogs trotted in, she gently shut it behind her.

The disorder was impressive, by any standards. Bookshelves overflowing, piles of journals and manuscripts stuffed into every crevice, stacks of paper everywhere. She noted the gun rack next to one of the bookshelves. Almost full. It struck her as odd that the men had taken so few of the rifles with them, given the potential danger.

Stacey shivered at the thought. She had read about these poaching gangs, terrorists, actually. Wildlife terrorists, well-funded and well-armed, capable of anything—rape, murder. Automatic weapons, souped-up all-terrain vehicles. The ability to move in, wreak carnage, then sweep away, leaving smoldering campsites and enormous, mutilated corpses in their wake. Stacey thought of Flora and Flossie—how differently it might have turned out. She'd heard the orphan sanctuaries were filled to bursting with young, malnourished, injured, emotionally traumatized babies and juveniles. This African adventure was proving to be a real downer. She'd taken to checking her airline tickets throughout the day, just to be sure she hadn't misplaced them, and was counting the hours until her departure. Nothing she could do but worry—and worrying about baby rhinos and elephants wouldn't change a thing.

"Let's get to work here," she said to no one in particular.

The dogs thumped their tails in apparent agreement, then curled up on the woven grass rug and fell deeply asleep. Stacey frowned as she surveyed the immense wooden desk. How anyone could work in such disarray, let alone do world-class research, was beyond her. Surely Eric would appreciate a bit of tidying up. That way, she would earn computer rights. Maybe. She began to stack papers in one pile. Books in another. And magazines in yet another. Big on the bottom, small on the top. That, at least, made generic sense. Eric would know where to look for what accordingly.

Once the desk had been organized to Stacey's satisfaction, she sat and turned on the hard drive. It began to hum and blink satisfyingly. Scarlet let out a particularly redolent fart, so Stacey rose to open the window. In the distance she saw a cloud of dust unfurling. It must be Hosea, returning from his shopping trip. Stacey sincerely hoped that he had been able to obtain more Evian spritzers. She especially longed for the rose-scented ones but would settle for any, even plain. She hoped he hadn't forgotten and patted her pocket holding one of the last precious canisters.

"Good grief, dog!" she exclaimed as she waved her arms about and wrinkled her nose. "Whew! No more sausage for you, you little stinker!" Then she sat back at the computer, leaning forward to scan the icons crowding the screen.

She was interrupted by a low growl. Both dogs were awake, their ears stiff and eyes wide. Surely, they wouldn't react to Hosea in such a manner. Or any of the camp vehicles. One of the most profound joys of their canine lives, aside from treats, was greeting returning friends. But perhaps it wasn't a camp vehicle. Perhaps it was reinforcements, dispatched to help with the poaching menace.

"Shhh. Quiet!" she ordered as she rose again to look out the window at the approaching Jeep. Eric hadn't said anything about visitors. But then, Stacey could scarcely be considered Eric's confidant. Odd, however, that Zahara hadn't mentioned any visit. Surely, Eric would have given Zahara a heads-up.

As the Jeep got closer, Stacey's heart sank. It didn't look official at all. Beat-up, with tires hanging from the sides, dents, a cracked windshield. She could barely make out the driver and passenger, two shadowy men, as the Jeep rolled slowly up the drive. When it parked a short distance from the front terrace, Stacey hushed the dogs once more and withdrew to the side of the window so she wouldn't be visible from below.

When she peered out again, she froze.

The two men had gotten out of the Jeep and were standing next to it in the drive. Both were quite tall, unlike the familiar peoples of Damaraland. They more resembled skeletal wraiths than humans. The clothes they wore were tattered and filthy. Ill-fitting camouflage pants, far too short. Ragged T-shirts. High, sculpted, hollow cheekbones and deep, sunken eyes. Stacey watched in mounting horror as the men nodded to each other, surveyed the area, then turned toward the stairs. After a few steps, however, they stopped.

"What do you men want? Are you lost? Hungry?" Zahara was using her big voice, sonorous, defiant. Incredibly brave.

One of the men, the taller, stepped forward and smiled. Even from the window, Stacey could see his sharp yellow teeth —what was left of them.

"This be Rhino Camp?" he inquired, his head cocked, his smile wolfish.

The dogs were now clearly agitated, their lips curled and hackles raised. They growled steadily, emitting occasional furious yips. "Quiet!" she commanded in a whisper. Chastened, though clearly reluctant, they obeyed. Pieter had trained them well.

Zahara hesitated, then answered, "Yes. You have business here?"

"Why . . . yes. I would like to speak with—uh—the boss, please." He spoke slowly.

"The boss is out," Zahara snapped. "Back shortly. I can give you food. Water. I'll tell him you will return tomorrow. He's a very busy man."

The tall stranger stroked his chin, his head still cocked. "I, too, am a very busy man. Perhaps I could speak to . . . another boss."

"Impossible," Zahara barked.

Stacey could hear the strain, the panic rising in Zahara's voice as she stood there on the porch, unyielding. As she peered out the window, she noted the second stranger scoping out the premises. Thankfully, he had not yet scanned the second-floor windows.

"Rhino Camp," the man declared absently. "You have ivory, perhaps? You must have ivory." He smiled. "Maybe even rhino?"

"This is a research facility, not a warehouse." Zahara stood her ground. "No ivory here. Nothing of value. Not a thing. If you don't leave, now, there will be trouble. Many people are here. Working. Come back tomorrow."

Stacey was trembling as she realized each was calling the other's bluff. There was more at risk here than simple robbery. Plenty of ivory, contraband, secured under lock and key. But Zahara would never give any of it up. And Flossie. Even her little horn nubs held value on the black market. And who knew what else these men were capable of, especially if they discovered the two women were here alone. She had to save them. But how? The dogs? These two tiny, overfed dogs? They would die trying, of course, but could do little more. Surely the men were armed.

Her mind racing, she conjured every Hollywood siege she had ever watched. Westerns. War movies. Well then, if the men were armed, Stacey would be too. Dragging a chair toward the window, she furiously piled two stacks of books as high as the bottom ledge with smaller stacks slightly higher, creating a stabilizing valley between them. She rushed to the gun rack and grabbed the rifle with the biggest bore, sliding it ever so slowly into the slot and just out the window. Then she elevated the butt of the rifle slightly with a couple more books. All the while, she prayed that the men were too occupied with Zahara to notice.

She crept back to the gun rack. She could hear the mounting tension in the exchanges below. She had to act. Now.

Seizing the next largest rifle, she went to the door. The dogs, eager to take part in the unfolding drama, rushed to her side, crowding her and pawing at the door as if possessed.

"No! Stay! Back!"

She opened the door slightly, kicking them aside. But they wouldn't obey. Not this time. "No!" she shrieked as they struggled past her and streaked down the hall for the stairs.

Stacey tore after them, her heart pounding. *Oh, please,* she begged, *please don't let them hurt Zahara or the dogs. Please.*

A riot of barking erupted. Stacey could hear Zahara call out in the confusion. One of the dogs yelped, a shrill cry of pain. Then silence.

Stacey tiptoed just out of range near the front door. To her amazement, she saw Zahara kneeling, both dogs struggling as she restrained them, choking and gagging.

"I will let them go if you do not leave now," she threatened, her voice cracking, clearly playing her last card.

The men chuckled. "Yes. I would like to see that," the tall one said as he reached slowly behind his back.

"No, you would not." Stacey stepped out from the shadows, leveling her rifle at the man. "You would not like to see that at all."

He slowly returned his hand to his side and regarded her.

"Ah, so I see two dogs and a rifle. But there are two of us. Should we be afraid?" His voice had a singsong lilt to it. Stacey looked into his blank gaze.

"No. Two dogs and two rifles." She jerked the nose of her weapon toward the window upstairs, at least she hoped in the direction of the window, where she prayed the rifle would be visible—and not ridiculously askew.

The dogs twisted and strained in Zahara's grip.

Stacey gulped, then shouted upward, "Don't shoot until I give the signal!"

The man drew a sharp breath.

Stacey gained courage. With her eyes narrowed and, she hoped, inscrutable, she addressed the pair, her voice sober and low. "If two rifles aren't enough, I'm sure the others have heard the dogs. They will be here soon. With more rifles. Grenades even. Understand?" Then she tapped the metal canister in her packet. "Get out now! I'm not afraid to use one."

The two men, clearly uncomfortable with this unexpected development, exchanged nervous glances and edged toward their battered vehicle.

"Tomorrow, then," the tall one spat. They both turned and jumped in the Jeep, threw it into reverse, and sped away, dust coiling like an angry serpent behind them.

Both women seemed paralyzed, Zahara kneeling with the squirming dogs, Stacey still wielding the rifle that now wavered in her hands. When the intruders were sufficiently distant, Zahara released Scarlet and Rhett, who charged down the drive, then wheeled and trotted back in triumph. Stacey laid the weapon gingerly on a nearby chair. She realized she was shaking as she stumbled blindly forward, toward Zahara.

"Miss Stacey!" Zahara cried out, but Stacey couldn't hear, couldn't see. Darkness enveloped her in an immense, obliterating wave as she sank to the ground.

41.

Left on her own without even Clare to talk to, Stacey became a cruise director, aware of the most minute details concerning Rhino Camp. A natural-born gossip, she also knew the goings on of everyone, quietly stashing information in hopes Clare would come back, with the anticipation of their combing through it like a jewelry sale at Bloomingdale's. But as the days went by and Eric became even more possessed—with poachers or Clare, who knew?—she decided it was time to quit her role as observer and take action, so she set up an ambush for him near his tent. Adept though he might be at dodging lions and rhinos, she was confident he could not dodge her. The few times he'd been forced to talk with her, he'd pasted a smile on his face, but the effect was more that he had indigestion.

"Hi!"

Eric jumped, clearly jolted. "Hi?"

"Over here. I'm not going to eat you, you know." She laughed and slapped his arm. "I might like to, but I'm not." Up close, she noticed how gaunt he'd become, dark circles under his eyes, his tanned face now ashen.

Eric straightened his shoulders. "Can I help you with something?"

"No, but I might be able to help *you* with something. Invite me in?"

"Well, we better go to my office. By the way, nice work with the intruders." He glanced at his tent.

"Thanks. No, we're here. This is good." She loved the storm sweeping across his face as he looked at his tent, the compound, the sky—anywhere but at her.

Eric sighed heavily. Inside, he cleared a teetering stack of papers off a chair. "Kind of messy. Sorry."

Stacey looked around the tent, every flat surface, including the bed, covered with books or papers or empty teacups. "It is. I could help you organize this. Like I helped with your office." Stacey noticed Eric glowering at her. "You know, when I saved the camp?"

"I'm still recovering from your organizing. Here at least I know exactly where everything is. Well, almost everything." Eric fussed with a stack of papers. "I work here at night sometimes. Actually, Stacey, I was just about to work. So tell me how you can help me. I know the researchers haven't been very—"

"Nice? No, they haven't." She picked at her nails and spread her fingers to admire them.

"I'm not sure I can change that."

"Oh! Silly you. You think I'm here to tattle on someone." She had so little power at Rhino Camp compared to her relative status stateside that she enjoyed this brief toying with him. "No. I'm here about Clare."

"Clare? What about Clare?" Eric bristled.

"Yes. Clare. The woman you love? The woman you're about to lose?" She smiled brightly up at him. "Got anything to drink?"

Eric just stared at her. "Drink? Yes, uh, whiskey." He wiped two glasses with the hem of his T-shirt, poured a finger of Jameson in each, and handed one to Stacey.

"Thanks." She took a tiny sip and, like a cat, delicately licked her lips. "I'm making you nervous. That's not what I want. I mean, it's kind of fun, but it's not why I came. It's just hard to see you two so in love—and so blowing it."

"Have you talked with her? Since she left, I mean."

"No. I talked to her before the explosion, whatever that was about." She studied him. "What *was* that about? I doubt she'd leave willingly with Daniel. I would, but she doesn't like him, and that's putting it mildly."

"She doesn't?" Eric turned back to his desk and picked up a book. "You need to talk to her, not me."

"I have, of course, or I wouldn't be here. Not since she left— or rather, you let her leave. She's in love with you. But you're doing this schizoid combo: *You've done me wrong* and *I'll die if you leave me* shtick, so naturally, she's confused. You might want to soften that a tad because you study shit, among other things, and you and I both know there's no truth in any of that crap. You're just too scared to go after her. Poachers? No problemo. But love? Ew, spooky."

"Wait. She told you she loves me?"

"Head over heels."

Eric sank onto his bed and slugged down the whiskey. His face darkened. "You didn't see what I saw when Daniel came here. And I did not say I'd die if she left. She tell you that?"

"I seriously doubt *you* saw what your weak male ego and overactive imagination think you saw, Mr. Scientist. Actually, you're kind of being a jerk to a girl who's great. The only female, maybe the only female in the world, who would stay here with you."

Eric sat, head in his hands.

"So what are you going to do about it?"

42.

Eric cruised along the base of the Kaokoveld Range to the west of Rhino Camp. As usual, he had risen before dawn, knocked back a few cups of black coffee, and stuffed a cooler full of water bottles and sandwiches Zahara had prepared the night before.

As not so usual, earlier he had retrieved one of the two Remington 870 pump shotguns as well as a .40 caliber Smith & Wesson service pistol from his office. He winced as he removed them from the rack, as he always counted it a point of honor seldom to carry any weapons beyond a flare gun and a much smaller pistol. To him, lethal weapons constituted a breach of faith with the natural world—and a sign of incompetence, of compensatory masculinity. The kind trophy hunters, miserable bastards, every one of them, represented.

But with the recent spate of poaching incidents, especially the near catastrophic one at camp that Stacey and Zahara just faced, the situation had changed, mightily.

Consumed with grim thoughts, he had stuffed boxes of cartridges and bullets into a rucksack and left the room.

As Eric drove west on the highway, the black night bled into dark gray. Apart from the tires humming on the asphalt, he was alone in the silence, alone with the thoughts thronging his mind, strangely at odds with the peaceful predawn sky. He shook his head violently, as if to erase them, but to no avail.

Clenching the steering wheel, he followed the bright

points of his headlamps cutting a narrow swath through the darkness. If only he could see his own course as clearly.

The poachers. Pieter and he'd had words, repeatedly, over Eric's fixation on hunting them down and bringing them to justice. The night before, just after dinner, Pieter had grown uncharacteristically strident, banging his fist on the table, shouting, "And just what do you intend, once you have cornered these villains, Eric? Do you intend to stun them with your charisma? Disarm them with your conservationist zeal? Convert the murdering scum to a life of farming? Wood carving? Or perhaps they'll join you, renouncing their past crimes. I can see it now. Eric's army. The Rhino Corps."

Eric had glowered at his empty plate in response. It was true. Other than locating the most recent intruders, he had little in the way of a follow-up plan. At least Pieter had strength in numbers, as he had enlisted most of the graduate students in his search. Eric, typically, had refused to let any of the researchers tag along. He didn't want the burden of inane conversation—or the responsibility of a budding career in wildlife management cut short by an AK-47.

Eric had scowled. "I'm not insane. I'll just pinpoint their whereabouts. Contact you. Then we'll decide. Together." He realized the plan sounded muddled. He didn't care.

"You could contact the authorities, you know."

"Don't trust them. Not a one. Too much money changing hands. Too high up."

"Well then, man—what difference do you think we could possibly make?"

"Drive them off. Destroy their camps. Let them know this territory is defended."

"By a delusional PhD and an assortment of scrawny bookworms?" Pieter's lips curled in a sardonic grin. "Terrifying!"

Eric felt the heat rising to his face recalling the conversation as he raced along the two-lane highway. The Jeep was bucking dangerously. He looked at the speedometer, then eased off the gas pedal and took a number of deep breaths.

Of course, Pieter was right. But it wasn't as if Eric had a choice. He wasn't there merely to chronicle the obscene slaughter and inevitable extinction of this ancient species. He had to do something. Self-appointed guardian? No one else had stepped up. "Not on my watch," he muttered. "Not on my watch!" He repeated this mantra as he stared into the fugitive darkness.

Slowly, the gray sky faded into a dull blue.

Eric laughed softly at the sight. *Blue. Am I blue? Decidedly.* It had been a horrible mistake to have allowed Clare to stay at camp. Stacey was little more than a migraine-inducing annoyance. But Clare—Clare was lethal. How could he have fallen for it, the whole bungled affair? Allowing her to play nursemaid-mommy to little Flossie. To insinuate herself into his camp. His work. His life. His heart.

Eric groaned as he relived their brief, intense encounters. He had only to look at her to ache for her. But when his lips touched hers. When his fingers slipped across her silken skin. He had tasted the honeyed warmth of her neck, her shoulders. And hungered for so much more. He imagined his mouth exploring every delicious valley, crest, and hill of her body. Imagined her green eyes, dilated and limpid with desire. Her laughter, gentle as an evening breeze and as refreshing. He could hear her murmuring his name as she gathered him to her, enfolding him. Engulfing him.

But that dream had been severed as savagely as if by a

poacher's snare. She was just playing at caring about the rhino. Like Marie Antoinette playing the little milkmaid with her Meissen porcelain and silken petticoats. A game. A charade. She'd go back to the States, to all her money and privilege. No other explanation for that helicopter charge. Perhaps if she was feeling nostalgic, she might write a check to some rhino rescue organization or another around Christmas. But why prostitute herself to Sypher at Lodge at Damara? That made no sense. She could probably buy the place and have change left over.

No. He could forgive her her wealth. He could even forgive her concealing it from him—unless, of course, that was all part of the masquerade. What he could not forgive was the scene in his office. Her betrayal. Her surrender to Sypher and all that he stood for.

Eric realized with a kind of grim pleasure that the Jeep had accelerated again. It didn't matter. She didn't matter. She was gone. He gunned the engine and plummeted into the shadows.

43.

The drive had been uneventful for over an hour but became more challenging after leaving the well-worn roads and off-road tracks. Now the Jeep heaved and hurtled over rocky desert, along washed-out riverbeds. At last Eric reached his destination, a long, low, coastal range riddled with valleys, dead-end gulches, plateaus, and escarpments. A dream hideaway for poachers. He thought he had seen a thin ribbon of smoke yesterday as he was heading home from a tour of some of the nearby water holes. He had marked the location in his mind and now was keying in on it as best memory served.

The bright morning sun threw everything into sharp relief. Every rock, every shrub cast a long, crisp shadow. Even the grains of sand took on particulate identities. As Eric drove slowly along the outermost edge of a sheer wall of red and ivory stone, he ground the Jeep to a slow halt and slowly stepped from the cab. He took in the scene, stretching his aching arms and back. Other vehicles had been here before. And recently, so defined were their tracks. How many, he couldn't tell. He decided to radio Pieter with the information.

"Rhino Man to Rhino Camp. Come in, please." No response. He waited, then repeated the call.

"Rhino Camp here. Where the hell are you?"

"Pieter, I think I've found something, a site."

"Good God, man! How close?"

"No idea. No visual contact. Only tire tracks."

"Any idea—" The connection was breaking up. "Look, send me your coordinates. I'll be there as soon as I can." Pieter paused. "Eric, want me to contact the police and wildlife management?"

"No. Don't." Eric's voice was cold, removed.

Pieter countered, "We have no idea what we're getting into."

Eric responded without emotion. "They wouldn't be here for hours. And there might be collusion. Higher up. Lower down. I'm not going to risk an alert. Or an ambush."

"Eric, we can't risk a massacre. And since you have no idea what you're dealing with—Eric, are you armed?"

"Roger that."

"Sit tight until we get there. Nothing rash."

"Roger. Out," Eric answered in a hollow voice. He turned off the radio, hesitated, then nosed his way into the deep shadows of the gulch.

Inside the towering walls, the terrain, which before had been inhospitable, now became positively hostile. The chassis scraped and screeched over boulders. Occasionally, all four of the wheels were airborne, leaving the Jeep tipping precariously until gravity chose a smashing point.

The going was so difficult that Eric began to wonder whether he had miscalculated, whether the tire tracks had actually entered the inlet from this point. Perhaps it was a ruse, to throw off pursuers. Eric heard a painful metallic crunch, closed his eyes, and whispered a fierce curse. Perhaps this wasn't where he had observed the smoke after all. His tracking instincts, though honed over years, were certainly fallible.

The Jeep, its wheels spinning and grinding, at last turned a sharp corner. There, spread before him, a wasteland of garbage, meat-drying racks, and a large blackened fire pit. No signs of life. No vehicles. Probably abandoned. For now.

Satisfied the camp was deserted, Eric turned off the ignition. He tucked the pistol into his belt, nonetheless, and stepped out.

As he toed the ashes, his eyes narrowed, and his jaw clenched. Cold. Overturned wooden boxes, camp seats no doubt, circled the ring of stones. Eric surveyed the closest. With a sickening rush, he noted curls of cut wire littering the area around it. No question. Snares. Perhaps the very metal that had come so close to ending Flora's life. And Flossie's.

Eric tried to control his revulsion as he sank onto a box and put his face in his hands. There was nothing else to do. Pieter would be here soon enough.

IN LESS THAN two hours, Pieter strode into the camp, florid and breathing hard, Chuck trailing behind. He looked about at the heaps of empty cans, the mounds of brown beer bottles glinting in the bright sun. At Eric, sitting on an overturned box, seemingly oblivious to the scene—and to the arrival of his friend.

Pieter bellowed, "Left the Land Rover near the cliffs. After wasting a good half hour looking for you. What in God's name were you thinking, driving into a potential ambush! I've known you years, but you've never struck me as suicidal. Until now."

Eric looked at him blankly. "I suppose I wasn't thinking."

"What if you had stumbled on a live camp? What would you have done then?" Pieter was shaking. "All I can say is you are one lucky son of a bitch."

Eric nodded, still abstracted.

Pieter approached a pile of empty bottles and gave them a wild kick. They rattled and clinked as they rolled about, but Eric just stared into the charred center of the fire pit. Chuck instinctively hung back. Pieter swung an arm, encompassing the camp. "Just look at this shit. Bastards! I'd say five to ten, and probably quite recent." He jerked his head in Eric's direction. "You know, one of these days you will wake up to find you aren't actually bulletproof. I just hope you survive that little lesson."

Getting no response, Pieter took a deep breath and jammed his hands into his pockets. Then he turned to Chuck, who seemed to shrink under his gaze. "There's no sense taking any more risks today. We've already exceeded our quota. For a lifetime. Chuck, I want you on that ridge. Watch for any sign of activity. Any dust plumes. I don't care if it's a herd of wildebeest or an ostrich. Anything. I don't want to be caught in this death trap. You have a signaling mirror?"

Chuck shook his head.

"Then take mine. We'll be leaving soon. I just want to have a short chat with our friend here."

Chuck trudged off and began the steep, rocky climb.

Pieter watched the khaki figure, nearly invisible against the dusty hillside. He turned to Eric, who still sat slumped on his box. "You can't go on like this. You're here to study the rhino—that's your mission. Not some one-man vigilante squad."

Eric didn't respond, so Pieter continued, increasingly strident. "You know what I think, *Doctor*? For someone who professes to be so damned intelligent, you strike me as pretty damned stupid." With that, he picked up a nearby bottle and hurled it at a large rock.

This pronouncement jolted Eric out of his private thoughts. "Stupid? How so?" He brushed his hair from his brow. "Enlighten me."

Pieter coughed and crossed his arms. "This whole poacher nonsense. It has consumed you. Beyond reason. Has it occurred to you that this fixation might be some kind of sub—sub—Damn it!"

"Sublimation? Is that the word you're thinking of? I don't see how—"

"Precisely," Pieter interrupted. "Have you considered that perhaps it's not the poachers after all? You've been scouring this part of the country like a mad man. A mad man chasing even crazier phantoms." He paused. "But I tell you this—in truth. I don't think you're so much chasing. You're running."

Eric spread his arms. "You call this phantom?" He began to chuckle wildly. "Running, you say. And what, pray tell, am I running after?"

"Not after! From!" Pieter was practically bellowing. "Damn it, man. It's as clear as the nose on your face. Clare. You're in love with her. And she you. Any fool can see you two belong together. But you're not just any fool, are you? A god-damned stubborn, blind, over-educated, moralistic fool. It's not the poachers at all. It's your goddamned heart."

Pieter whistled toward the crest of the hill and summoned Chuck with a fierce wave. Then he turned toward Eric and announced, "Let's get out of here. I'm driving you back to camp. You seem rather—rather foggy to me. To be honest."

"Pieter, have you ever been anything but?" Eric laughed weakly.

Pieter answered the dig with a loud harrumph. "Let's get out of this godforsaken place." He reached out a hand and pulled his friend to his feet. "Perhaps the trip will return you to your senses." He snorted. "If it isn't too late."

44.

Back at camp, Eric couldn't shake the feeling that he was being hunted, haunted. Pieter and Stacey's unrelenting intrusions into his personal life, his heart, had left him unsettled and agitated. Even the long walks about the compound with Flossie and Elvis scampering beside him couldn't lift his spirits. Ever since Pieter had forbidden him from further poacher patrols, these walks were a necessary outlet for the ungovernable feelings that possessed him.

Before all this nonsense, Eric had been comfortably attached to the idea that bachelorhood was his lot in life. At least a kind of bachelorhood. In truth, he was wed to his research. The emotions surging within him recently were an altogether unwelcome distraction. Clare's image floated and danced, inescapable in sleep or awake, a bewitching, confounding mirage. Eric could smell the honeyed warmth of her hair, and he would tremble as he imagined it pooling across his naked chest as she lay her head against him. He could see her dancing green eyes probe his very soul. Those luscious lips. Her radiant laughter. He ached as he conjured her elegant hands caressing his body, lingering, toying, teasing.

He just couldn't shake the image of Clare's anguished face when he'd burst in on her and Sypher. Was it possible Stacey was right? And that he'd been unspeakably wrong?

"Damn it! Enough!" he shouted. Flossie and Elvis skidded to a halt and turned toward him, quizzical, alert. Elvis emitted a concerned bleat.

"Sorry. Didn't mean to spook you. I was just—just remembering our old friend." He sighed. "Let's get back to the office. Get some work done. That a plan?"

Apparently the suggestion was agreeable to his ungainly companions. Rhino and goat merrily gamboled their way back toward the center of camp.

Once the two were ensconced in the boma, nestled in fragrant beds of hay and snoring heartily, Eric felt he should return to the more serious business of compiling data regarding population densities, birth rates, predation, and polishing up a paper he would soon be submitting for publication. Work. That was the only antidote to these fevered hallucinations.

Zahara greeted him as he entered the great room. "I know it's early, Doctor Eric. I've made a tasty ragout, just the way you like." Apparently she too had joined the multitude of worriers obsessing over Eric's emotional and physical health.

"No, thank you, Zahara." He cringed inwardly at the disappointed look in her eyes. "Save some for me. Perhaps a bit later. Thank you very much."

He climbed the stairs. Stacey was locked in her room with the dogs, whom she had appropriated entirely since the snake incident. Just as well, Eric concluded with a low chuckle. He couldn't help but wonder what these two animals, raised in the harsh environs of Rhino Camp, thought of Evian spritzers and fashion magazines, but with Stacey's blandishments they took to their new life with gusto.

Eric entered his office, his inner sanctum, smiling as he recalled Stacey's incredible resourcefulness and courage in dealing with the poachers. Fortunately, these qualities had absolved her from the immense violation she had wrought upon his workspace. It had taken hours to dismantle her piles, but at last the organized chaos of his paperwork was restored. He pulled a thick file from the shelf, "De-Horning: Risks and Management," and settled down at his desk. But the words, the tables, the graphs shimmered and swirled, then faded before him. Furious with himself over his lack of focus, he shoved his chair away from the desk and turned toward the window. All he could see was Clare, melting into his ardent embrace.

These visions, these passions were unendurable. Not eating, not sleeping, not able to work. He couldn't go on like this. Something snapped inside him. Suddenly he was filled with resolve. One way or another—he had to know the truth.

Eric opened a small notebook, riffled through its pages, picked up his phone, and began to dial the Lodge. Then he stopped and thrust his phone into his pocket. No. He had to see her. To hear it from her own lips. To hold her. To tell her he would never leave her, never doubt her, if only she would be his.

He bounded down the stairs. As he strode toward the main door, Zahara peered from the kitchen. "Doctor Eric, everything all right?"

"Never better!" Eric beamed as he grabbed his hat, planted it firmly on his head, and dashed down the steps to the truck.

The miles unspooled beneath his tires as he raced across the red, dusty plain. He barely noticed the barren, arid landscape that he loved with almost religious fervor, so fixed was he on his decision, so elated with desire and resolve. He lost all sense of time, and before he knew it, he began the sloping ascent toward the main gates of Lodge at Damara. Revulsion overcame him at the sight. More amusement park than anything. He swept those thoughts aside as he sped through the gate, saluting an obviously bewildered guard. Thank God, he would be liberating Clare from Sypher's lewd advances, from this nightmare of crass commercialism. Together, they would save the rhino for posterity. As a team. A loving partnership that would change the world.

Eric pulled up to the entrance and jumped from the truck. He raced into the enormous lobby and up to the reservation desk, where he pounded insistently on a small silver bell. A desk clerk emerged from a back room, looking somewhat askance at the dusty, disheveled man—so unlike the usual guests who arrived decked to the nines, as if they had stepped from some pricey outfitting catalog. And this guest had not arrived by shuttle as guests invariably did. The next wasn't due for an hour.

"Yes, sir? How may I help you?"

"I'm here to see Clare. Um, Miss Rainbow-Dashell," Eric stuttered, pulling his hat off and running his fingers through his unkempt hair.

The clerk faltered. "Was she expecting you, Mr.—Mr.—"

"Bolton. The name's Bolton."

The clerk hesitated. "I'm very sorry, Mr. Bolton. Miss Rainbow-Dashell left us this morning. Had a flight to catch."

Eric's heart gave a painful kick. This couldn't be happening. Desperate, he stammered, "Do you know which flight?"

"Not for certain, sir." He tapped a few keys on his computer. "I imagine the three fifteen to Johannesburg. But I really can't say for certain." The clerk scanned the empty lobby.

Eric looked at his watch. Was there time? Only if he drove as if the devil himself were on his tail. He spun toward the door.

"Good day, Mr. Bolton," the clerk warbled in Eric's retreating direction. "Thank you for visiting Lodge at Damara. Do come again."

As he clambered into the truck, Eric prayed that there was enough petrol in the tank to get him to Windhoek. The engine roared to life. Two drowsy porters started as tires squealed away from the curb.

45.

Eric glanced at the speedometer as the truck began to buck violently. Eighty-seven miles—and on this pavement. *Slow down, old boy, or you'll lose control. Lose control? I've lost my mind,* he mused wryly. No matter. He would not let Clare leave Namibia—or Africa—without begging her to be his. Forever. Warts and all. Warthogs and baby rhinos and Pieter and all. If he couldn't catch up with her at Kutako International, he'd simply have to charter something at Eos and get to Johannesburg. The flight was just under three hours. Surely she'd have a layover. Three flights daily to O.R. Tambo, assuming she'd take the same route home. Eric was calculating departures and distance madly. She would have to catch the second flight of the day, the 3:15, just as the clerk had mentioned. That made sense, given that she hadn't left the Lodge early enough for the 7:10. He shook his head in frustration. He could make the airport, assuming no delays, but could he catch her before boarding? He pressed down the accelerator and tightened his grip on the wheel. The landscape sped by, a monochrome blur of termite mounds and scrub.

Suddenly, it occurred to him. He couldn't just leave the truck running in front of the terminal while he looked for Clare. It wasn't his property but the camp's. Best-case scenario, it would be towed; worst, some opportunistic citizen would avail himself of free transportation. No, that would not do. Casting about for solutions, he would try contacting Dr. Sheldrake's compound by phone.

After dialing, he listened to the static, despair rising in his chest. At last, someone picked up.

"Allo?"

"Yes. Eric Bolton here. Dr. Sheldrake, please."

"Moment."

Eric heard footsteps and a screen door slam. It seemed minutes before the familiar voice answered.

"Bolton—everything all right?"

"Yes—going to be, I hope. It's—"

"You'll be delighted to know how well Flora is doing. Tried to hook me yesterday. Took a good charge at one of the keepers too. You should have seen him fly over the—"

"Wonderful, Doctor. It's just—I'm in a bit of a bind. Can you spare anyone to meet me at Kutako in, say, an hour? Actually, two people. I'll need a driver. Have to make a flight to Tambo. Emergency. Uh. Personal business. No time to park."

"Personal, eh? Anything to do with that leggy blonde?"

Eric sighed. "Afraid so." He could hear the veterinarian chuckling warmly.

"Delighted to hear. No worries, Bolton. We'll be waiting."

"Thank you. Again in your debt. Bye for now."

Eric laid the phone on the seat and again increased his pressure on the gas pedal. Was his attraction that obvious? And what of hers? What had Sheldrake sensed during the controlled chaos of Flora's rescue? What had everyone seen that he hadn't? Well, at least it wasn't too late. If she would only forgive him his outburst at Rhino Camp. He cringed at the memory. What had come over him, seeing her and Sypher like that? Blind rage. Nothing more. Of course, Clare would never have encouraged Sypher's advances. She had too much class for that oily snake. Eric just prayed she didn't have too much class for an oafish field biologist.

The highway began to even out, and Eric noted signs of civilization, however rudimentary, now dotting the landscape. Small cinder block hovels squatting just off the shoulder, scrawny chickens milling about. Occasional barbed wire fencing stretching off into the distance—to enclose what? Anyone's guess. Then, at last, more homes, more fences. Now sturdier chickens. Goats. And Namibians, the women in their bright garb, men in faded work clothes. Children half-clad. Small stores. Then, a real petrol station. Eric checked the fuel. Getting low, but he would make it. He had to.

It seemed to him as if he were racing through time, modernity bearing down on him as he fled the familiar desert, so prehistoric and austere. Now clutter and combustion and claustrophobic construction assaulted his senses. He would never be tamed into living like this. He glanced in his rearview mirror, half in longing for his familiar desert and half in fear of a patrol car in pursuit. He had all but forgotten his speed.

At once, the exit was upon him. He swerved violently to the left. There it was: Hosea Kutako International Airport. Eric roared toward the departure area and slid to a stop. Sheldrake and an assistant were standing beside the hospital's white van, waving their arms. Eric waved back, swerved to the curb, and leapt from the truck.

Scarcely aware of the looks he generated, he galloped into the terminal, dodging travelers and porters alike. He skidded up to the Air Namibia ticket counter.

"Johannesburg," he blurted. He looked up at the schedule

board, panting, as he thrust his credit card at the wide-eyed agent. "Three fifteen."

"I'm afraid that flight is boarding, sir. It would be impossible—" She frowned at him across the counter.

"An emergency. Please, just sell me a bloody ticket. I've got to make that flight."

"Very well, sir," she sniffed. "We do have one seat available. You may purchase the ticket. Of course, you know that you might not—"

Eric stiffened and leaned over the counter, then regained his composure. No use threatening the silly woman. Another agent was already eyeing him warily.

Tapping deliberately at her console, she finally slid his receipt toward him, checked his signature, and handed him his boarding pass.

Thankfully, there was no line at the security checkpoint. Eric forced a lame smile as he resigned himself to the usual body scan. That procedure, too, seemed maddeningly extended.

"Forgive me, but I've got to make a flight that's leaving immediately. I know this looks odd, but I've got to—"

"One moment, sir," the guard responded, taking another leisurely swipe with his wand. "You may go."

Eric broke into a trot, then a run. As he approached the gate, he could hear the announcement: "Flight SW 727 to Johannesburg has boarded and is now—"

Eric groaned as he raced up to the boarding agent's counter. She was a lovely petite brunette, barely able to disguise her consternation at the late arrival.

"Sir, I'm afraid—"

"I must—um, it's my wife—a medical emergency. She's already boarded. I've got to make this flight."

His urgency moved her. "Let me see what I can do." She reached for the microphone and, turning from him, spoke softly into it.

Eric could only hear the pounding of his heart.

Moments later, the doors parted.

"They've held the flight, Mr. Bolton. On behalf of Air Namibia, we wish you and your wife all the best."

Eric reddened as he rushed past her onto the tarmac and clambered up the metal stairs toward the hatch where two crew members awaited.

"We're quite full today, sir. Let's get you seated as quickly as possible," announced what seemed to be the senior attendant.

"My wife is on the flight. She's, she's very ill," he stuttered in exhaustion. "Possibly weeks to live. I only just found out. I've got to sit with her. I'm begging you."

"Oh. I'm so very sorry." She touched his shoulder as they entered the cabin.

In a flash, Eric spotted her and motioned to the flight attendant. Clare was seated next to the window, gazing out. The large man beside her was dressed in a business suit and looked to be trying to engage her in conversation. She nodded occasionally but appeared preoccupied, listless.

The flight attendant approached their row, then leaned toward the man. "Excuse me, sir, but we have an urgent request for a seat exchange. A personal matter. Would you be so kind?" She waved her arm toward the aisle in a welcoming yet authoritative gesture.

The man glared at Eric, then fumbled with his seat belt and rose.

"You don't mind if I retrieve my briefcase, do you?" the

man grumbled at the attendant as he began digging in the overhead compartment.

Clare had leaned her brow against the window.

Eric pressed his hands together in silent thanks, then slid breathlessly into the vacant seat.

"Miss Rainbow-Dashell, I believe."

Hearing his voice, Clare let out a tiny cry. As she turned, her eyes welled up with tears.

"What—what are you doing here?" Her voice quavered. "I thought you despised me. That you never—"

He took her hand, opened it, and brushed the palm with his lips.

"What I'm doing is begging you to forgive me. For being so wrong." He raised his eyes to hers, grasped her shoulders gently, and pulled her toward him. "And to be my wife. Please say yes." He kissed her with fierce insistence. When she broke their embrace, a torrent of passionate declarations poured from him: "I love you, Clare. I adore you. I need you. I want you with me. Forever."

Clare seemed agitated, confused. She cast her gaze downward.

"You don't have to answer right away." Eric realized he was trembling. The craft had taxied to the runway, preparing for takeoff. They sat next to each other, he grasping her hand tightly as the plane rumbled and rose.

Once the aircraft had achieved cruising altitude, Clare, still looking at her lap, whispered, "I was reconciled to the thought we were over. Done. That there was no more—"

Eric took a deep breath. He pressed on, grasping for the perfect words. "Not over. Just beginning." Hope suffused him. "You know, Clare, Johannesburg is an astonishing city. Perhaps we could enjoy some time alone. A break from everything. I know I've been stressed. A bit overdue in terms of a vacation."

Clare lifted her head, smiling. More the Clare Eric had fallen in love with. She gave a bright, lilting laugh.

"Stressed? No, I hadn't noticed. Really, nobody noticed." She giggled. "So you'd like to show me the sights? While I consider your proposal?"

Eric realized she was teasing him, and he warmed to the notion. "We might consider it a honeymoon . . . of sorts."

"Really, Eric? Now I must consider your proposition as well?" Her green eyes twinkled. "Don't honeymoons usually take place *after* the wedding?"

Eric blushed at his forwardness but soon recovered. "We're in the southern hemisphere, Clare. Here everything is reversed."

And with that, laughing softly, she squeezed his thigh and kissed him. Over and over again. Then she nestled her head against his shoulder.

46.

On the veranda outside Rhino Camp's dining hall, Eric stood in growing agitation as he watched Pieter insistently shake his head.

"God," Eric chided, "you're so damned subtle. What's wrong? You don't find a wedding at Rhino Camp suitable? I don't have time to fly to California—or to England." Eric fought to overcome the urge to smack the wall in frustration. "Not now. Not when we're so busy. And will you, for the love of God, stop looking at me as if I've just soiled my pants?" He began to pace.

"That I could understand." Pieter lifted one bushy eyebrow while lowering the other, which only added to Eric's annoyance.

"You should have been a boarding school master. You've certainly perfected all the mannerisms."

The two stood in a silent standoff.

When Eric finally calmed down somewhat, he ventured, "So, oh genius with the vast store of experience in romance, where do *you* suggest I get married? The Vatican? Maybe the pope has space in his schedule. The Taj Mahal? Chartres?" He paused, trying to collect his thoughts. "Clare's not like that. She's down to earth."

"You sure she said yes when you proposed? She understood you *were* proposing marriage?"

"Okay, that's it. You're wasting my time." Eric stomped off toward his office.

"The Skeleton Coast!" bellowed Pieter.

Eric stopped but didn't turn.

Pieter walked up to him and grasped his shoulder. "It's all arranged. A gift from me and Spacey Stacey and some anonymous Californian admirer who's bloody generous. And, by the by, that Stacey has turned out to have talent. Nothing remotely useful to Rhino Camp—Christ, she didn't even know those rifles weren't loaded." He paused. "But she sure is hell on wheels about weddings."

"Skeleton Coast. Brilliant," said Eric soberly. He turned to face Pieter. "Perfect. Clare will love that. I will love it."

"Seriously?" Pieter paused. "Well, then good. Yes. A fine start to a long and happy marriage." He slapped Eric on the arm. "Clare might allow you to forget she's not just one of the guys, maybe more often than she should, but she is a woman, and this is her wedding day. Her one wedding day, might I add," he said, raising an emphatic eyebrow.

"Now that we've determined the location, I suppose I'll need a best man." Eric gazed at the researchers as they filed in for lunch. "I suppose Hosea could accommodate." A smile crept across his face. "Unless you might happen to be free?"

"Already cleared my calendar for the occasion. Best man? My honor. You do have a suit?"

"A suit? No idea. Doubt it."

"Really? Why not have one of the Herero women sew up a colorful ceremonial robe, trim it with lizard, add a few chicken feathers? Or you could just ask your mum to send you one."

"Wasn't planning to tell them. Not until later. They'll make a fuss."

Pieter clucked and shook his head again.

"Don't start that! I was going to tell them, take Clare to

visit next year. But I didn't want any drama—any complications—more than necessary." He realized he was perspiring.

"God, you're right. They're just the kind to go off the deep end and send a card—or would they be so daft as to send a gift? Good heavens, that'd be intolerable. I mean for a busy man such as yourself, taking time to open an envelope, unwrap a gift. Good Lord, the demands people make these days."

"You're enjoying the hell out of this, aren't you?"

"Trying to, my friend. And so should you."

WHEN CLARE HEARD the wedding was to be on the Skeleton Coast, her spirits soared. She'd attempted to be pleased with Eric's suggestion of a small ceremony at Rhino Camp, imagining Flossie and Elvis as attendants, and she'd tried to ignore the look of acute disappointment on Stacey's face at the news. Then Pieter and Stacey had come up with this Skeleton Coast idea. *Bless you both, a million times over,* she thought. The least romantic man and most manic woman on earth had partnered to concoct the most romantic wedding on earth. This reversal took a bit of adjustment, of course, but Clare was elated that she wasn't going to be married in the dining hall, Eric wearing a clean white T-shirt and she the one sundress she had in her closet.

Meanwhile, Stacey had become a runaway train, impossible to stop. Several times a day, she brought Clare new photos of floral arrangements, of dresses, of cakes, of bouquets.

Clare had written her parents, before the change of venue, saying the wedding would be very small, very informal, and that she and Eric would visit next year to celebrate with them in California. Now, she thought they might actually come.

Now, she felt like a real bride. Almost. And when Stacey showed up with photo 1,038, another gown printed from Internet, Clare instantly knew what this wedding would look like.

"See? The neckline has those little beaded scallops. See? Just here." Stacey traced the photo with her perfectly manicured red fingernail. She'd tried unrelentingly to convince Clare to consider various styles without much success.

"That's it."

"What? What's it?"

"That dress. It's perfect." Clare took the photo from Stacey as she hugged her. "Oh, Stace, help me order it."

Stacey hesitated. "Um, Clare, did you see the price? It's um—"

"Yup, saw it. Let's see if Zahara has a tape measure."

"We could try to find a knockoff?" But Stacey looked at Clare. "Oh, my God! You are going to be the most beautiful bride of all time." She sniffled and dabbed at her nose. "You going to have bridesmaids? I mean, you might think about it. Maybe some California friends?"

"You and Flossie are the only girlfriends I'd consider. A gown for Floss? Well, the cost for that would be prohibitive. You, on the other hand—"

Stacey looked bewildered and anxious.

"So, would you be my maid of honor, Stacey?"

"Me? Yes! Yes!" She jumped up and down squealing, then took Clare by the hand. "Oh, you won't regret this. I'll get a dress. A beautiful dress." Stacey took a deep breath. "But quiet. A quiet, beautiful little dress. I'll just be a quiet little flower in your bouquet."

47.

For weeks, boxes of every size and description had been arriving at Rhino Camp in unprecedented numbers, which Eric found alarming.

One contained the bespoke suit Eric's mother had ordered from Savile Row. Stacey and Pieter had delivered it in triumph to his tent. Eric shook his head as he watched them walk away, side by side, the most unlikely alliance, perhaps, on the planet. The relationship between Flossie and Elvis was positively sensible compared to Stacey and Pieter's. Eric doubted it would endure after the wedding but was pleased there was peace for now.

With some trepidation, he unpacked the suit and tried on the pants and jacket, first straightening his shoulders and sucking in his already flat stomach. But that was not necessary. In fact, the suit was a bit big. His recent bout of what Pieter had declared "lunacy" had apparently taken off some weight. He was scrutinizing the effect in the mirror when Clare walked in.

"Oh, my, now that's a new look." She walked over to him, put her hands on his shoulders, and turned him around. "Pants and jacket, very nice. And it is, after all, Africa, so I don't think you are required to wear a shirt." She ran her hands under his jacket and up his muscled bare back, pulling him close for a kiss.

The kiss lingered as he embraced her, pulling her off her feet.

"Stop that! You're getting me all hot and bothered." She

nibbled at his neck. "We've come this far with our virtue intact. Let's wait for the proper wedding night bliss."

"God, woman—you'd better leave. Quickly. Besides, I need my beauty sleep." He took off the jacket and, in his consternation, made a mess of folding it.

"Here, let me." Clare hugged it to herself and hung it up. She paused before turning. "Eric, if I forget, in the excitement tomorrow, I just want to say I feel like the luckiest woman in the world to have found you, to be being marrying you."

Eric nestled her into him. "Who's the lucky one, I'd like to know." He felt as if he would never release her. "You sure you don't want to stay? What if tomorrow we get run down by a herd of elephants on our way to the coast and this was our last chance?"

Her musical laughter washed over him. She blew him a kiss as she slipped out of his arms. "'Night."

THE WINDING DRIVE from Rhino Camp to White Whale Lodge on the Skeleton Coast took about four hours. Eric had ushered Clare and Stacey off early the morning before the day of the wedding. Clare silent, Stacey chattering away. Today, he and Pieter drove among looming ocher sand dunes and across undulating dry washes, at last cresting a high dune overlooking the ocean. Below lay the White Whale Lodge, named for a massive bleached whale skeleton imbedded in the sand nearby. Notorious for wildly unpredictable currents, the coast was littered not only with whales washed off course and killed but with the rusted hulks of ships. Not all of them old. The coast still had her wiles and could entice even a modern vessel with sophisticated navigational devices to her treacherous shoals and bars. Still, the site was gloriously scenic, the salty wind crisp and invigorating. The dark aquamarine expanse laced with whitecaps ceaselessly rushing the shore.

The lodge itself had been meticulously designed to complement its remarkable natural surroundings. Voluminous white canvas sails, like gulls' wings, mirrored the round dunes and provided dramatic shelter for the floor-to-ceiling glass cottages overlooking the ocean. A short distance away stood a much larger, similar structure, over which arced three sides of brilliant white sails protecting the long dinner tables from the bracing ocean wind. The effect struck Clare as if it were some exotic canvas version of the Sydney Opera House. Drinking in the panorama, the women retired to their suite to unpack.

The men had needed to conclude arrangements at Rhino Camp and arrived much later in the afternoon. They checked in and were shown to their elegantly appointed glass "tent."

"They have a pool here," observed Eric dryly.

"I know. How environmentally insensitive. Eric, for the love of God, could you once, just once?" Pieter took a deep breath. "Knowing you, my friend, I inquired. They assured me that it's salt water. We could make them take it out. See the error of their ways. Later. After the wedding."

Eric nodded. In truth, he felt the venue would do nicely. Luxurious, yes, but tastefully so. And this celebration merited a certain degree of luxury.

In an effort at conciliation, Eric announced, "Actually, I'd enjoy a dip right now. You in?"

The suggestion resulted in a tornado of shed clothing, and the two friends raced across the sand toward the welcoming water.

The following day, Eric would stay with Pieter until the

ceremony, Clare holding firm to the superstition of the groom not seeing the bride before the wedding.

As the hour approached, Pieter said, "I'm going to head over. Check that they've set up and everything's in order for the ceremony and dinner. Don't want anything going wrong." He fussed with his tie and scrutinized himself in the mirror.

"I have to say, Pieter, you look quite fine in that suit. I had no idea you owned one. I had no idea you'd become a wedding planner either. You've turned into someone I scarcely recognize. When was the last time you cared about dinner? Zahara could put a can of beans and a can opener out, and you'd be happy as hell."

Pieter harrumphed at the charge. "Just get ready, will you? And don't be late."

Eric fiddled with his shirt, his tie, his jacket. It'd been a long while since he'd completely donned a formal suit, and he felt restricted, the clothing binding him, the tie symbolically cutting his head from his body. Would he ever be able to return to a life that required this dress code, even occasionally? Would Clare ever desire that? He banished the thought.

Satisfied with his appearance, Eric took his time, walking slowly from the bungalow to the dining tent. Barely visible from the path, huge candles in festive hurricane lanterns set the canvas aglow, and the pool in front reflected the opalescent sky. After kicking the breakers into a fury, the trade winds had calmed down as they often did at sunset. Wisps of clouds drifted on the horizon. Farther down the beach, he could see the skeletons of wrecked ships strewn across the sand or listing in the water. These half-buried rusty hulks looming in the distance were eerie testament to the power of nature. They cast sobering shadows on the pristine landscape.

Since he was twelve years old, pouring over a treasured book on Africa that his grandfather had given him on one of their weekly visits to the zoo, the rhino particularly had captured his imagination. He'd set his heart on living here in Namibia. Never had it let go. But there had also been a growing sense that he could be like one of these ships, albeit smashed by different waves on a different shore. Nevertheless, a ridiculous wreck. Alone.

Now there was Clare. The moment he'd seen her at the Windhoek airport, he sensed she could change his life. He'd almost given up hope, could feel himself solidifying, calcifying. The miracle of her love would keep him connected to a life outside himself and outside the rhino. They would fight that fight together, saving the rhino so that their children and their children's children could marvel at them, share the same awe of them. But they would create a new life for themselves, too.

He stood for a moment reflecting on the beauty around him. To smell the ocean, feel the moist salty freshness. He must remember to bring Clare here often. Pieter and Stacey had been wise to choose this magical site for the start of a new life.

When he entered the lodge, he was overcome with emotion and delight. There stood his mother and father, his sister and her husband. Eric had finally convinced Hosea and Zahara to attend after repeated assurances that Rhino Camp would not fall into ruin at the hands of the researchers during their absence. He wouldn't have believed his eyes at this remarkable gathering except they were all soon embracing each other and chatting with sincere cordiality.

Pieter led two people over. A man dressed not in a suit but an intricately embroidered guayabera and loose pants, a woman in a diaphanous, brightly patterned dress, reminiscent of American hippies. "Eric, I'd like to introduce you to Clare's parents, Rainbow and Theodore."

Eric appreciated the father's enthusiastic grip and intense, joyous gaze. "Pleased to meet you, Theodore. Still having some trouble believing you've come all this way. We're so happy."

"Trip, everyone calls me Trip. Clare writes that you walk on water. Perhaps after dinner you could teach me."

"She may exaggerate a bit."

Clare's mother held his hand, tears of joy rolling down her cheeks. "We've never seen our daughter so happy, so peaceful. Even if you don't walk on water."

Soon English and Africans and Americans were laughing and talking. Eric stood to the side, basking in the happy energy filling the room with a warm glow.

THE WEDDING WOULD take place soon, just before sunset. Stacey had spent an exhausting afternoon poking and twisting Clare's hair and fussing with her makeup, Clare protesting all the while about wanting to look natural. And Stacey saying poop was natural but you didn't want to look like it, and on and on. At last, Stacey left her alone, satisfied with the compromise. Clare regarded her reflection in the mirror. She could not deny Stacey had done well. Her hair was braided and wrapped like a golden crown, which she hoped would stay secure in the evening breeze. The light application of makeup heightened the dazzling green of her eyes. Placing her fingertips gently on her cheek, Clare couldn't believe how luminous her skin was, whether because of Stacey's spritzer magic or her own happiness. It didn't matter.

She looked like a bride, though still dressed only in a slip because Stacey warned her in no uncertain terms the dress would "wrinkle like an elephant's butt" if she even thought of sitting in it.

It occurred to her that, much like the makeup had accomplished, she was herself but different, better. She saw reflected in her eyes a confidence she'd not seen before. All that she was and all that she had experienced had been for this day. A fragment of Robert Browning's poetry entered her thoughts: "Grow old along with me! The best is yet to be, the last of life, for which the first was made." Her life had so often been one of slipping and sliding. But this life she was about to embark upon with Eric, this life in Africa, this was the perfect life, the perfect union.

Stacey bounded back into the room with a fruit drink. "Use the straw. You'll ruin your lipstick otherwise." She admired her handiwork. "You look beautiful. If I do say so myself."

"Thank you, Stacey, for everything."

"Nervous?"

"Yes, a little." Clare turned in her seat to look out the window. The ocean lapped at the dunes, stealing the sand, which at high tide it would return. "Well, it's almost time. We might want to tack this veil to my head. With this breeze, I'm worried it will sail across Africa and land on some bewildered person in Mumbai."

Stacey helped Clare step into the gown, carefully arranging the long train of exquisite silk.

ALTHOUGH THE WEDDING dinner would be held in the vast canopied veranda of the lodge, Clare and Eric wanted the ceremony on the beach. Stacey and Pieter had plotted a route for

Clare so that she would be hidden from sight until just the right moment.

Eric and Pieter stood waiting high on the beach with the minister. The guests clustered nearby. Groom and best man were dressed stiffly in black suits and starched shirts, the African clergyman in his ceremonial robe, a peacock array of blues and greens. Eric had raised concerns whether the marriage would be legal with this particular minister officiating, but Pieter had assured him it would be fine. Even so, Eric was thinking that as insurance, he and Clare should later be married in Windhoek by the government clerk.

Gasps of wonder and surprise brought his mind back to the moment.

There, at the top of a nearby dune, he saw Clare, a vision he would never forget. Above her head, feathery pink clouds streaked the azure sky. Her veil fluttering behind her in the breeze. Her white silk dress shimmering pink and cream in the sunset. Her train billowing gently across the sand far behind, making it appear that she was not walking on the sand but was suspended, floating above it. Floating toward him, smiling. Eric had never seen anything more beautiful.

Stacey struggled a few feet before her, her high heels sinking deeper into the sand with each step, until she stopped in utter frustration and flung them as far as she could. Clare must have been barefoot, gliding with such simple grace.

They approached, Stacey taking her place next to Pieter, Clare joining Eric.

Eric took Clare's hand, looking deep into her eyes, stunned by the overwhelming force of his love.

"Forever," he whispered, as they turned toward the minister. "Forever."

ACKNOWLEDGMENTS

To our infinitely patient and generous husbands, Rolf and Richard.

To our editors Adam Russ, Kate Montieth, and Susan Hodgson, as well as the Davis writing community.

To She Writes Press for their guidance and support.

And, of course, to each other.

ABOUT THE AUTHORS

photo credit: Richard Williams

Raised in the high plains (mining towns) of Wyoming and Montana, **Kathryn Williams** couldn't wait to see the world. After serving as a Peace Corps English teacher in Afghanistan, then traveling across India, Turkey, and Greece, she returned to the US, where she began teaching college composition in Northern California, using summers to continue traveling throughout South America, Mexico, Canada, and Europe. *Rhino Dreams*, set in far-flung Namibia, seemed a perfect locale for her first book. Kathryn lives in Northern California with her husband and their very demanding Sheltie, and is currently finishing a book of short stories set in the least exotic locale imaginable: a down-at-the-heels trailer park in hurricane-prone Florida.

Carolyn Waggoner has been caring for and about animals her entire life. She currently lives in Davis, California, with a sizeable menagerie of rescue creatures—and an indulgent veterinarian husband. Carolyn devotes her days to throwing sticks, scooping litter boxes, preparing meals, and, on rare occasions, even writing.

Learn more about the authors at www.rhinodreams.net.